Trust Me

Isabel Jolie

TRUST ME

Poem by Becca Lee First edition
ISBN: 978-1-7343291-6-2

Contents

And as she fell apart
her shattered pieces began to bloom -
blossoming until she became herself,
exactly as she was meant to be.

-Becca Lee

Chapter 1

Olivia

New York hums with a frenetic energy. I've missed this city, its buoyancy and the constant whirr of life more than I ever thought possible. Others might see grit and grime, but when the sun bounces back from the skyscrapers, I see the rainbows. To me, this island belongs to dreamers.

When I fled, I didn't have a plan. No idea where I wanted to go or what I wanted to do. I simply had to get far away from a painful reminder and public scrutiny. As a stranger in an adopted country, I had time to do some soul searching. Time to regroup. Heal. The woman stepping off the plane and into the JFK terminal returned home with focus and a plan.

I've been back for two weeks. I'm following my plan. The past is behind me. That's what they say, right? Onward bound. Game on.

On my first day back, I was a little lost, wandering down Edgecombe Avenue. The spotted gold lettering on the window of Manhattanville Coffee caught my eye. Everything about the coffee shop called to me, the brick wall behind the bar and the thick marble slab counter as aesthetically appealing as any café in Prague. One side is a wall of windows that can open into doors in warm weather. A row of five tables for two line up alongside the windows. I've only been in the business school program for two weeks, but I've already staked a claim to the fourth table by the second window toward the front.

Today, I'm sitting at my table, reveling in the delectable coffee aroma when I should be studying. We first-years have this crazy intensive accounting focus that kicks off the semester. As an advertising major, I passed through undergrad without ever taking an accounting course. I'd thought of it as a class for mathematically-challenged students.

That's so not what it is. I'm not sure what it is, but none of it makes sense to me. I should be focusing on accounting. Instead, I'm mindlessly flipping through the "40 Under 40" *Fortune* article. Procrastinating.

The large wooden door opens, and a gorgeous male specimen meanders up to the marble counter. We're talking Abercrombie model. Wavy brown hair, not so long that it falls below the ear, but long enough that you can see actual waves dusted with natural blond highlights. He's wearing faded jeans and a dark navy sports jacket with a white pressed shirt. Something about him looks like Texas, but I can't put my finger on what, exactly. His sunbaked skin? The cowboy boots? Maybe it's the way he walks? Kind of like he just dismounted from a horse. Yeah, horseback riding in Manhattan. *Pull it together, Olivia.*

I drag my attention away from Mr. Gorgeous, drop the magazine on the table, and pull out my accounting textbook. The giant, heavy, eight-hundred-page textbook that could double as a weight when working out.

I'm on chapter two but should be on chapter ten. In one hour, my accounting professor's open office hours start. My plan is to drop in and either convince him to commit to meeting with me each week or recommend a tutor.

Paige, the blue-haired barista with hoop earrings lining her entire right ear, giggles. Her cheeks turn pink as she delivers Mr. Gorgeous his coffee. I refrain from rolling my eyes. The girl has a star tattoo on her nose. Mr. Texas doesn't at all look like her type, but she can't stop herself from flirting. Because, yes, he is that attractive. Women probably throw themselves at him in fits of giggles and a mindless fluttering of eyelashes all the time.

Mr. Gorgeous settles in a leather chair one row over, directly in my line of sight. Without so much as a glance my way, he pulls out a folded *Wall Street Journal* from a thin, dark brown metro briefcase. Oh, my. How am I supposed to read accounting with that eye candy sitting right there? He sips his coffee, adjusts his paper, and quick as lightning, his eyes meet mine. He flips out the paper with one hand, concealing his face. The one-handed paper manipulation move. Talent. Gorgeous and talented.

Since his paper blocks his vision, I'm free to stare. He has thick wrists, muscular forearms, and I can see what looks like a silver band bracelet. No wedding band. Intriguing. I'd guess he's in his thirties.

As he reads, one brown leather cowboy boot resting over a knee, he gives off a laidback vibe. The kind of guy I'd hoped to run into in Prague but never did. His persona is reminiscent of Matthew McConaughey from one of his roles as a relaxed business guy or lawyer in the south.

Maybe it's his Southern aura—his leisurely gait, unpolished brown leather belt, and of course, the brown leather cowboy boots. Texas would be a good bet. He might be a better fit for Delilah, my old roommate Anna's colleague. She's as deep south as they come and plans to

8

return to New Orleans. You could take this guy back home to New Orleans. Delilah's parents would take one look at those well-worn boots, slap him on the back, and drawl, "Welcome home, son."

Yet I saw him first. He's my daydream. I sit back, coffee mug hovering over my lips, and let my mind roam. How would it start between us?

He'd put his paper down and smile at me. A warm smile. He'd focus on me so I could see the color of his irises. From this distance, I can't tell. But, no, if this were to happen, he'd look up and notice me.

Then he'd walk over and politely ask to sit with me after telling me his name. I'd flip my hair back off my shoulder in a seductive manner and smile with a gracious and casual air. I'd tell him I was finishing up, and I'd close this mammoth book so he'd have room to set his coffee cup on our table.

As we talked, he'd reach out to hold my hand, and his fingers would play with mine. It would turn out that we both like business. He's older, so he already has his M.B.A. He'd be impressed that I had this amazing job offer but decided to take a step back to pursue a graduate degree so I wouldn't hit a ceiling in the future. He'd find my goal-oriented sensibility appealing.

We'd talk all afternoon. Maybe eat lunch here, sharing fresh bread and cheese, and then as the sun was setting, he'd ask me if I had dinner plans. After dinner, we'd walk back to his nearby apartment, and we'd know. We would both know we had found our other half. The person who brought out our best. It would be easy. Everything would be easy between us.

I'm so happy in my daydream, staring at his sinewy forearms, that I don't even hear *Take It Easy* by The Eagles

9

blaring. Mr. Gorgeous flicks one corner of his paper down to eyeball me about the same time I hear my ringtone. My coffee splatters onto my black slacks as I startle from my comatose state. The loud ringtone blasts through the low hum of coffee shop noise.

The contents of my backpack pour out onto the wooden floor and into the aisle as I search for my cell. Heat radiates off my face. Not one to sit and chat on the phone in a coffee shop, I snatch my phone up and press decline.

Mr. Gorgeous flicks his paper and shifts it to remove me and my offensive song from his view. The snap of his paper hits my ears like a scolding. I reload my backpack, throwing the pens, lip gloss, random coins, and Post-it Notes back in with more than a little annoyance. This isn't a library. A ringtone isn't a personal affront. Noise is all around.

I pick up my phone from the table to text Delilah back. Glancing up as I type, I catch the backside of Mr. Coffee Shop Beautiful rambling out the door.

Bye-bye, Mr. Coffee Shop Love. *C'est la vie.*

These are my years to get a degree, redirect my career, and find my success. And tempting as daydreaming is, I need to focus on the most boring subject I've ever encountered, accounting. This might be an island of dreamers, but it's also an island of doers. We achieve our dreams by working toward them every single day.

******

Less than an hour later, I wander down the long hallway of offices searching for the number I scribbled on my Post-it Note. I pause after locating office number 222. The door stands slightly ajar, and I peer through the opening onto a nondescript wall, high ceilings, and dated fluorescent lighting. I push it wide open without knocking, expecting a hallway to other offices. Professor Longevite's head lifts, and he peers at me over his laptop. His shoulders slump, his skin is pale, and dark circles are visible beneath his eyes. He looks as happy as I feel when I read accounting.

"Hi. Um, I'm sorry. Is it your open office hours? I'm in your accounting class."

He stares at me. A moment passes, and I wonder if he heard me. I open my mouth to repeat my question when he deadpans, "Office hours start next week. You can close the door on your way out."

"But the first-year accounting exam is next Friday. I need help. Next Friday will be too late. Could you recommend a tutor?" I've made many attempts over many days trying to read my accounting textbook like a book, and it doesn't jive.

He shifts the spectacles from his nose to his forehead then points to the chair across from the desk. "Sit."

He scratches along the side of his floppy, lopsided mop of reddish hair, and when he pulls his hand back, it looks like a few pieces of hair remain on his palm. He stares at it for a brief moment. "Actually, here, pull your chair by mine. I'll give you a quick overview."

"Thank you so much. I didn't take accounting in undergrad, and I'm a little lost."

He nods like this does not surprise him. "What chapter are you on?"

"Two," I say, a little ashamed.

He tilts his head to the side and leans back in his chair. "Here's the deal. For next week, you need to be thinking of it as learning to analyze how a business is doing. Income statement, balance sheet, statement of cashflow. You need to make sure you know how those work."

I pull out my pen to take notes. A shadow crosses his office doorway, and I glance up. For a minute, I think I see Mr. Coffee Shop's back walking away, but I shake my head. *No way. Accounting. Focus.*

Professor Longevite stops speaking and looks to the door as if he's expecting someone to walk through it.

I follow his gaze out into the empty hallway. "I know you weren't expecting to have office hours right now. If you need for me to come back at a different time, I can do that."

His attention returns to me. "A friend was supposed to meet me here, but he probably got caught up with work. If he shows, we can schedule a time. For now, let's get through this."

He opens the accounting textbook that had been lying on his desk and pushes it to me. "Don't try to read the textbook like a book. It's a reference book, explaining to you how to get answers. Let's start with understanding debits and credits."

I sit there for the next hour taking notes, absorbing his monotone voice. More than once, I squelch the desire to ask him if everything is okay.

I leave his office a much calmer person. I'm getting it. More than that, he helped this strange view of math make sense. He might be the most boring professor I have ever encountered, and he might also need antidepressants, but Professor Longevite knows how to explain the material. I make a mental note to make cookies and bring them for him next week as I head out the door.

My internship this semester is at Esprit Transactions. The founders started it as a way to make it easier for businesses to accept credit card transactions. Esprit revolutionized online payments when they made open source code available to developers, and they're now the number one backend source for commerce websites in the world.

I hop into a cab so I won't be late to the first orientation meeting. As the cab bounces along the avenue, I pull up my favorites list. Ten minutes to kill.

I tap Anna's name. Voicemail.

I tap Delilah's name. On the second ring, she answers.

"Hey, there!" her cheery voice sounds through the line.

"Hi. Guess what? I saw a Matthew McConaughey lookalike."

"Maybe it was him. Maybe he's filming around here. You never know." She's such an optimist.

"While that would be lovely, it wasn't him."

"No, you never know," she insists. "It could be. Celebrities can be hard to spot."

"I know. But it wasn't him."

"No, you never—"

"Stop it. Are we meeting up tonight?" I love Delilah, but the girl would have continued that circular conversation for at least five more minutes if I didn't nip it.

I barely knew Delilah before I moved away, but I've seen her more than anyone since I returned two weeks ago. Anna, my best friend and college roommate, found the love of her life while I was in Prague. She still makes time for me, but Anna's a bit of a workaholic, and between Jackson and the office, she's pretty scheduled.

Delilah, a New Orleans blondie, seems to always be available. She's a creative director with Anna at the Evolve ad agency. It feels a bit like Anna set us up knowing she wouldn't have adequate time for the two of us now that she's in the throes of romantic bliss.

I exit the cab and head into the tall glass building with the green Esprit Transactions logo at the top. I check my watch. Fifteen minutes early. Good.

I stop in at the front desk, and they check my license before letting me pass to the elevator bank. As the elevator starts to close, a suited arm catches the door. The dark suit nods at me as he walks in and puts an arm out to hold the door for another man. My mouth opens into an "oh."

Mr. Coffee Shop steps in the elevator.

Mr. Suit asks me what floor, and, speechless, I point at the panel to show I've already pushed my button.

Mr. Coffee Shop frowns and stares at me. He steps to the far side of the elevator and doesn't stop watching me.

I nod acknowledgement, because he's not going crazy, he has seen me before, and I offer a soft, polite smile. Mr. Suit pushed the twenty-eighth floor, so they must be together.

I keep looking at Mr. Coffee Shop, then away from him. Every time I glance his way, he's blatantly staring at me. I rub my tongue across my teeth as a quick check for lingering food particles, then swipe through my hair to check that it's vertical. He never looks away.

I want to say something like, "Were you at Manhattanville Coffee earlier today?" but every time I go to open my mouth, something stops me. He's not saying anything. I shift my feet, an uncomfortable sensation rising underneath his blatant stare. He must know he's seen me but can't place me. I tend to stare at people when I'm in that situation, trying to figure out how I know them. I swallow, and the noise is too loud. My toe taps as discomfort threatens to engulf me.

The doors open onto the eighteenth floor, and I rush out, glancing back at Mr. Coffee Shop Man. He stares without apology. I offer one more timid smile to him before the elevator door closes. Does he work here? What are the chances of seeing him twice in one day?

I breathe to get my bearings. I see a restroom at the end of the hall and enter. I run a brush through the long, wavy mass on my head and rinse with mouthwash. I'm dressed professionally in black heels, black slacks and a white wraparound blouse. I dressed today aiming to bridge the gap between a college campus and corporate America. I apply lip gloss, decide I don't need any blush after my run-in with Mr. Coffee Shop, and zip up my little make-up bag. One last check in the mirror, and I head out.

A receptionist with her dark hair pulled back into a low bun smiles at me, offers me a clipboard, and directs me to the conference room. She explains this afternoon's session will be with HR. We'll complete the required paperwork and have a brief orientation. On Monday, we will be assigned to our departments.

I head toward the conference room as a man in a security uniform approaches. He nods a greeting to the front desk but continues toward me.

His long legs carry him across the floor in a quick and deliberate manner. He heads straight to me. The silver bar on his right breast pocket bears the name Bill Withers. "Ma'am, can you please come with me? We have some questions for you."

He's stiff and formal, and my eyes focus on the gun in his holster. The gun is solid and dark, and if it's fake, it is a quality reproduction. *Am I in trouble?* I want to ask him, but I feel like in TV shows, when people ask that question it's a

15

sure sign they are guilty, so I refrain. I watch a lot of crime TV.

"Ma'am?"

I pull my shoulders back to address him, puzzled as to why he has singled me out. "Yes, sir. I was just heading into the conference room. Are you joining us?"

"No, ma'am. I need you to walk with me to my office." He places his hand on my elbow. On reflex, I yank my arm away. *What in the world?*

He ushers me to the elevator, and we ride down to the third floor. From there, he directs me to a room with a rectangular table and four chairs. One wall holds a window that looks into the hall. There is a long mirror on the opposite wall. I can't help but wonder if people are watching on the other side. But then I dismiss the thought as ridiculous. Way too many crime dramas.

He points to a chair on one side of the table. "Please sit."

I do as he instructs. I know I haven't done anything wrong. My brow wrinkles, as confusion ripples through me. In Prague, I learned to be more vocal and to present myself as a leader, but here, I'm an intern and am unsure. I'd prefer not to lose this internship on day one. I exhale and lower myself into the chair then cross my legs and arms to await more information.

"What brings you to this office, Ms. Grayson?"

Okay. So, Bill knows my name. "I have an internship here."

He pulls out his phone and starts reading. "This says you applied two months ago online. And you had an in-person interview two weeks ago."

"Yes, that is correct." This guy can't be HR. He has a gun in a holster around his waist.

"Why did you decide to interview at this company?" The man is steel, expressionless and formal.

I rub my forehead to alleviate the mild tension headache forming. "Is this part of the interviewing process? I was offered an internship here, and I already accepted it?" My statement comes out sounding like a question.

"Ms. Grayson, I need you to answer my questions. No, this is not part of the interview process. I'm part of the security team, and you have come to our attention as a potential security risk."

"A security risk? What kind of security risk?" I sit straighter in my chair, alert. Annoyance and anger simmer, and my grip tightens on the edge of my seat.

"Please answer my questions. We'll go through this process much more quickly if you do." He leans back in his chair. He has coal-black eyes and a chiseled jaw. His broad shoulders swallow the back of the chair, and his forearms relax on the armrests. His fingers flex ever so slightly, as if he's ensuring he can reach his holster in a nanosecond.

I breathe deeply to clear my head and focus, then clarify, "Why did I interview here? Is that the question?"

"Yes, ma'am."

"Esprit Transactions is a relatively new company. Less than ten years old, with explosive growth. The merger and acquisition division in particular appeals to me. I'm hoping to work at a venture capital firm after I graduate from business school. The experience here will be invaluable."

"Did you apply for internships anywhere else?"

"Yes." My knee bounces below the desk, but my hands and fingers remain still while I look my interrogator in the eye.

"Where?"

"Several other VC firms I identified through the Columbia University internship program."

"Why did you choose this internship?"

I pause and glance around the room as I formulate my answer. This is not an interview. This is not HR. He's assessing risk. This guy isn't here for bullshit. I decide to play it straight. "I didn't get the VC internships. I only applied for three, total. I was living in Prague and didn't have time to focus on finding an internship. Columbia University had a link to the job posting for this position."

"You returned from Prague recently." His matter-of-fact voice makes a statement. He isn't accusing me of anything, but his attitude is antagonistic. A simmering blend of annoyance and anger continues to rise within me, approaching a boiling point. Nothing riles me more than to be accused of something. But he hasn't accused me of anything, so I inhale deeply to calm myself.

"Yes, about two weeks ago." He flips through some pages in a folder, and I wonder if he's double-checking my answer. Should I ask for a lawyer? But that would be absurd. He's building security.

He glances up from his folder and asks, "How long did you live there?"

"Around eighteen months." My gaze centers on him.

"Why did you choose to move to Prague?"

Because my ex fucked everything up, and I wanted to get the fuck away. I glare at Bill and exhale. "An excellent job opportunity. I also wanted the international experience."

"Why were you in Professor Longevite's office this afternoon?"

I narrow my eyes and tilt my head. "How did you know I was there?" I sit up straighter and pull my shoulders back. Did someone follow me? *What the ever-loving fuck?*

He repeats his question in a stern, commanding voice. "Why were you there?"

I still my knee and grip the armrests. "He's my professor. That has to make sense to you, because I'm in the *M.B.A.* program. What doesn't make sense to me is why you know I was in his office this afternoon." I can hear the anger in my tone, but at this point, I no longer care. It's an internship. They can fucking fire me. This is insane.

Mr. Security nods. He shifts in his seat and looks like he is recognizing that maybe he has overstepped, but maybe not, because he continues with his questions. "In Manhattanville Coffee, you were doing some research. Can you tell me what you were researching?"

"You know I was in a coffee shop earlier today too?" This is beyond freaky. This is offensive. Intolerable. I slide my chair back away from the desk.

At this point, the conference room door opens. Mr. Coffee Shop walks in. "Bill, it's okay. She's clear."

Mr. Security nods and stands, his lips a firm, straight line.

Mr. Coffee Shop turns to me and extends his hand. "Sam Duke."

I squint and angle my head in a cloud of confusion. Anger courses through me, but some sense of professionalism forces my arm forward. "Olivia Grayson." Sam Duke. The name sounds familiar, but I can't place it.

He has a firm, warm grip, and his eyes meet mine. My palm is clammy, and I yank it back quickly. "What's going on? I'm confused. Do you work here?"

A smile crinkles his lips, and a soft, barely audible laugh escapes. "Yes, I work here. Sorry about the confusion, Ms. Grayson. We've had some security issues. I asked Bill's team to check everything out. We're good." He turns to Bill. "Can you escort Ms. Grayson back to the orientation?"

Bill nods in acquiescence. He still isn't smiling.

Coffee Shop man, a.k.a. Sam Duke, looks me in the eye as he says, "Have a good afternoon, Ms. Grayson." He turns on his cowboy boot heel and lumbers down the hall out of my sight.

I face Bill. "Can you please explain this?" Security issues? Me?

"Mr. Duke saw you at the coffee shop reading an article on him. Later, he saw you at Columbia, then he saw you here and found out you were an intern. We've had some issues in the past, and in an abundance of caution, his personal security detail requested I talk to you."

"Personal security? What does he do?"

The corners of Bill's lips turn up into a slight smile. "He's one of the founders of Esprit Transactions. He's also the CEO."

Chapter 2

Sam

From the twenty-eighth floor, the boats floating by on the Hudson River look like toy ships. A lone sailboat catches my attention, and I watch as it swings to the right of a ferry. Needing to burn some energy, I grab a soft basketball from my shelf, give it squeeze, and aim for the goal that hangs on the back of my closed office door.

I take a few shots to relieve the tension coursing through my muscles and to take my mind off what just happened. We grilled a young intern all because of some random coincidences. *What the hell?* Paranoia is eating away at me, and I don't like it. Things have to change. I might be a programming geek—my brother's words, not mine—but damn if I need to be scared of my own shadow.

I open my door and catch Janet's eye. "Can you call down to Bill Withers and ask him to come to my office?"

"Certainly." She smiles. The thin silver metal piece from her headset reflects the overhead light as she shifts her head and immediately dials. I used to tease her about looking like a telephone operator, but appearances aren't something she seems to care too much about. She's a few decades older than I am and the most on-the-ball assistant a guy could ever ask for. She wears her auburn hair in a neat chin-length bob, but it wouldn't shock me at all if one day she walked in sporting a grandma-like poodle perm. Something about her reminds me of my Aunt Dottie.

I return to my desk, open my laptop, and start going through emails. There's a light tap on my doorframe. Bill Withers stands in the doorway.

"You asked to see me, sir?"

"Yeah. Come have a seat." I gesture to the two open chairs across from my desk. He sits down, back flagpole erect. Between his posture and his buzz cut, he's classic military. He's wearing a suit, but he looks like he should be in uniform. A well-decorated uniform with brass pins of all types along the pockets and arms.

We both sit as I begin the conversation we need to have. "I don't want what happened today to happen again."

"I don't follow, sir."

"We interrogated an intern. A goddamn intern, Bill." I run my fingers through my hair, partially out of habit. Partially to emphasize my point to the stone wall in front of me.

"Sir, we cannot be too cautious. It was highly unusual for you to run into her three times. You know that."

"Bill, this whole situation is making me paranoid, and I don't like it. First, I'm running a business here. I can't be pulling people into an interrogation room because they run into me a few times. That intern is in my buddy's class. I was right near the school. It really wasn't that odd that we'd run into each other on campus. If you guys had done your homework, today would not have happened. You could've checked her resume and application and seen she wasn't a threat. If your team wants to be on the lookout for risks, that's fine. But I need you to do your research thoroughly before pulling this kind of thing again. Got it?"

"Sir, my first concern is your safety. I can't do my job if you try to place parameters around how I do my job. She entered the building. We took necessary precautions."

"All right, all right, all right. Look, I get it. I know you take your job very seriously. And I appreciate it. I do. There's been some weird shit, and I know you're doing your job. I'm asking that you take a moment before interacting with any *suspects*." I put air quotes around the word, hoping it makes him realize how ridiculous this whole thing is. Something tells me that nuance is lost on Bill. "Because, Bill, chances are any *suspect* in this building is an employee. I'd like to believe our employees are emotionally stable. I'd like to trust that security and HR can work together to weed out psychopaths. *Comprende?*"

"Mr. Duke, you brought her to our attention. As you should have. Her activities were unusual and warranted additional investigation. We needed to meet with her, given she was already in the building."

I huff. He's right. That's the part that burns me up. His security detail has me on edge. They stay well away from me, but I know they are there. If they aren't, then there's a camera nearby. I'm at the point now where I can't enter a restaurant or even a blasted deli without searching for security cameras. Locating the camera or the security guy is becoming my obsession. I twist in my chair. "I didn't know you'd go and interrogate her. I wanted to make you aware so you could do a background check. Look into her. I mean, did you see her? She's remarkable. Dark hair. She's…she stands out, so I noticed her. But you should have——" I halt, realizing I'm spending too much time on this. I flatten my palms on the desk and look Bill in the eye. "My expectations are that you will proceed with caution before interacting with employees."

I return my attention to my laptop. Message delivered.

I hear Bill respond with a military, "Yes, sir." Then he drops a manila folder on my desk. "Here's the information on Ms. Grayson, sir. I assure you we will take more care with Esprit employees moving forward." He starts to walk away then pivots on his foot. "Sir, please remember. You cannot be too cautious. Your safety is our top priority, and it is a matter of grave concern for the board."

"Thank you, Bill." I nod and give what I hope is a warm smile. I don't like to question Bill's expertise. But what kind of business interrogates interns? Jesus. Bill's good at his job. I don't doubt our business is secure. The man has done time in Iraq. He's Blackwater elite. He knows what he's doing. The man's a human equivalent of a German shepherd attack dog. Unfortunately, he's a bit like a German shepherd that's still going through training.

I flip through the file after he leaves. Ms. Grayson is twenty-eight years old. Back in that coffee shop, I would have pegged her for younger than that. Her breeze-tousled dark hair caught my attention the moment I opened the door. She sat poised, in a crisp white shirt with a magazine draped over some sort of encyclopedia. As I walked by, she glanced up, and those eyes…the cobalt-blue a stark contrast to the dark. Like an exotic minx. If I'd known she wasn't in undergrad, I might've actually talked to her when she was staring me down. Her suspected youth held me back. That, and the fact she was reading a magazine I knew I was in. Even so, I still chose to plant my ass in the club chair across from her. I slide the folder into my briefcase to take it home and read later.

I pick up my phone to glance through my texts before folks start coming into my office for my next meeting.

Jason Longevite: What happened? Thought you were stopping by?

Crap. I type in a quick response.

Me: Stopped by after my meeting, but you had a student in your office. Want to grab dinner tonight?

Jason Longevite: Yeah. Sounds good. Text me where.

I pick up my phone. "Janet, can you find a place for me and Jason to get dinner? And once it's scheduled, send a car to pick him up? Coordinate with him. Thanks."

Ted, the director of my pet project, our VC group, walks into the office. I signal to him to walk over to the round conference table at the corner of my office. He's got a few thick files. He's going to update me on some of the small businesses we've decided to back. This, right here, is the best part of my day.

Now that we're the leaders in our field, our core business doesn't get my blood pumping like it used to. I miss the thrill of growing a start-up. Picking out small companies starting to make a go of it interests me. Helping them along, figuring out the best business plan, that's my passion.

Ted passes me a folder. Dark shadows color the skin below his bloodshot eyes, dark enough to make me take a second glance to make sure he's not sporting injuries from a fistfight. "You doing okay, there?"

He sighs. "Yeah. Just tired. Which, actually, before we start going through the folders," he taps the table lightly with his knuckles, "I saw the conference room filled with interns here for orientation. Have they all been assigned? Can I get one or two?"

I pull at my chin, taking in his haggard appearance. I could suggest we hire some more staff, but one of the things I like about our little VC group is that it's small. Streamlined. Efficient. I have no idea if all the interns are assigned, but I can definitely request one. A certain dark-haired beauty comes to mind.

I walk back over to my desk and press the intercom for Janet. "Yes, sir?" her voice rings out into the air.

"Janet, can you please have an intern assigned to the VC group? Actually, have two interns assigned to Ted. And then have Olivia Grayson assigned to me. She can help Ted and me in the VC group, but I have a project I could use some extra help on."

Ted's eyebrows raise in response to my request. Yeah, so what? I'm the CEO. I can pick my intern. After what we did to her this afternoon, treating her like a potential criminal, she should get to work with the CEO. Makes sense to me.

He hasn't seen Olivia yet. There's no reason for him to be suspicious. Of course, Ted's wife works in the marketing department. It's possible I deserve a raised eyebrow. The man might know more about where I'm coming from than I do.

Chapter 3

Olivia

I push open the door to White Horse Tavern. Almost all the wooden booths are full, and several patrons hover around the bar area, as expected on a Friday evening. Delilah waves above the crowd of heads to catch my attention. Her signature blonde bun bounces a bit on the top of her head. I head straight over.

"Hey, there, lady!" She bounds over, wraps me in a warm hug, and smiles as she leads the way back to our table.

I sit across from her and scan the tavern for a waitress. Any waitress will do, but after the day I've had, I want a drink, stat.

"Hi, girlie. What are you doing? I'm right here." Her hands float in the air, gesticulating as she speaks.

"Looking for a waitress. Maybe I should just walk up to the bar?"

"That kind of day, huh? Here, you can have my wine. I'm not too crazy about it. I should have remembered to stick to beer."

I understand what she's saying. The wine selection at the White Horse, while typical for a pub, could be mistaken for a two-buck chuck on most days. Palatable, but it's pretty much a guaranteed hangover in a glass.

I don't care. I take her glass and drink.

The waitress makes her way over, and Delilah orders us two pale ales then turns her attention to me. "What's going on? Bad day?"

"I don't know if I'd say it was bad. A bit stressful, I guess? Peculiar. Remember that guy I told you about?"

"The guy who might have been Matthew McConaughey?"

I huff and finish off her wine. "The guy who was *not* Matthew McConaughey. It turns out he's one of the founders of Esprit Transactions, where I have my internship."

"No shit! Oh, that is so cool! You guys are going to get to do naughty, awesome intern-boss sex stuff," she responds in loud rapid-fire while bouncing enough on the booth seat that the mass of hair on the top of her head wobbles back and forth.

I rest my forehead on my palm. I should probably order a bottle of wine. It doesn't matter if it's cheap crap. I'm gonna need it. "No, Delilah. No." I shake my head, emphasizing my answer while trying to refocus on what I was saying. "Not at all. I was actually taken into some room by security and interrogated. It seems he was at Columbia too. They thought I was a risk! As in, dangerous." The complete absurdity of the situation has me riled up. Yes, sometimes I'm mistaken for being ethnic, but come on, now.

"No shit. So, what happened?"

"This security dude pulled me into a room and asked me a lot of questions. I'm pretty sure he had a real gun in his holster. Which, is that normal?" I pound my fist on the table for effect. "Anyway, coffee shop guy came in and said I checked out."

"Did you get to talk to him?"

"Who?"

"Matthew McConaughey!"

"For the last time. He. Was. Not. Matthew McConaughey. His name's Sam Duke. Shook my hand and left. I was so flustered and angry by the time he walked in. I was, like, this close to quitting." I put my thumb and index finger together with little space between to be sure she got the point. "What kind of company treats its employees like that?" I toy with the empty wine glass while searching for the beer that has yet to arrive. "Do you think I'm overreacting?"

"Nope. Not at all. That's weird. Nothing about you says 'danger.'"

"Right?"

"Well, forget about today. It's Friday. And you are a grad student. An internship should not be getting you down, my friend. I do have a surprise for tonight." She flashes a row of pearly whites with her eager smile, bouncing a little as if she's trying to contain her excitement.

The waitress delivers our beers, and we pause our conversation until she's moved along to another table. "Let's hear it. What are we doing?"

"Scores!" she shouts and shoots her arms out into the air like a cheerleader.

I take a large gulp of my pale ale. A strip club? She cannot be serious.

"Got you." She points at me, laughing, sending her blonde bun jiggling all around the top of her head.

"Funny. Very funny."

"Nah, Anna and Jackson are joining us. That's my news. I don't have anything more exciting than that."

"Oh, well, that's cool. It'll be good to see them. I haven't seen them since that day we helped them move into their apartment." We'd spent the day up on their rooftop terrace, the only space Anna decorated since they'd had the place painted after closing. Anna, always a happy sort, radiated joy on moving day. Jackson and Anna moved the day after I returned from Prague. And the next day, Delilah helped me with my suitcases and got me settled into their old apartment, a.k.a. my pre-Prague apartment, vacated just in time. Kismet.

"Yeah. I'm stoked they live in Chelsea now. They're practically my neighbors."

"It might be time for me to look for a new apartment. Living on the east side isn't ideal when school and work are on the west side."

"You could move in with me. My place has plenty of room."

I play with the top of my drink. My girl is not lying. Blondie has an enormous, gorgeous apartment. There's no way she's not relying on parentals for that spacious pad. "While I do love your place, I think I've hit the stage where I want to live alone."

Her luminescent teeth shine under the overhead light. "Oh, I know. I love living by myself."

"Well, then, why did you ask?" I reach across the table and tap her arm to tease. "What if I had said yes?"

"Oh, I'd deal. I don't even know how much longer I'm going to be in New York, you know?"

"No! I didn't know this." I reach out and tap her elbow again to scold her.

"Yeah, my parents. And, well, my entire family, which consists of a boatload of people, expect me to move back to New Orleans. My mom keeps reminding me that my move to New York was about me *spreading my wings*." She air quotes the words.

Before I can respond, Anna surfaces through the crowded pub, wrapping her arms around Delilah from behind. "Hey, you guys!"

I move my beer and empty wine glass over beside Delilah so we can let the couple sit together. I was away when Anna found Jackson, so thinking of her as a couple is new to me, but it's a wonderful thing. Jackson slides in the booth across from me, while Anna and Delilah sit across from each other to chat about a campaign at Evolve, the ad agency where they work together.

Jackson absentmindedly rubs Anna's back and plays with her hair. He and I don't know each other well. "How's b-school treating you?"

"It's good so far. We're still in the first few weeks with kind of an overview focus. But after next week, our regular classes start, and I think I'll like it a lot. It's interesting. Good people. A lot of the professors have real-world experience, which I like."

"Yeah, I know what you mean. My favorite law professors were the ones who had actually practiced law. Are you doing an internship?"

I give him a dramatic sigh as thoughts of my afternoon in an interrogation room return. Delilah leans over with a wide smile. "Yeah, she is. Tell him what happened today." She nudges my arm as if she's trying to push me forward.

I roll my eyes. I doubt Jackson wants to hear all about my day. I shrug, and Jackson leans back, waiting for one of us to explain. "It's nothing, really. I didn't get great vibes from my internship today. We had orientation this afternoon. Paperwork, plus some general HR videos."

Delilah breaks in again. "They thought she was dangerous and pulled her into an interrogation room."

Now she has Anna's attention. "What?" Anna asks, eyes wide with disbelief.

I focus on Delilah, hoping to silently convey to her to stop talking about this, as I answer, "Yeah. It was just a strange coincidence. I ran into someone several times that day, and the security team seemed to read into it. It was odd but fine."

The waitress comes over to take our order, perfectly timed to transition the conversation. I'd have no issue sharing everything with Anna, but I don't really know Jackson. And I don't want Delilah relaying the story in a way that makes me look like some adolescent. She can be harebrained. In the last few weeks, I've grown to love her, but I don't trust her to be super aware of what might be embarrassing to her friends. Like mentioning my coffee shop fantasy.

After the waitress leaves, Jackson takes a sip of his beer. With an arm still behind Anna's back, he continues the conversation. "I wish I'd known you were looking for an internship. I could use an intern for the mergers and acquisitions consultancy group I'm heading up at my law firm. I'm kind of behind the eight ball on reaching out to the business schools."

"Why are you looking at business schools? Wouldn't you want interns from law schools?"

"Well, we have a full intern program for law students. But I'd like to get a business school student in who understands some of the business aspects of an M&A deal. A lot of what I need is someone to do research and complete reports."

Anna beams at Jackson. "This is a group Jackson's starting up on his own. He sees it as a business opportunity for the firm to offer more than just legal expertise."

I twist in my seat, a new interest in Jackson forming. I've been debating between business and law to some degree. And I've been wanting to do M&A and VC work. I catch Jackson's eye, aiming to address him the way I'd address a business colleague, not my old roommate's boyfriend. "First, I don't think you are too late to recruit interns. I do know some students are still searching for a good internship opportunity. But, if you'd consider me, I'd be very interested. I could email you my resume and come in to interview with anyone you'd like."

Jackson rubs his chin like he's thinking. "It's my group. There's no one you'd need to interview with. Do you think you could come in on Monday? You can bring your resume, and I can introduce you and take you through some of the work I'll need done. Then you can decide for sure."

"My classes are over by two p.m. Monday. I could head to your office right after that."

Jackson resumes playing with Anna's hair, but his brow wrinkles a bit. "So, would you do both internships? How much time could you give me?"

I sip my beer as I consider his question. I'm not feeling particularly loyal to Esprit Corp. "I'd drop the other internship. I hadn't actually started. They haven't even assigned me to a group yet. Today was an HR intro session for all new interns, and next week I'm supposed to find out what I'd be doing. It's a financial services company. I'm interested in M&A, so what you're considering doing is actually much more in line with my goals."

Anna leans in, putting her arm around Jackson and eliminating any space between the two of them. I can't stop myself from grinning at seeing her so happy. She kisses him on the check then says, "Okay, guys. Enough business. No more shop talk. It's Friday night."

"Hey, I'm done. No more shop talk. I just got myself a highly qualified and experienced intern, so I'm good." He raises an eyebrow and points at me. "But Monday, when you come in, we do need to talk about compensation."

"Yeah, no worries. I'm sure whatever you generally pay interns will work. It's the experience, not the money I'm after." My company paid for my apartment when I was abroad, and I had minimal living expenses, so I have a sizeable savings stockpiled now. My grandmother has a fund to pay for all her grandchildren's tuition expenses, so I'm not at all worried about my internship income. It's the experience I need if I'm going to pivot to another career.

Jackson bites his lower lip as he smirks. "You may need to work on your negotiating skills."

Anna softly punches his arm. "Hey, enough. What are you two doing tomorrow night? It's supposed to be a nice night, and we were thinking we'd grill out. Would you guys like to come over? Chase is gonna come."

I sip my beer. "Sounds good to me. I'm in."

Delilah shakes her head. "Sorry. I've actually got a date."

I turn to her in surprise. "With who?"

She shrugs nonchalantly. "A guy I met in the gym. No big deal."

Anna tilts her head and studies her for a moment. "Wait. This is, like, the third date with the guy from the gym."

"Oh, no. Third guy from the gym. All different guys. No third date." Delilah plays with the square drink coaster as she answers Anna.

Now it's my turn to continue asking questions. "You've had three different guys from the gym ask you out? What do you wear to the gym?"

Delilah scans the room, looking away from me, as if she's bored with the conversation. "Normal gym clothes. No make-up." She turns back to me, as if something just occurred to her. "What gym do you go to? Are the gyms in the upper east side filled with married guys? Why aren't you meeting guys at the gym?"

"I go to yoga. There aren't that many men in yoga," I answer. Everyone at our table is studying me. "What? I'm not looking for guys when I'm working out."

Delilah drones on, not willing to drop it. "Where do you lift weights?"

"I don't lift weights," I answer, annoyed.

"You really need to lift weights. It's important. You should do that at least three times a week," Delilah says as she holds up three fingers for extra clarification.

"I'm thinking about taking up kickboxing." There's a new place that opened two blocks from me.

Delilah wrinkles her nose. "That could work. You're still in your twenties. Hey, I know. I'll ask my date tomorrow night if he has any friends. Then we can double date. That would be fun."

I shake my head. "No. No, Delilah. I'm good. No blind dates needed. Trust me."

"Oh, no." She taps the side of her head. "I'm on it. You are beautiful. Stunning, in this striking what-tropical-island-is-she-from kind of way. I'm gonna find a guy for you."

I catch Anna's eye, and we both start laughing. "Fabulous." It's my olive skin. I've grown up standing out from my fair-skinned family. Throwback genes, my mom says. Or she had an affair. In my family, anything is possible.

Anna sits back and runs her finger up and down her pint, smearing the condensation. "You know, I don't think you have to worry about Olivia. Back when I lived with her, she had dates all the time."

"Come on. Not all the time. You're making me sound bad."

"No, really. Do you not remember? Pretty much every weekend. You also had several boyfriends."

"Several? Like, two or three," I bite back.

Anna grins, and everyone around the table sits back like they're at a comedy show, about to hear the big joke. Anna starts to count on her fingers. "Julian."

"No." I shake my head, resolute. "He doesn't count. We were never serious. Never *exclusive*." I emphasize *exclusive* to illustrate my point.

"Will. Damien." Ah, Damien. There's the rub. Yeah, I used to date guys every now and then. Before Damien.

I search the restaurant for our waitress. Shouldn't our food be here now?

Jackson, empty pint in hand, also scans for our absentee waitress. "That's three. Maybe we shouldn't put Olivia in the spotlight, guys? What do you say?"

Delilah tilts her head like she's studying me. It feels like she's about to embrace me or comfort me. What kind of vibes am I sending out? "Don't worry, darling. We'll get you back in the game."

Back in the game? Yeah, I haven't been dating, but I've been a frequent business traveler for the better part of the last two years. Nonbusiness travelers have romantic visions of business trips. Yes, I've visited major cities all over

36

Europe. But the trips eventually become a blur of hotels, conference rooms, and airports.

Anna taps me. "What's that smirk on your face for?"

I laugh. "I was just thinking about the last time a guy asked me out."

"Tell. Tell," Delilah chants, looking a bit like an excitable sorority girl eager to bond on a girls' night.

The memory has me rolling my eyes. Looking around the table, I grin, knowing this story will entertain. "Well, I was at this bar in London. I was about thirty minutes early before a business dinner, and so it's not like it was even late at night." Everyone is nodding, waiting for it. "This guy comes up, offers to buy me another drink, which I decline, but we talk. We do the small talk, you know." Everyone nods. They know how it goes. "I live in Prague. Yada, yada. Leaving soon for business school."

Delilah has a huge grin on her face and says, "Yeah," to prod the story on.

I sit back and take another swig of my beer. This is a good one. "He says he's an MBA too. So, I say, 'Yeah?' You know, being nice?" Everyone nods because, of course, what else would you say? "And then he grins and says, 'Married but available.'"

Delilah pulls back so far she's at risk of falling off the edge of the booth. "No."

I laugh at her dramatic reaction. "Yes. He goes on to tell me he's happy to meet up with me after my business dinner. In my hotel room."

At this point, everyone is shaking their heads.

"And, yes, my friends," I pause and pound the table for a drum roll effect, "that's been my dating life abroad."

Anna turns to Delilah. "Okay. We're both working on introducing her to some decent guys. It's time she gets back in the saddle stateside."

Back in the saddle, huh? Do I want to go through that again? I think I'd rather daydream.

Chapter 4

Olivia

On Monday morning, I find myself sitting at Manhattanville Coffee staring at my phone. The first item on my to-do list is to call Esprit and resign from my internship. Friday night, my decision came easily. Then my conscience had to wake up and weigh in.

On one hand, I'm completely within my rights to resign. I'm certain they can replace me without issue. The conference room had been packed with interns. I haven't even been assigned to a group, nor have I met anyone I'd be working with. Zero investment on anyone's part outside HR.

On the other hand, I committed to a semester internship. Quitting kind of goes against everything that's been ingrained into me since fifth grade. That year, I wanted to sign up for basketball, and after joining the team, I discovered my balls only met air. I spent every game seated, humiliated, on the bench. I begged to quit but was told "you made a commitment."

All weekend, I weighed the pros and cons. And it came down to it's just an internship. A low paying, menial job designed to let subservient peons get a glimpse into a company or industry. All the while doing grunt work no one else wants to do at minimum wage or for free.

Esprit seemed to think I looked like a psycho criminal. Yes, Sam Duke was lust-worthy, but the intern-boss thing never really happens in real life. And no matter how great it ends up in romance novels, there's no respect for colleagues who cross the line. It's a situation I'd be smart to not put myself into. Not that Sam Duke was interested in me. But if I worked there, wondering if I'd run into him in the halls and then did once in a while? I'd lose my dignity and flip into a giggly, starry-eyed schoolgirl. No, thank you. I've already traveled that path.

"You're new here, aren't you?" Damien asks, pulling out the chair and sitting down at the gray six-top circular table. I'm sitting with my supervisor and two women from the media department. My food sits on an orange tray. Damien doesn't notice the other women at the table, but out of the corner of my eye, my boss frowns.

I hold out my hand and say, "Yes. I'm an assistant account executive. This is my first week. I'm Olivia."

When he shakes my hand, he holds it firmly and rubs his thumb across the back. The movement sends tingles down my spine, and my cheeks warm. Damien's suit fits him well, and I have no idea if he's my level or falls much higher in the organization.

"I'm a designer in the studio. I'm Damien. I'll keep an eye out for you." He stares at me like a hungry predator, and I can't look away. Before he leaves, I giggle. In front of my new boss, I giggle and bat my eyelashes.

The memory floods me with mortification. Back then, I was fresh out of college and had no idea how to handle a handsome man flirting with me. I had no idea what other women would think of me or how the gossip mill within a business worked. Now, I'm older and more experienced.

I tap my phone and call my contact at Esprit HR, a lovely woman named Ms. Merryman. "Oh, I understand. No problem. Can you tell me your name again? Thank you for letting us know." Then, nothing. I hold my phone out to view the screen and double-check that the call disconnected. Who knew turning down an internship is easier than canceling a credit card?

Almost instantaneously, I feel better. Lighter. Stress-free. After classes, I take the subway down to Chambers Street to get to Jackson's offices. Goldwater, Brooke, and Associates occupies four floors in a building on 195 Broadway. The building once housed the headquarters for American Telephone and Telegraph. I learned that tidbit when searching for the location.

I'm not sure what to expect when I open the door, but I definitely didn't expect the modern lobby that greets me. An elaborate structure of thin brass pipes covers the ceiling. Edison lightbulbs adorn the ends of the pipes. The polished concrete floor and iron stairwell are industrial. Light pours in through the windows. I could definitely get used to working here.

The elevator opens on the fifteenth floor. As I greet the curly redhead behind the reception desk, Jackson steps around the corner. "Hey, there, great timing."

I give Jackson a polite hug, the kind of restrained courtesy hug common in the workplace. He's looking at me like we're friends, but I'd prefer everyone here not know we are. Although, it's an internship. I need to remember that too. It doesn't really matter. I'm here for the experience, not to climb a ladder. I'm not even a lawyer.

I follow Jackson into a conference room. The walls are glass, so the only privacy offered in the room is sound.

41

Jackson sits down and looks at his watch. "We have about thirty minutes before a client is coming in. What do you say I take you through an overview of the kinds of reports I need help with? If you feel ready, then I'll introduce you to the client."

"Sounds good."

Jackson's entire career has centered on mergers and acquisitions. He's not the kind of lawyer you call when you get a speeding ticket or a DUI. Acquisitions are his specialty, and he's kind of made a name for himself. He dives deeper than most lawyers by thinking through all the business angles. Sometimes he arrives at a completely different solution for the client or a novel and unexpected way to acquire a company.

Jackson walks me through the folders on the table. In a nutshell, he wants me to do the legwork for a client. Collect and analyze extensive data on the GPS market and industry. Complete an analysis of financial performance.

One of his clients is considering either investing in or acquiring the company. The client's interested in emerging tracking technologies, but he's not so enamored with the hardware business. The first step is understanding the company's strategic position in the marketplace. More or less an MBA student's wet dream.

If the client wants to move forward, I'd start working on valuations and financial forecasts. It's the business angle Jackson loves. It's no surprise he's campaigned to create this M&A consultancy within his firm.

He's impassioned as he takes me through everything. He's animated, and there's an understated excitement to his words. I can see why he puts in long hours. He loves what he does. I want that.

A knock sounds at the door. "Ah, Olivia, meet our client."

My mouth drops open. No way. Sam Duke. Mr. Coffee Shop Man.

His head angles sideways, like maybe he's surprised too. He rubs his palm over his mouth. He's definitely caught off guard, because he doesn't speak.

I can't stop staring at him. The tips of my fingers chill. I rub my hands together to warm them and notice they feel clammy.

Jackson breaks the awkward moment. "Hey, Sam. Are you such a regular now they don't even have us greet you at reception?"

Jackson's grinning. He walks around the table to shake Sam's hand. Sam glances at Jackson but keeps his focus on me. He unabashedly inspects me, seemingly oblivious to Jackson's presence. "I'm sorry to interrupt. Should I wait outside?"

Jackson raps Sam's shoulder the way a quarterback would pat the back of a teammate. "Yeah, man, if you'd give me a minute. I've got to finish things up. It will only take a minute."

Sam backs into the hall, Jackson closes the conference room door, and I catch his eye. "I'm in. If that's what you want to ask me, I'm in."

Jackson stretches his shoulders back, a huge grin on his face. "That's great. We'll talk details later." Then he opens the door for Sam, standing in the hall, watching us through the glass, and welcomes him back into the conference room. "Sam, meet the newest addition to our team, Olivia Grayson."

Sam rubs his chin. He smirks. Is he aware I resigned from his company today? After last week, he could be wondering if I'm an ultra-sophisticated stalker. Like I somehow knew he had a meeting here today and wormed my way in. As if.

He holds out his hand to shake mine. A self-conscious wave floats over me as he holds on a tad longer than necessary and tilts his head to the side. "Ms. Grayson, we meet again."

Jackson asks, "Do you guys know each other?"

I want to tell Jackson that this is Mr. Coffee Shop, but I don't think he'd get the reference. He won't get it because I never told him and Anna the whole story. Did I? I can't remember. I try to avoid oversharing.

As I'm standing there trying to figure out the best way to explain to Jackson, Sam speaks up. "Well, yes. I thought she was going to be interning with us, but I found out from HR she resigned." He turns to question me. "Is this why you resigned? To come and work here?"

Sam has taken a seat at the head of the conference table. He looks amused. Not angry.

Sam's wearing jeans and the same cowboy boots. He doesn't sound like he's from Texas, but he speaks slower than New Yorkers. He's a business guy, but he looks like he'd be at home on a baseball field, or on a horse, or anywhere outside. It's that sunbaked skin and dimples and care-free, wavy hair.

Jackson squints and pointedly looks down at me. A little too late, I realize they were both expecting me to answer. "Olivia, did I steal you from Esprit Corp?" He's grinning, so he doesn't seem annoyed. Bastard looks entertained.

I lift my chin and attempt a courteous answer. "Yes, my original internship was with Esprit Transactions. Mr. Duke,

I do apologize. When this internship came through, it felt like an ideal opportunity. I couldn't turn it down. Since I hadn't yet been assigned to a group in your company, I felt I could resign without any—"

Sam raises his arm and interrupts. "Wait, now. You hadn't been assigned to a group yet?" I stare back, uncertainty rising with his ire. As I brace myself for the worst, he throws his hands in the air. "Look, never mind. I'm not angry. This guy probably offered you better pay. I haven't checked on what we're paying out interns, but I'm sure it's chicken feed. You're still gonna be working for me." He looks between Jackson and me. "Didn't mean to put you guys on the defensive. I'm good. This may be even better, actually." He studies me, and one dimple appears with a slight smile.

My cheeks are on fire. For once, I am grateful for my olive skin. Otherwise, I'm sure my cheeks would be flaming red.

Jackson sits at the table and pulls up a folder. It's one of the folders he hasn't yet shared with me. He directs Sam's attention to a piece of paper that lists several items on it as I pull out a chair to join them at the table. "These are some of the first steps I'm proposing. Olivia's going to be point person on research, and if we get to it, the evaluation."

Jackson sits back in his chair, waiting to see what Sam says to that.

Sam reads the list and looks up. "Sounds good to me. I'll have some of my interns doing similar work, so we can compare. If you hadn't stolen this one, she'd be the one doing the work on my end."

His smile is big. Those dimples might be the end of me. Sitting here, so close to him, bathed in natural light, for the first time I see the color of his eyes. A smoky blue. Insane. I've never seen that color blue before. He runs his hand through his hair and gives me a knowing look, as if he knows my thoughts aren't professional. Women probably fawn over this man everywhere he goes, and that thought has me sitting straighter and reaching for a pen to take notes.

After the two men further discuss all items to be uncovered during the research phase, Jackson taps his fist twice on the table. "Sounds like a plan. Olivia, let me introduce you to Joel, one of our paralegals. He can get you acquainted with Westlaw and LexisNexis." Then he directs his attention to Sam. "Do you mind waiting for a minute in my office?"

Sam stands and says, "No problem. I have a call I need to make. Nice to see you again, Olivia. Good to have you on the team, even if it is on my legal team."

I stand and look him in the eye and give a professional, curt nod. "Thank you, Mr. Duke."

He raises his arm with a stop motion. "No, call me Sam." He visibly peruses my body, and almost to himself, he mutters, "You should definitely call me Sam."

My skin tingles as if he physically touched me. I turn my attention to the table and the folders. He takes three steps toward the door, and I find it easier to breathe.

Sam reaches the door and turns, rubbing the back of his neck. "Ahm, Jackson, do you mind if I take a minute to speak to Olivia?"

Jackson looks between us. The request catches him off guard, and I can tell from the look he's giving me, he's trying to decide if I'm okay with it.

I speak up to put Jackson at ease. "It's fine." I'm uncertain what Sam will say, but I expect further questions about why I quit his company.

"Okay. I'll be down the hall in my office." Jackson exits, but I notice he leaves the conference room door open. Maybe he's listening to see if he needs to come save me.

Sam takes a couple of steps in my direction. His right dimple pops as he kind of chews on his lower lip. I brace myself. He puts both palms down flat on the table and leans toward me.

"So, you were gonna be on my team. Just so you know. I requested you. But I wasn't bullshitting when I said I think I like this better."

I shift my shoulders back to display perfect posture and hold my breath.

"I like this better, because it'll make asking you out on a date a whole lot easier."

Fuck me. Not at all what I thought he was going to say.

He tilts his head, and his dimple disappears. "I know we didn't get off to a great start. I would have talked to you back at that coffee shop, but you looked too young. Now I know your age. And I'd really like to take you to dinner."

I swallow. I breathe. Sure, he's a good-looking guy. But is this okay? I bite my thumbnail as I consider the potential ramifications of saying yes. We might have some great dates. But then I'd come out of a restroom while the waitress is giving him her number. Or I'd turn the corner at a dance club, and he'd be in the hall receiving a blow job.

He steps back from the table and stands tall. "You can let me know later if you want. I don't want to pressure you."

I focus on my breathing to rebound from his direct question. "Does this mean you no longer believe I'm a threat?"

He smiles in a way that disarms. "No threat. At least, not in a way that's gonna require security."

I return his smile as I lean down to grip the edge of the table. "Dinner sounds…" I pause, searching for the right word, "nice. Let me check with Jackson. I've no idea what the company policy would be, if they have stipulations regarding dating clients." I exhale. There. That sounds like a solid response. I'll tell Jackson to say he doesn't think it's a good idea. Working together won't be an issue. It's not me turning him down.

A grin spreads across his face, and both dimples are back. I forget to breathe for a moment. He's so freaking gorgeous. "Let me handle Jackson. He'll be fine with it. How's this Friday?"

A dizzy sensation hits me. I blurt, "I'm busy this weekend." Where did that come from? It's only Monday, and I haven't given the weekend any thought whatsoever. But Sam's too gorgeous. He's probably right; Jackson will likely be fine with us going out on a date. But after my past experience, next time around I plan to aim for men a little lower down the hotness scale. Find someone who isn't a master on the playing field.

Sam bites the corner of his lip and studies me, like he's trying to decide if he's going to let me get away with stalling. "Okay. Well, maybe one night next week." He winks at me as he exits.

Chapter 5

Sam

Three soft taps on my office door break my attention from my laptop. My vision blurs as it adjusts from staring at code on my computer screen.

"Jan, it's okay. Come on in." I know it's my assistant because she's the only one who knocks at my door. Anyone else would be announced by Janet via my desk telephone. Janet's the only reason I still have a desk phone. I can push one button and speak to her, and she can respond via intercom.

Janet walks up to my desk and stands, holding a file, notepad, and pen. She's the most efficient executive assistant I've ever had. All business, she taps her pen against the notepad. I'd bet a hundred bucks that notebook has a list in it, and she's tapping the first item on her list.

"I made reservations for you and Jason at Pisticci. Six-thirty. Is that okay?" She's asking because that's earlier than I'd normally meet him. It will take at least thirty minutes to make it up to Harlem.

"Yeah, that's fine. Pisticci, though? I figured he'd just want to meet at Mel's. And I'm surprised we need reservations, anyway. This was his idea? Did you speak to him?"

She pulls her shoulders back and immediately looks like she's about to face a firing squad.

I stop her before she can answer by putting my hand up and saying, "Don't get defensive, Jan. I don't care where we eat. I want to know, though, did you speak to him? Or was this all via text?"

"Yes, I spoke to him." Wrinkles line up along her upper lip, her tell that she wants to bop me upside my head.

"How did he sound?" I ask. Her lips instantly relax.

"He didn't sound good."

I rub the underlying tight muscles on my temples. This isn't an easy situation. Jason finished post-remission therapy some time back, and we've been waiting to hear if he's in full remission. I'm optimistic, but Jason is one pessimistic guy.

"Okay. What else you got for me?"

Janet's pen moves a little farther down the page before she stops. In a voice that makes her sound like a concerned mother, she asks, "Is he doing okay?"

Janet isn't one to pry. I like her for that. But over the years she's gotten to know my family. My mom sends her a Christmas gift each year. My brothers sometimes take her to lunch when they come to town. And Jason, well, he's like a brother to me. He's pretty fond of Janet too.

My brothers and I met Jason during a ski trip one Christmas break. We were in Vail. My dad overheard an instructor telling Jason's dad ski school had no openings. My dad must've seen that Jason was around the same age as his gaggle of boys, so he told him he could put his son in with us. The four of us skied together that day and then every day for the rest of the break. For years, Jason skied with us, even once we stopped skiing with instructors.

Jason's parents both passed away his sophomore year of high school. Skiing, of all things. Some people were skiing where they shouldn't and caused an avalanche. He was a boarding school kid, so that part of his life didn't change after his parents' death. But my parents stepped in and made sure he spent every break with us. Summers too. During college, he came back to my house more than I did for breaks, because, well, my parents' home is his home now too.

Freshman year of college, Jason was diagnosed with non-Hodgkin's lymphoma. He's been through one crazy bull ride. He's been in partial remission at times, then had to go through another whole round of chemo, radiation. I can see he's in a down cycle. Even with all that crap, he has his PhD and is an assistant professor at Columbia University. Pretty fucking impressive, if you ask me.

I look Janet in the eye. No need to sugar coat it. "I don't know if he's doing okay or not. That's why I wanted to hear how he sounded. He's seemed so…" I rub my hand through my hair, trying to come up with the right words. "It's like he's given up. If he gets bad results, I found a clinical trial for him, but he's not so into it. It's like he's ready to throw in the towel, and we are nowhere near the end of the game."

It's so frustrating. I want to shake him sometimes. Things I control are so much easier to deal with, and I have absolutely no control here. Helpless isn't a feeling that sits right with me.

"Sam, did you hear me?" My blank expression must serve as an answer, because she continues. "I said there's no point in either of you worrying until you get those results back. If they aren't good, make sure he brings you in with him when he meets with his doctor to discuss next steps. That's all you can do."

She then proceeds to check off her list as I half-listen.

The plan was to meet at the restaurant, but I notify my driver I need him now, then shoot off a text to security to let them know I'll be on the move. I grimace when I contact security. The whole situation pisses me off, but as long as they stay out of my way, I can deal. After all required parties are notified, I head on up to Columbia. I can't wait any longer. If he got bad news, he'll want to tell me face to face, so I'll bring my face to him.

******

Jason's office is rather small, and the whole room has a sterile feel. The standard issue metal desk he's sitting behind might be from the sixties. The off-white walls are marred by light gray scratches and smudges. Supposedly, there are security cameras throughout campus, but I have yet to locate one in the halls of this building, and there's definitely not one in Jason's hole of an office. I tap on his half-open door, and his head jerks up from the papers he's grading.

I put a big smile on my face. The smile does not reflect my inner turmoil, anxiety, or worry, but it's what I think he needs, so I smile. "Hey, man!" I walk right on in like I own the place and plop myself down in one of two wooden chairs across from his desk.

"I thought we were meeting at six-thirty? At the restaurant." His brow wrinkles in confusion.

"Yep, that was the plan. But I wanted to get out of my office. Figured I'd come down and see if I could convince you to swing by Ten Twenty for a drink before dinner."

He lifts his arm off the desk and checks the watch on his wrist, shoulders slouched forward in a defeatist position. All his movements are slow. Damn. "If you need to stay here and finish grading papers, that's fine. I have my laptop with me. I can work right from here, and we can head over to Pisticci's whenever you're ready."

Jason stares vacantly in my general direction. It's too much for me, so I peer down at his desk and notice the black and white name holder. The white font reads "Dr. Longevite," but someone has taken a pencil and darkened parts of the loops of the o and e's. "Someone's been messing with your nameplate, man."

"What?" He sounds somewhat confused.

"This nameplate right here." I pick it up and turn it to him so he can see.

Jason taps the eraser end of a pencil on the desk, apathetic to what I'm showing him. "Probably a student. Probably did it while I was sitting right here talking to them, and I didn't even realize it." He leans back into his bulky wooden office chair. It's on wheels, which is the chair's only redeeming feature that I can see. Nothing about that chair is ergonomically correct. He sighs. "If you're here to find out if I've gotten the results back, I haven't. I promise I'll tell you when I do. Should be any day."

"Hey, man, I know you'll tell me. You seemed a little down, so I thought my smiling face might cheer you up."

A blank face stares back at me. No emotion. It's like he didn't even hear me. I don't know what's going on with him, but I know it's not good. I'm on the verge of carrying him out of this sad-as-fuck interior office when he speaks. "You don't need to worry about me. There's nothing you can do, anyway, so don't expend the energy."

"Are you out of your goddamn mind? That makes no sense."

He looks away from me to the blank wall. Stacks of books and piles and piles of folders sit along the floor. A good gift might be hiring someone to come in and organize all those messy piles.

"Enough about me." He taps his desk with his knuckle. "Really. Enough. Can we not talk about me tonight? Please?" His eyes glisten, and more emotion rings through his voice than I've heard from him in ages.

"You got it, man." My first instinct is to reach down and pull out my laptop. Scan through to look and see if there's a game I can put on to watch while he grades papers. But then I think about a certain student of his, and I grin. "Did you know that one of your students is an intern of mine?"

He studies me while shaking his head. I can tell he's wondering where I'm going with this.

"Olivia Grayson. Do you know her?"

His fingers flick over the corner of one of the stacks of papers on his desk. "Yeah, I know her."

I think he's going to say more, but he doesn't. He rests his arms on the chair while he stares at one of the haphazard piles on his desk.

"What's she like?" I ask. Might as well see what information I can get out of him. Anything to keep a conversation going on something other than his health.

He looks up and squints. "Is that why you're asking me about her? I thought you might be preparing to ask me to do something nefarious."

I laugh out loud. "Nefarious? What the…? What do you mean by that?"

"She's having trouble with accounting." A smile breaks out on his face, the first one I've seen in ages. "You planning to hit on your intern?"

"That sounds bad, doesn't it?" I smirk. "She's not actually my intern. We hired her, but she quit. Turns out she took a job working for one of the law firms I work with. Small fucking world, huh?"

54

Jason puts both elbows on the table again, but this time he actually looks entertained. Alive. "Yeah. But you work with half the law firms in Manhattan. I guess odds were she'd end up working with one that works for you in some capacity."

I point at him. "That is a huge exaggeration."

"I doubt it. Anyway, you asked about her. She's smart. Good student. Doesn't have an accounting background. I haven't paid much attention to her, but now that I know she's your love interest, I will."

This guy must be seriously in his head these days if he didn't take more notice of Olivia. She's stunning. Those eyes. Showstoppers. "Well, I've only asked her out on a date. And when I did, she told me she was busy. All fucking weekend. I asked her out on a Monday."

"You losing your charm?" The smirk on his face makes me grin too.

"Nah. I've still got game. And you know me, I love a challenge. I'll float some date ideas by you over dinner. I'll get her to give me a chance. Eventually. I'm not one to give up." Out of all my buddies, Jason comes up with some of the most unique date plans. Or at least he used to. Back in the day, before cancer hit him, he was known for memorable dates. Things like painting dates, horseback riding, planetarium. Never an ordinary dinner and a movie. Always something out of the ballpark.

Yep, shoot two birds with one stone. Make Jason think about something else. Simultaneously plan an unforgettable date with a dark-haired stunner. My kind of night.

Chapter 6

Olivia

Standing outside Anna and Jackson's doorway Saturday evening, I struggle like a circus juggler with a loaded grocery bag, wine, and cake. Grappling with it all, I almost spill the bourbon salted caramel cake I purchased from Billy's Bakery. I can't get a hand free, so I bang my elbow on the door, creating a low thud. Sharp pain shoots through the bone in my arm, so I switch to kicking the door.

Minutes pass before the door swings open. "Hey, whoa." Jackson springs into action, lifting the cake box first.

"Hey, I know I'm early. I bought all the stuff for the charcuterie, but I need to put it together. Do you mind if I head to your kitchen?" I shake my right hand to encourage blood flow to return.

"No problem. Anna will be out in a minute. I'm gonna jump in the shower. Chewie needed to go for a walk." Anna and Jackson have the most adorable labradoodle. She was Anna's, and if it wasn't for Chewie, they probably wouldn't have ended up together. Jackson encouraged Anna to transition from walking Chewie to running with the apartment-bound dog. I was in Prague during all of this, but even from afar, it quickly became apparent that Jackson was more than a running coach.

I head into the kitchen and start pulling out my ingredients for the charcuterie. Anna has a dream kitchen. The countertops are all Carrera marble. The white shaker cabinets with antiqued brass knobs are my favorite, although

I covet her sea glass tile backsplash. The kitchen opens up into the great room with a pass-through bar. After I unpack my bags, I survey everything spread out on the counter and decide I might have gone a little overboard at Zabar's today.

"Hey, you!" I hear Anna's cheerful voice before I see her. She comes around the corner and wraps me in a warm hug. Taking a step back, she peers into the bag I brought. "What all did you bring?"

I pull out my board, a large slab of walnut hand-hewn by an artisan from the Hudson Valley. I love the deep, rich browns along the grain pattern and the curved, natural flowing edges. "Well, I kind of did the normal. Prosciutto, pate, salami, olives, found some fresh figs, dried pears, jam, brie, a golden cheese." I artfully arrange thin peppered crackers in one section of the board while I talk. "And I know not everyone loves foie gras, but Zabar's had the most gorgeous terrine. Sound good?"

"Sounds delicious. I have lasagna in the oven but haven't started it yet. Needs a little over an hour in the oven, but figured I'd wait until everyone is here to start it." She picks up the wine I brought over and studies it.

"I didn't go fancy on wine. Zabar's had the Decoy cab on sale for, like, twenty bucks, so I figured I'd go for quantity tonight."

"You brought four bottles?" Her gaze runs along the counter, and she sees the cake box. "And cake? You know, you don't have to bring so much food when you come here. You make me feel bad."

"Well, I know how our group can get. I want to contribute so you and Jackson don't start turning us away." Truthfully, I kind of live for these weekend nights at their place. It's more lowkey than a restaurant. We've been enjoying their amazing rooftop, but tonight the weather has turned chilly. October is letting us know winter is on its way. I'm kind of hoping we stay inside, at least until I've had a couple of glasses of wine.

"Tonight, it's only four of us, and it looks like you brought enough for eight. But it's okay." Anna pulls out salad ingredients from the refrigerator and lines them up on the island. "We'll just save any leftovers for next weekend. Most of your charcuterie stuff saves."

"Who's coming tonight?" I hadn't asked, but I'd assumed it would be our normal crew.

"It's just us and this guy Jackson has been working with. A client." I pause from layering the three different kinds of salami. I turn to Anna, but her back's to me as she chops away, so she doesn't know my mouth dropped open. She continues. "Delilah and Chase had other plans. They both have dates. First date dates." She turns her head with a smile, sees my face, and whips around. "What's wrong?"

"Who is the guy coming over?"

Her smile goes from normal to enormous. "Someone you know. And someone who asked Jackson if it's okay if he asks you out."

"Motherfucker!" A mixture of annoyance and panic rises within me. Anna starts laughing but turns her back to me, dismissing my alarm in favor of finishing up her salad.

"I haven't met him yet, but Jackson has talked so much about him I feel like I already know him. He seems to love working on his projects. I don't exactly understand everything they do, but I can tell Jackson's happy. And it's awesome he told Jackson he wants to date you. He likes you. It's so sweet."

"Anna! You couldn't have given me a heads up? Told me he was coming? Asked if I was okay with it?"

Anna spins around. "Are you not okay with it? Do you not like him?"

I resume work on my board and huff. This is fucking crazy. I don't like being set up on dates, and Anna, of all people, knows this. I've gone years being her one friend who didn't annoy the crap out of her by trying to force her on bad blind dates. "It's not that. I would have liked a heads up. That's all."

Anna brushes past me and opens a bottle of wine. Smart move. The buzzer sounds, and she sets the wine bottle on the counter and heads to the door so she can buzz him up. I get to work on unwrapping the cheeses. The last plastic cheese wrapper won't unwrap. Frustrated, I toss the block of cheese on the counter then pour myself a large glass of wine since Anna never finished the task. I give myself what I like to call an "American" pour, filling the glass far too close to the rim. Then I swallow a large gulp.

As I drink my wine, I stare out through the window. Lights flicker in random apartments, a scene not too different from the view from my place in Prague. How many nights had I sat, staring out my window there? Sort of wishing I had friends to go out with. Feeling like a bit of a lame ass on a Saturday night, weighing my option of staying in or going out alone. So many months, I stayed in. Ordered in. Then, one night, I'd had enough of the solitary confinement.

I got dressed, did my hair, and headed out, Kindle in tow. Ordered wine, similar to what I'm drinking now, and ordered dinner. Simply being surrounded by other human beings had felt cathartic. That first day, I'd felt awkward and self-conscious. Like people were looking at me and wondering what was wrong with the friendless woman alone on a Saturday night. The more I did it, the less I cared what anyone else thought. The sensation of judgmental gazes on my back diminished as I came to realize *no one cared*. And I even met people. Interesting people of all ages. All on my own.

I set my wine glass down and resume work on unwrapping the last block of cheese, using my knife to pierce the thick plastic wrapping. Had I known he'd be here tonight, I might have had my hair blown out or spent a little more time on my make-up. I'm wearing jeans and a somewhat thick sweater, and I'm in my socks because I took my shoes off at the door. My hair has been in a ponytail for hours, and if I let it down now, it won't hang straight. This is not exactly putting my best foot forward. In fact, he may see me and think I'm trying to communicate a lack of interest. *Stellar friendship, Anna.* It's all fine. Perhaps it's for the best if he loses interest. Sam's gorgeous, confident, and has articles written about him in major magazines. The last good-looking, confident guy I dated ended up being a lying cheat. And he was a fraction as successful in business as Sam.

Sam's deep Texan timbre echoes through the hall. Jackson's heavy footsteps resonate from the other end of the apartment and continue down the hall to the entry.

After a few more minutes, as I'm finishing up, the three of them exit the entry hall and enter the great room. I'm in the kitchen, and Sam and I lock eyes through the opening between the two rooms. I hold my breath, caught off guard. Sam's wearing faded jeans, cowboy boots, and a waffled cotton Henley that shows off shapely pecs and biceps. The Henley sleeves are pulled up a bit, revealing light hair on his forearms and a leather wrapped bracelet on his right wrist. Weekend Sam. An electrical charge surges through me, and I hold the counter, suddenly uncertain about how to greet him or what to say.

His white teeth glimmer in the kitchen light as he smiles. "Olivia? It's so good to see you again." He steps up to me and places a light kiss on my cheek. My stomach flutters, and heat cascades from my cheeks down to my chest. "Seeing you again makes my weekend."

I cast a glance down to his boots and swallow, then remember my wine and search the counter for it.

Sam takes a step back. "Damn! Look at this spread. Did you do this?" His expression is one of wonder, like he can't believe I could put this together. It's really the easiest thing in the world to prepare, which is why I always do it. But his reaction makes me feel like I'm Julia Child.

I nod and look up at him, feeling self-conscious. "It's kind of my thing."

"The charcuterie board is completely her thing. No one rocks a charcuterie like Olivia," Anna comments as she bypasses us to push buttons on the stove. "Here, why don't you guys put that on the table? We can munch on it while we drink wine. We have a little over an hour before the lasagna will be ready."

Sam picks up the board and leads us to the kitchen table, calling over his shoulder, "I brought wine too. Let's finish the bottle you guys are drinking and then we'll open up one of mine."

I gather the wine glasses and see the two bottles he brought over. Stag's Leap. I recognize the label. He has solid taste in wine.

The rectangular table seats eight, but Anna has pulled some chairs away. It's clear from the place settings the four of us will be sitting at the center of the table, two on each side. Anna and Jackson sit together on one side, and Sam and I are on the other. It feels like we are having that first date this weekend after all.

Sam's light brown hair looks darker, maybe a little damp, and the skin on his jaw looks especially smooth. A hint of cedar floats past when he leans in. The Henley he's wearing hugs his biceps, and he straddles the seat with his legs wide. He's a city boy, but so much about him says country. A cowboy hat is the only thing missing from his ensemble.

"Sam, where are you from?"

He grins as he cocks his head at me. "You don't think I'm from here?"

I shake my head and take a sip of wine. My eyes are locked on his smoky blues, and my body temperature rises.

"Well, you got me. I'm from Texas."

"I knew it!"

He chuckles. "What do you mean, you knew it? I've worked hard to hide that accent."

I twirl the wine in my glass, a wide smile on my face. "I don't know. I can't really tell you exactly what says Texas. The moment I saw you in that coffee bar, it was the first thing that came to mind. That you were from Texas. That you looked like you should be on a horse. And you know, the ever-present cowboy boots."

"Well, you're right. I should be on a horse. It's one of my happy places. Grew up on a ranch outside of Austin. And after another glass of wine my Texas twang will come right on out. In terms of the boots, you can't knock 'em until you try 'em. Once you wear a pair in, about the only thing more comfortable is flip flops."

I stare at the worn brown leather on his feet. "I like that you're so comfortable in casual clothes." Some men—my uncle, for example—are lost when it comes to dressing in anything other than a suit. I've seen my uncle in pressed shorts and black dress socks on a weekend summer afternoon.

He sips his wine. "Yeah, I guess I do tend to be pretty casual. You've got to remember, though, I started as a coder, and no one cares what programmers wear. And, as we grew, other casual tech leaders gained prominence. You know, Steve Jobs, Mark Zuckerberg. My company is successful. I have yet to find an investor or board member or client with more interest in what I'm wearing than in what I can do for them. But for years up here in New York, I did try to temper my accent."

"I don't think there's any reason to hide your natural accent." My cheeks burn as I stare at him. It's like we are the only two people in the room, but we are not, and I don't want to be rude, so I turn to Anna. "Don't you both agree?"

Anna grins, a knowing, teasing look directed at me, while Jackson responds. "I can see why you'd hide it at first. My Virginia accent isn't quite as noticeable as a Texas accent, but it still stands out. I kind of keep it in check too." Jackson swirls the wine in his glass. "But now, you've made it. I would think you could speak with any accent you chose."

"Yeah, you're probably right. But now it's habit." Sam shifts and taps his wine glass lightly to mine. "So, where are you from? Somewhere I'm guessing there was no accent to hide."

"Connecticut."

"I coulda pegged that."

"Why?"

"You're clean cut, elegant."

"You think this outfit is elegant?" That thought makes me laugh. Elegant is the last thing I'm feeling.

Anna breaks into the conversation. "Oh, Olivia, he has you so pegged. You're the most elegant woman I know. I always feel like I'm a hippie chick next to you."

"Bohemian is your style. That doesn't make me elegant."

She grins and points at me. "No. You make you elegant. You don't even realize you do it. Even when you dress down, you're put together. Everything fits. That sweater you're wearing fits you perfectly at the hips. Your hair might be in a ponytail, but you don't have a single stray hair out of place. And even though you aren't wearing make-up, you have a natural glow. You could have just finished a photo shoot."

I sip my wine while listening to Anna's heated diatribe. "It sounds like you've thought a lot about this."

Anna laughs. "I have!"

Jackson picks up Anna's hand and lays a gentle kiss on it. "You each have a distinct sense of style. Both of you are beautiful." His hand slides below the table, and Anna's cheeks flush.

Sam holds up his wine glass. "I'll toast to that. To the two most beautiful, stunning women I've seen in quite a long time."

"Now I can hear the Texas twang coming out. I guess that means the BS starts flowing too," I tease.

"Oh, no. Honesty. Ply me with alcohol, and you get honest Sam."

We stare at each other, grinning. This time it's Jackson who chooses to break into the conversation. "So, Olivia, I don't think I've heard much about your trip to Prague. You traveled all around, right? Any favorite places?"

Everyone directs their attention to me. "Yes, I loved Prague. But my favorite place?" I gaze up to the ceiling while I mentally run through all the places I went. "I kind of love Edinburgh most. But, in all fairness, that's the only place I went for holiday, not work. And, you know, when you're in a place for work, I don't think you give it a fair go. And I traveled so much for business, all the places kind of blend together at a certain point, you know?"

Sam leans back in his chair, positioning himself so he's close to me yet can see me entirely, even my socked feet. "I completely get that. I've been on so many dog and pony shows through the years." He twirls the rich red liquid in his glass. "Where all did you go? And when was this?"

Anna jumps in. "Oh, she just got back. She was away for almost two years."

"Why Prague?" He doesn't sound surprised, more curious, like it's a question he's been wondering for a while. It's on my resume. I doubt seriously the CEO ever sees the interns' resumes, though.

I brush off the Prague question because I'm not proud of the answer. My uncle set me up with the job. Instead, I choose to answer the *where* question. "Let's see. My list." I start counting on my fingers. "Paris, London, Dublin, Budapest, Berlin, Madrid, Lisbon, Barcelona, Rome, Moscow, Amsterdam, Stockholm, Copenhagen, Vienna." I know I'm leaving some out, but at a certain point, it sounds too pompous.

"You did a regular European tour, huh?"

"Yeah. It was kind of nonstop." I tap my short, polished nails against the wine glass. "Sometimes it was new business, sometimes existing clients. Sometimes meeting with other people within our agency. The agency I worked in is part of a worldwide conglomerate."

We all continue talking, swapping stories about trips we've taken.

The oven buzzer rings. Anna jumps up, and I follow her to help. Jackson clears away the charcuterie while Sam opens another bottle of wine. As I put the salad bowl down in the middle of the table, Sam hovers near my side, and a current runs between us. In a hushed voice, not quite a whisper, he says, "When we go out on our date, I want to hear a lot more."

His lips are so close I'm tempted to brush mine against his. He tilts his head down, his blues closer to mine than they've ever been, our bodies almost touching.

Jackson walks around the corner, oven mitts on, carrying the lasagna. Sam and I break apart like two kids caught in a kissing game. Anna brushes past Jackson with a hot plate to set down on the table.

Sam pulls my chair back for me to sit down. Ever so briefly, after pushing the seat under me, he squeezes my shoulder. A tender caress. A quick moment that once again takes my breath away and leaves me tingling and warm.

The melted cheese on the lasagna bubbles. Marinara sauce drips over the sides of the thick, white casserole dish. Like a good hostess, Anna suggests we start with the salad while the lasagna settles. She stands and spoons salad into bowls for each of us.

Jackson holds a glass up. "To spending time with friends, old and new. And may we spend much more time together in the future."

We all clink glasses, and I watch Sam as I sip my wine. He returns my gaze. A warmth permeates my body. His knee rubs against mine. I have an urge to stroke his thigh, but I refrain. Instead, I relish each time we innocently brush up against one another. His attention makes me feel beautiful and wanted. The conversation flows easily between business and personal interests and stories from our past. He's the perfect gentleman and mixes with my friends with ease. This might be the best non-date I've ever had.

Five bottles of wine are empty, and it's almost midnight before I notice the time. Anna and Jackson live in Chelsea, which isn't exactly close to my apartment in the upper east side. I could stay in their guest room, but I'd much rather wake up in my own bed and have a lazy Sunday morning with a bagel, coffee, and the *New York Times*.

"Guys, I've got to call it a night," I announce.

Anna squeals, "Noooooo. We've still got another bottle of wine to drink. And I have a new card game I didn't even get a chance to pull out."

"Sorry, babe. You guys continue." I stumble as I go to get my pocketbook out of the coat closet. Yes, I've definitely had enough. As I catch myself on the doorframe, Sam comes up behind me and places his hand on my elbow, and that tingling sensation filters down my arm.

"I've got you. I'm gonna head out too." Sam texts as we wait for the elevator after saying our goodbyes. When the elevator door opens, he rests his arm on my lower back. Electricity zaps between us. I risk glances up at him, and when he's not on his phone, he returns my gaze.

A sleek, black Tesla S waits outside the building. Sam guides me to the car and opens the door. "A car for the lady."

I hesitate on the sidewalk, uncertain why he's offering this car. "I can take a cab."

"I insist." He holds the door and waits.

"What about you?"

He points left as another identical black Tesla pulls up behind this one. A man in a suit stands by the streetlamp watching. I notice his expressionless face for a brief moment before Sam's body blocks my view. He brushes a kiss on my cheek as he asks me about my plans for tomorrow. The soft kiss sends every part of me fluttering, and I agree to see him tomorrow as I tilt my head up, asking for more. Under the streetlight, his smoky-blues are dark, and he hesitates for only a second before he dips down and places his lips on mine. A soft, demure, tantalizing kiss. He toys with my hair for a moment then whispers his promise, so close his breath brushes my ear. "Tomorrow." I slide into the back seat, and he closes the car door and taps the top of the car twice. Warmth surrounds me the entire ride home.

Chapter 7

Olivia

At our girls' brunch earlier today, Anna pulled it out of me that Sam asked me out for tonight. Within minutes, Delilah had nail appointments booked for all of us, a blowout for me, and she returned to my apartment with me so she could help select my first date outfit. Yes, my nerves are sending my insides tumbling, but overall, thanks to my friend's support, I'm feeling prepared and attractive.

At 5:55 p.m., I gather my pocketbook and phone and head to the lobby. Meeting him outside feels gracious, and it avoids him seeing my apartment. It's not that I'm ashamed of my apartment, but I know I'm going to be moving at some point, so I haven't yet put forth any effort into decorating since returning. Anna left the furniture when she moved out. I just moved my stuff back into the closet.

The place doesn't feel like me yet. It's more representative of my pre-Prague self. A girl with a roommate. First apartment after college. The apartment I was preparing to leave before I found out about Damien's cheating ways and then catapulted across the ocean.

As I push open the glass door, there in the circular drive in front of the lobby sits the black Tesla from last night. Sam is leaning against the side of the car, waiting.

A brisk wind blows a few stray leaves down the street. A pedestrian pulls her coat closed tight as she hustles past us on the sidewalk. Overhead, a cloud-free sky forecasts a rain-free evening.

Wearing jeans, cowboy boots, and a navy crewneck sweater below a tan suede car coat, casual Sam looks as delectable today as he did last night. His tousled hair shifts in the breeze, and I have an urge to reach up and run my fingers through it.

He told me to dress casually, which is a description I always find to be a touch ambiguous. I send a mental thank you to Delilah for helping to pull together my outfit. I'm in a brown suede mini skirt, matching tall heeled boots, and a winter white sweater. I have a short Barbour jacket in my arms to block the wind in case it gets chilly later.

After catching the time, he squints and says, "I was waiting so I wouldn't be too early. I was about to go in and buzz you."

I giggle then cringe at the nervous, schoolgirl sound. "Oh, I didn't want you to have to do that. I thought I'd wait outside for you."

He brushes a kiss across my cheek in greeting. Once again, my skin comes alive with his touch. Ever the gentleman, he opens the back passenger door for me. A different driver from yesterday sits behind the wheel. Sam walks around the car and joins me in the back seat.

He leans toward me and reaches for my hand, running his fingers through mine as if we've held hands a thousand times in the past. An energy pulses between us. "Olivia, I'd like you to meet Wes. He works with me, and he's going to be driving us around tonight."

"Nice to meet you, Wes."

Wes turns his head so he can see me and nods in a formal way. "Nice to meet you, ma'am." Ma'am? He has a rather strong southern accent, and it makes me wonder if Sam relocated him from Texas. Sam's hand caresses mine, and all thoughts of Wes the driver fly away.

"I brainstormed a hundred good first date ideas the other night with my buddy." Sam's smoky gray-blue eyes shine under the streetlight through the car window, and his smirk is subtle enough that only one dimple shows.

"Yeah? Am I in for a great treat tonight?" I ask, feeling unsure because he looks like he's about to tell a joke.

"Well, now, I hope you have a great time tonight. An unforgettable time. But let's just say that tonight I stuck with what I feel comfortable with. I have a couple of pages of ideas written down for later on when we've been dating a while. You know, for when I'm trying to spice things up and surprise you."

He squeezes my hand and grins. He's too perfect. Oh, my. The electrical tingle from his touch wars with vexing apprehension. *For when we've been dating a while.* Is he for real? I want his words to be genuine, but how many guys open up right from the start? Players. Players will say whatever you want to hear. Damien greeted me after work that first day with, "Hello, beautiful."

We pull up outside the McKittrick Hotel in Chelsea. He climbs out of the car the moment the wheels stop to open my door for me. "I had originally planned for us to take a walk along the High Line. But those boots don't look like they're made for walking. We can do that another time." He winks as he leads me along the sidewalk. He is correct. These boots aren't made for distance. I do appreciate his thoughtfulness. Damien would never have cared. As a matter of fact, more than once we'd wandered the streets of Manhattan perusing menus, walking for blocks as my feet ached, so he could find a menu he liked.

I eye the genteel hotel sign. For some reason, the name is familiar to me. Sam leans down to talk to me as he guides me indoors. "I like this place. I like it in winter too, but my favorite is summer, and I don't know how many more weeks they'll have it open for summer. When they transform it for winter, it's like a different place."

We step onto the elevator, and I realize we're going to Gallow Green. It's a restaurant I've read about but have never been to. Other people join us in the elevator, and Sam graciously pulls us to the side to make room. He lightly caresses my hips and pulls me close to him, my back to his front. Again, it feels natural, which is odd. It's like I'm in this weird state of paradox. I'm excited and nervous, but at the same time, it feels like this is exactly where I belong. I remind myself to take it slow, to learn from the past.

As the elevator rises, Sam whispers in my ear. I don't catch what he says, but as I glance up, he brushes his lips to my cheek, and he strokes my hips and along my lower back. My body lights up, electricity zinging through all my body parts.

The door opens, and the other passengers step forward to the hostess stand. A woman standing to the side of the stand seems to recognize Sam and walks toward us. "Mr. Duke?"

"Yes. Are you Karen?"

She's in black, which seems to be the uniform of the staff here. "Yes. We have your table ready for you, Mr. Duke. Please follow me."

We follow her through the restaurant. A table for two rests below a tree filled with twinkling lights and a direct view over the city. No other table resides beneath our shimmering tree. Tall, trimmed bushes have been set around our table, creating a natural privacy screen between us and all the other diners. Before we sit, Sam sends a quick text to someone, then slides his phone into his coat pocket.

Finished with whatever he needed to take care of, he graciously slides my chair out for me. "I thought we could have dinner while enjoying the night below twinkling lights surrounded by the comfort of heat lamps."

"Sounds perfect."

"Tell me, what's your poison? Do you prefer to start with Prosecco, champagne, white, red or a cocktail?"

"I'm flexible. Whatever you prefer."

He rubs his chin as he studies me. "So, you like for me to make the decisions?"

"Ah, maybe not always." I grin and cross my legs. "But for tonight?"

He chuckles a bit at that and turns to the waiter and orders one Southern Pines and one Wild Turkey on the rocks. He looks a bit mischievous as he says, "We'll start with bourbon to calm my nerves. Then we'll switch to a nice cab."

I pull back and decide to call him on his over-the-top flirtations. "Are you nervous?"

He smiles just enough that only his right dimple reveals itself once again. "A little bit. I'd like to see you again. I don't take that many women out on dates."

I scoff at that. "I find that hard to believe. You're gorgeous. Earlier today, my girlfriend told me you're on the *Post*'s most wanted bachelor list. And that you make *Page Six* with some regularity."

He sits up straight, and his smile disappears. His chest rises and falls while he studies the canopy of lights. When he speaks, it's as if he's made a decision. "Tell you what. I'm gonna focus on the fact you think I'm gorgeous. And I'll tell

73

you a little secret. I think you're gorgeous too. The sexiest thing I've ever seen." My breath catches as he leans over and whispers in my ear, "And I absolutely love this short suede skirt."

Both of us glance at my legs. My skirt sits high, exposing a good amount of thigh. At that moment, what I want more than anything is for his hand to rest along my skin. Instead, he adjusts the napkin in his lap.

"So, Prague. Tell me about it." His demeanor is more reserved, and I can't help but notice he has shifted back in his chair, away from me. He sips his water. "What was your favorite place?"

I adjust my position in the seat and pull my skirt down a bit. "Well, I used to love going to Grand Cafe Orient for lunch or coffee. When it's warm, I'd love to sit outside and people watch a bit on their upstairs balcony. There's a place called the American Bar that I went to quite a few times. I had a friend who used to hang out with Tom Waits there. How cool is that?" I grin at him as I sip my drink.

"Did you ever meet him?"

"Nah. I'm not sure he even still lived in Prague when I lived there. But I used to like to sit at the bar, or in one of the corner booths, and think about Tom Waits hanging out there. Just kinda cool."

"Coffee shops and bars are your favorite places in Prague?" he asks with a raised eyebrow.

"A favorite place speaks to your soul. Or, at least, that's true of my favorite places. And a placed packed with tourists isn't going to be my favorite place."

The sunset catches my attention. Pinks and peaches color the sky above glittering city lights. It's gorgeous. I point it out. He agrees and visibly relaxes, setting a forearm on the table and leaning forward, closer to me. "Is it true what they say about the expat experience?" I tilt my head, questioning what he means, and he explains. "A character and confidence building experience?"

"Yes. Definitely. I'm much more confident now. I had to do so much by myself. Some of that might have more to do with working in a smaller, less bureaucratic company than being in another country, though."

"I hear you. When we started out, it was a skeleton crew. Everyone wore many hats, and we accomplished so much so quickly. Now I'm blown away by how many people it takes to change a lightbulb. I miss those early days. Maybe that's why I'm starting up this VC group now." He sips his wine and sets it down, rubbing his fingers along the glass base. "Favorite museum?"

"In Prague? Or anywhere?"

"Anywhere," he responds playfully while holding his arms out wide to indicate the world.

I laugh and think. "Museum of Natural History. Right here in NYC. All my nannies used to take me there. I love art. Tate Modern. But my favorite memories are at the Museum of Natural History. You?"

He slides closer, placing both elbows on the table. "Can't say I've ever been a huge museum guy. But I like the architecture at the Guggenheim. No, my favorite places—you know, the places that speak to my soul," he winks at me as he says this, "are outside." He sits back in his chair again, stretches out his legs, and smiles.

I cock my head and ask, "And yet here you are in the concrete jungle?"

He smiles. "For now. But I get away quite a bit. That's why I rushed to have this date tonight. I leave tomorrow for a week. Business in San Fran, weekend in Texas. When I get back, though, I'd like to see you again."

"Are you ending our date already?" I ask in a teasing tone.

"Not at all. I'm not ready for this date to end. But I go after what I want, and I want time with you. So, I guess you could say I'm workin' the fields with a plan for tomorrow." He adds the last part with a strong hint of southern twang that makes me smile.

"Well, you can stop working so hard. I'd love to go out with you again." I'm not sure where those words come from, but I know it's the truth. Scary and a tad frightening, but it's true.

He clasps my hand, his other hand on his bourbon. He lifts my fingers to his lips, sending electric tendrils through me. Goosebumps form all along my arm. "I'm glad we're on the same page."

Dinner arrives along with a bottle of pinot. After the waitress leaves, Sam lifts his glass to toast. "To new beginnings." We clink glasses, eyes on each other. The moment feels intense. I fidget with the napkin on my lap.

"You said you like living in the concrete jungle for now. Are you planning on moving?"

"Nah. At this point, it's not just me. We have over fifteen hundred employees. Relocating would be an enormous strain on their families. New York is the financial center. It makes sense to be here. I have freedom. I can leave." He takes a sip of wine and continues, taking me in. "Now, one day when I have a family of my own, I might need to reevaluate, but for now, I'm good here."

The cavalier mention of a family of his own throws me, maybe because I don't allow myself to think along those lines since it might not happen for me. Finding someone good isn't easy, and my own parents are a clear example of what happens when a bad choice is made. I can't think of any other questions to ask him, so I sip my wine and eat. I ordered grilled swordfish, and it's delicious, and I tell him so. We taste each other's food. He ordered the charred octopus. It's delicious too, but I feel a bit smug because I out-ordered him, and as if he can read my mind, he tells me I did. We dig into business a bit, but he pulls us right back out of it.

"I love that I can talk to you about business, but this is our first date. Let's try to keep it work-free." He smiles and taps his knuckles on the table. "To re-cap. Prague. It seems you lived there like any normal city. Your favorite places were coffee shops and bars, and you spent a lot of time traveling on business. Which, you and I both agree, business travel is different than traveling to explore." He pauses. "Did I get all that right?"

"Yes, you did. Very nice job."

"Now, why Prague?"

I sigh out loud and stare at the dark, curly hair scattered on his muscular forearms for a minute, trying to collect my thoughts. "I can't really say." I shrug. "I don't have a good reason. It's kind of a crazy story."

He grins. "I like crazy stories."

"Well, I had a bad day one day and called my uncle. He had just had lunch with a friend who was looking for someone to fill a spot in Prague. My uncle has always wanted me to see more of the world, and before the end of the day, I had the job."

His finger taps the side of his wine glass as he looks at me thoughtfully. He holds up his index finger and says, "Two things I wanna know. One, more about that bad day. I have this feeling you're leaving something out."

"You are astute." I chew on the corner of my lower lip. This is an embarrassing story, not something I'm eager to share, but there's no harm in being open. His reaction might be telling. "I walked in on my boyfriend with someone else." He looks a tad surprised, but motions for me to continue. "She was giving him a blow job. In the office."

He swirls his drink contemplatively. The lights cast a glow in the amber liquid, forming a hypnotic swirl of gold. "So, you're a runner."

"What?" I ask in confusion.

"When things get tough, you run. Like a skittish wild horse." I sit up straighter in my chair and put my wine glass down. He immediately attempts to placate me. "It's okay. No problem. Just good to know you better. And know that upfront."

"I wouldn't say I'm like a wild horse." I roll my eyes at his comparison.

"That's fine. We can agree to disagree." He gives a lopsided smile. "Tell me about your uncle. What's he do? He an important part of your life?"

"I was completely justified in leaving my ex. He was cheating on me."

"I know. I know. I know."

I'm seething inside, but with each calm repeat of "I know," the anger dissipates.

He continues. "I didn't mean to insinuate you should have stayed with him. I was referencing the move to Prague. Now, your uncle. Important to you?"

I exhale and let the runner comment go. "Yeah, he is. I don't see him that often now. But when I was a kid, he was always looking out for me."

"What do you mean?"

"My parents kind of had their own lives." I try to word my explanation so I don't drum up sympathy. "They both had consuming careers. Nannies pretty much raised me. Later, boarding school. My uncle stepped in a lot when I was growing up. I always felt like he was checking in on me, making sure I was okay."

"Sounds like a good man."

We continue to talk through dinner. I share a bit more about my parents, and he gushes about his parents, brothers, and the ranch back home.

After the waiter takes away our plates, Sam looks down at his watch and grimaces. "Man, I had tickets to the show they put on here. But it's already started. I lost track of time."

"That's okay. I'd rather sit here and talk to you."

He tilts his head, questioning. "Are you sure? I wanted to have a memorable first date. The show here is supposed to be amazing."

The wine makes me bolder, and I take his hand. "I'm sure. I couldn't think of a way I'd rather spend tonight than getting to know you. If we were watching a show, we couldn't talk."

He brushes his lips across my knuckles. As he holds my hand, he studies me, a tender smile playing across his lips. He reaches out and runs his fingers through my hair and sighs.

"What?"

"You know our children will have blue eyes?"

His question isn't what I'm expecting at all, and I laugh. He's smiling, but there's a seriousness to his posture and expression, so I bite. "Because we both have blue eyes?"

With a shit-eating grin, he responds, "Yes, ma'am. If you ever cheat on me, it better be with a blue-eyed man."

I sit up straight and look him directly in the eye. "I'm not a cheater."

He nods, drops the grin, and looks me directly in the eye. "Neither am I."

My heart stutters. Can I trust him? This gorgeous *Page Six* playboy? Wouldn't all men claim to never cheat?

A jazz band has been playing for about the last thirty minutes in the back corner of the patio. Sam stands and pulls me to him. "Dance with me."

I look around the patio and don't see anywhere to dance. It's a romantic rooftop restaurant. There's no dance floor. "Where?"

He stands and pushes a few of the bushes away, creating a space for us to dance in our own private area. Bright twinkling lights adorn all the limbs and branches. In this one private secret area, we dance. Or rather, he holds me close, and we barely move, pressed against each other and swaying to the rich, soulful music. I breathe him in. Cedar. Forest. We sway together as the saxophonist, trumpet, and piano man find their groove.

We dance that way for a couple of songs, and then the band announces they are wrapping up for the night. Sam leans down and kisses me beneath the canopy of twinkling lights. His arms pull me close as the kiss deepens. He tastes like bourbon, something that must be taken in moderation. My sex pulses. First date jitters are now gone, replaced by something else. Need. My fingers run through his hair while his hands roam my back and over the curve of my ass. He grasps my hips, and steps back, creating distance. We're both breathing heavily. He gives a slight shake of his head, then places my hand in the crook of his arm to lead me out.

As we step onto the sidewalk, the familiar black Tesla awaits. The driver, like the last two times, remains in the car. Sam guides me to the passenger door.

Anticipation makes me speechless. He could ask me to his house. It's only 11:00 p.m. Not too late for a nightcap. Or he could send me home like he did before.

He pulls me in for a deep, possessive kiss. My arms wrap around his neck, and I finally get to run my fingers through his hair. He deepens the kiss. His firm, hard body presses me against the car. He moans, or maybe it's me, but all I want is him. He strokes my back down to my ass and pulls me closer to him. I raise my leg to wrap it around him to try to bring us closer, an attempt to bring friction where I so desperately need it.

Someone on the sidewalk cackles, "Get a room." The sound breaks the moment. I don't care that we're on a sidewalk, in public, with people walking by, but Sam takes a step back. His arms are straight, and he's using them to hold me back from him, as if he's pushing me away. His eyes are dark. Keeping his distance from me, as if I'll burn him, he opens the passenger door for me to enter the car.

"I get back Sunday. A week from today. Can I make dinner for you?"

"You want to cook?"

"Don't worry about who's cooking. Will you come to my place for dinner on Sunday?"

"I'd love to." I sit in the car, and he leans in to give me a soft kiss before closing the door. I roll the window down as soon as the door closes. He's standing on the sidewalk, waiting for us to drive away. "Why don't you ride with me? Or let us drop you off at your home so you don't have to walk?"

He leans against the window frame and bends down, so his face is close to mine. "Darlin', I'm trying to be good. Take this slowly. And unless we say goodnight right now— and I mean right now—all hope of me being good will get thrown out the window." He presses his lips to my forehead, backs away, and taps the roof twice as a signal to the driver. "Until Sunday." And he blows me a kiss.

For the second time, Sam sends me away with a warmth permeating my entire being. Have I ever felt this happy after a date? I don't think so. The city lights coalesce outside the window as the car speeds uptown. I close my eyes to savor these emotions. Yes, I'll probably find out he's a total playboy, but right now, I want to revel in my euphoria.

Chapter 8

Sam

I stand on the sidewalk as my driver pulls away to take Olivia home. I watch until the car reaches the end of the street and turns onto the avenue. Putting Olivia in that car took a world of willpower. All night, visions of those long legs wrapped around me floated through my head. Her thin sweater draped over the curve of her breasts. The outline of a low-cut lace bra showed through. Damn. The woman exudes sex, and I'd bet she has no clue.

I turn toward Tenth Avenue. I'm nine blocks from my apartment. I see available cabs on the avenue, but I need the walk to calm down. In my current frame of mind, I might be tempted to jack off to my Olivia fantasies in the back of the cab.

As I round the corner from 27th Street to Tenth Avenue, I see a tall guy about fifteen feet behind me in a dark suit. He's following me. I've had full security for almost two years now. I'm still not used to it, and it still puts me on edge.

Out of habit, I pull out my phone and text while I walk.

Me: Bill, can you do a full background check on Olivia Grayson?

It's after eleven at night on a Sunday. I don't expect a response. I continue to thumb through my texts, noticing a few I missed when I was with Olivia.

Mom: I'm thinking of throwing a small barbecue for family and friends Saturday. Would you like for me to invite Sandra?

I reply immediately.

Me: No.

The next text I choose to read is from my brother Ollie.

Oliver: Mom's inviting Sandra over.

Me: No, she's not.

He responds almost immediately.

Oliver: 😀

Me: Emoticon?

Oliver: I typed LOL, and it popped up as an option

My brother can be such a goofball. I place my phone back in my coat pocket and breathe in deeply at the wrong time. The garbage can I'm passing smells fierce. That's one good thing about temperatures dropping. Colder weather will diminish the foul city odors.

My phone rings, and I check it before answering. Bill Withers, my head security guy. It's after eleven at night, and the guy can't respond via text to a text?

"Hello." He's caught me when I'm in a good mood. Scratch that, I'm in an optimistic mood, so I don't answer in my normal clipped business tone.

"Hi. I saw your request. We did a level one background check. To clarify, you want me to dig deeper?"

"Yes."

"Anything in particular you want me to look out for?"

"Well, I don't know, Bill. I'm going to be dating her. You are the one always telling me I have to be cautious. Do whatever checking you need to do."

"I take it the date went well tonight?"

"Bill." I say his name in warning. I know his security guys report back to him. I know he knows everything I do. But he knows it pisses me off to have my face rubbed in that shit. When we went public, I didn't realize my security would become such a priority to the board of directors. Never occurred to me. I fought a personal security detail tooth and nail, but when shit hit the fan, I had to cave.

"When do you need it?" Bill understands my tonal warning.

"Our next date is Sunday, so I guess that's your deadline."

Bill coughs into the phone. "Sir, I didn't see any red flags with her. I'm sure she'll check out. But if you are planning on being seen with her, you may want to consider a security detail for her too."

"Jesus, Bill. I'm not the president of the fucking United States. Don't blow this out of proportion."

"Sam, you've had one date. It's not necessary. Yet. I'm reminding you it might become necessary. For her safety. Your safety is still at risk. Besides, if you're kissing her on public sidewalks, it's only a matter of time before her face hits the press."

"Fuck. Did security see paps out tonight?"

"No. But you know it doesn't have to be someone with a long lens."

I kick at a bent can tossed on the sidewalk. "Give PR a heads up. Tell them I want any photos pulled before they hit the paper. Or maybe I should call Cindy."

"I can handle it. I'll talk to Cindy first thing in the morning.

"Make it clear I do not want this relationship being used for media exposure."

"Relationship? Are you—"

I know where he's going and stop him. "Keep me updated. All right? Goodnight, Bill." I end the call before he can say more.

Chapter 9

Olivia

"I think one of your friends is waiting for you."

I'm in Professor Longevite's office. I seem to be the only student who takes advantage of his office hours. He's come to expect me. I now know how he likes his coffee and aim to arrive each Thursday at 2:00 p.m. sharp with his iced vanilla latte in hand.

I get up and peer around the door down the hall. I don't see anyone I know.

I step back into his office to grab my stuff. "It was probably someone who wanted to see you, and here I am, taking up all your office time."

"She wasn't my student. She was looking at you, so I assumed she was your friend." His disinterest is apparent as he taps away on his laptop.

I gather my notes and put things into my backpack. "I don't have any friends here." I'm not looking for sympathy, simply stating a fact. I show up to class, have a few projects, but I spend most of my extra time at my internship or with the friends I had before coming to business school. It's got to be one of the disadvantages of going to business school in your hometown. I haven't felt a drive to meet new people. I struggle to find the time to spend with the friends I do have.

The professor rubs his forehead, but as I prepare to leave, I notice he's studying me, for once observing me instead of his laptop. I pause and return his gaze, prompting him to speak. In a reprimanding tone, he asks, "What do you mean? Business school is for networking. You should be making friends."

I'm putting in about thirty hours a week at my internship while in full-time business school, so at first, I feel defensive. But then his words sink in. He cares. And he's not wrong. All I have to show for eighteen months abroad is two new non-work contacts, and I haven't reached out to either of them since my return to the States. "You're right. I should do a better job of meeting other students."

He nods and turns to his computer, seemingly satisfied with my answer. I heave my backpack over my shoulder and head toward the hall, silently beating myself up for being antisocial. My mom's nagging from my teenage years sounds in my head. *Why don't you have any friends? You're always home.* Never mind that I was home studying and most parents would have been proud. Of course, she didn't care about my grades. If she was home, she wanted me out of the house.

I round the corner into the hall, lost in the past, when I slam into a student about my height with straight black hair. I blurt, "Ow! Fuck!" She stumbles back, shell-shocked from a hit to her side out of nowhere. "I'm sorry. I wasn't looking."

She repositions her backpack and mumbles, "No problem. You scared me. That's all."

We stand staring at each other. She's not hurt, so I give her an apologetic smile and turn down the hall, running through my mental to-do list for the rest of the day.

She calls after me, "Do I know you? You look familiar."

I pause. I've never seen the girl before in my life, and I have a lot to do. But I remember Longevite's comment. I exhale and turn to face her.

I smile to hide a little of my annoyance at being stopped on my way to my destination. "No, I don't think so. I'm Olivia." She's attractive. Around my age, with stick straight bangs across her eyebrows. I've always wanted bangs like that but have too much body in my hair for them to lie straight without effort.

"Lindsey." She smiles a full smile as we shake hands, revealing brilliant, straight, white teeth. As she pulls her arm back, she points at me and says, "No, I know I've seen you before."

I shift my backpack strap on my shoulder. "Maybe around campus?"

"I doubt it. I'm in J-school. I'm here auditing a business class." She has her head cocked, and her eyes squint like she's thinking. She snaps her fingers. "I know! Manhattanville Coffee."

Given I basically live there, that's reasonable. I don't remember seeing her, but that doesn't mean anything. I have a tendency to live with blinders on. "Yeah, I'm there a lot. Headed there now, actually, to get some work done before heading home. Want to come with?"

She brightens and joins me. It turns out we both love Paige, the blue-haired barista. We both lived in Manhattan before attending Columbia so haven't met a ton of students here. She's getting her master's in journalism because she thinks it will help her get a better position at a magazine. I think that's a little crazy to spend so much money on a graduate degree to enter a field that doesn't pay well. But I keep that thought to myself given she's already in the program and not asking my opinion.

After we both get our coffees, I turn and settle at my table. Corporate finance homework first. Then my analysis for Jackson.

I look up and see Lindsey standing by my table, shifting from foot to foot. Crap. This is why I don't make new friends. Where are my social graces? "Hey, it was nice to meet you. Thanks for walking with me over here. It's nice to get to know another student."

"Yeah. Definitely. You look like you have lots to do, so I'm gonna get out of here." She turns to head out the door, then spins on her Doc Martens. She hesitates, and out of habit, I smile to make her feel more comfortable. She holds out her phone. "Do you want to exchange contact info? I don't want to be weird, but it'd be cool to plan to meet up sometime."

The New Yorker in me says *no*. I don't see a need to exchange contact info. But Longevite's face flashes before me and I say, "Sure." As we swap phones and enter our information, I push it a step further. "Ahm, I don't know if you have plans for Halloween, but I'm going out with some friends if you want to meet up with us."

Take that, Longevite. I'm a working, full-time MBA student, and I'm making friends.

Chapter 10

Sam

Ollie, one of my two younger brothers, and the only one of us who still lives at home, greets me in the foyer of our parents' home with a quick hug, slap on the back, and says, "Look what the cat drug in!" He's dusty and sweaty and looks like he's spent the whole day outside on the ranch.

"Hey, man, good to see you."

"You planning to go to Clifford's Halloween bash?"

I walk past him into the kitchen and pull out two cold bottles of water and pass him one. "Nah. I was in San Fran this past week, so figured I'd stop in to visit with Mom and Dad. It's starting to get cold up north. Came down for some heat." It's been years since I gave a damn about Halloween. Of course, if I was in New York, I could have taken Olivia out.

"If you don't go out tonight, do you know how many hearts you're gonna break?" Ollie tips the water bottle back and gulps over half of it down then wipes his mouth on the back of his hand.

My little brother. Such a ranch hand. I'm glad he's doing what he loves, and Mom and Dad couldn't be happier that at least one of their sons stayed home. Ian, my youngest brother, lives in Houston, which is still in Texas, but Texas is one big damn state.

Ollie loves going out to the area bars. I hate it. Here, everyone knows me. Even married women swarm around me. I've had married women back me in a corner and grab my crotch. What they really want to grab is my bank account.

I head outside onto my parents' covered porch and plop down on the sofa. "You are lookin' at what I'm plannin' on doing tonight. It's been a bitch of a week. And I bet Mom's invited thirty people to the barbecue tomorrow."

"You know it. I don't think she invited Sandra, though."

"Where the hell did that come from? That's so leftfield."

"You know Patty." He grins. "She wants to bring her boys home."

"Yeah, well, Sandra and I were over in college." Years of long-distance relationship. Should have ended it in high school; just didn't have the balls.

He bites his lip and squints. "It's not quite as leftfield as you think. She comes by at least once a week and brings cookies or cakes. At first, I thought she was trying to hit on yours truly, but all she'd ever talk about is you. Didn't take me long to see she's casting her line way out, like out to NYC."

"And if she'd been casting her line closer to home, would you've bitten?" I ask, a little leery of his answer. I guess it would be fine with me if they dated, but I'm not so sure I want my high school girlfriend to end up as my sister-in-law. She and I have done things, a lot of things. Things one shouldn't do with their sister-in-law.

Ollie looks at me like he can read my mind. "Nah, man. She was yours. No need to swap horses."

"Gotcha." A rare breeze whips across the porch, and I rest my head on the back of the sofa and close my eyes to enjoy it.

Ollie continues. "Tomorrow night, I'll introduce you to someone I am seeing, though."

I lift my head. "Seeing? As in more than once?" Ollie's been a player for as long as I can remember. He's probably run through every girl in Austin twice. Conventions have been his thing for the past few years because they bring in new blood outside of our high school circle of friends.

"Yep. Well, we'll see. I invited her to our family barbecue. So, there's that." He downs his water and leans forward to place his empty plastic bottle on the coffee table between us. "What about you? Any dates with hotties? I won't tell Patty." He gives me his trademark shit-eating grin. He loves to call our mom by her name. At least when she's not around. Wouldn't put it past her to go out in the yard and break off a limb to use as a switch on his ass if he pulled that in front of her.

I stare out into the back yard. Pasture and blue skies sprinkled with white clouds. Olivia's face comes to mind, with her dark, wavy hair, light olive skin, and stunning blue eyes. Darker than the sky overhead. "Yeah, I'm seeing someone."

Shock ripples across Ollie's face. "No shit! Hell has frozen over."

"Don't go gettin' crazy. We've been out on one date. But I'm flying back early Sunday so I can see her again." Hell, I should fly back tomorrow to get out of this barbecue. As if at this point that's an option. I run a company with over fifteen hundred employees, yet I still fear my mother's wrath.

Ollie gets up and grabs two beers out of the outdoor fridge. He hands me one, and we clink the tops before taking a sip. "Well, here's to your second date. I guess you've already done a background check and all that, huh?"

"Well, I mean," and here I can't stop a huge grin from breaking out, "she was my intern."

"You son of a bitch!" Ollie pounds his boot on the wooden deck. He looks like I announced I'm tapping an eighteen-year-old cheerleader.

I laugh out loud. "She *was* my intern," I say, placing emphasis on *was*. "She quit before she started."

"Damn! That would have been so hot if you were banging your intern."

"Yep. But she's twenty-eight. Don't let the word *intern* get you too hot and bothered."

"Why'd she quit? You come on too strong?"

"Better offer." I shrug and take a swallow of the ice-cold beer.

Ollie gets serious. "Man, if she's willing to walk away from you, that's a good sign."

"How do you figure?"

"It means it's less likely she's just after your money. If she was after you, she'd be aiming to spend every minute with you."

"Fuck you." It's all in jest, but his comment hits hard. My family is always worried someone is *just* after my money. I know they mean well, but they've been getting in my head. Just like Withers.

That's something that makes me envy Ollie. He'll inherit quite a bit from our parents, but most women see a ranch hand when they look at him. When he's with someone, he can be pretty certain it's because they like what they see, they like spending time with him. Not his bank account. He'll never need to look over his shoulder, question people's motives, or risk becoming a paranoid pansy.

Ollie keeps digging the hole. "As long as you wrap it up, you'll be fine. You wrap it up, she can't trap you."

I take a small square pillow from the sofa I'm sitting on and throw it at him. Bastard.

He laughs then takes a swallow from his beer. Leaning forward, elbows resting on his legs, he smirks. "Any woman who gets knocked up by you is coming after you with a horde of lawyers."

"As she should. If she's pregnant with my child and I'm not providing for it, I hope she does come after me. I'd be a shit human being if I didn't take care of my own children. The woman you're referencing by beating around the bush was a scam artist, and she was not the mother of my baby." I did hook up with the snake, though. But I also knew I had used a condom. And I always check my condoms before I toss them in the trash. Although my lawyer, through all of that bull, scared me into celibacy telling me stories of women who will retrieve used condoms to try to get themselves pregnant. I still don't get how that works, but I suppose it's conceivable.

Ollie kicks my leg to get my attention. "I'm fully aware she was a scam artist. But now that you've made the *Fortune* wealthiest list, or whatever magazine publishes that obnoxious list, you just gotta be careful. That's all I'm saying."

He chuckles then treats his longneck beer bottle like a microphone and starts singing about guitars and women. I grab my beer and stomp off toward the barn as he continues with his favorite Waylon Jennings song.

He shoots me with his finger and calls, "Be careful of those firm-feeling women, big bro!"

As I make my way through the back pasture, I pull out my phone to text Olivia, careful to keep an eye out for any manure piles lurking in the grass. Some habits die hard for good reasons.

Chapter 11

Olivia

I open the door, and Delilah screeches, "I love it!"

On reflex, I pull my blaring friend into my apartment and shut the door. She's wearing jeans and a sweater but has a large duffle bag slung over one shoulder. I'm in full-on Wonder Woman gear, sans make-up. My gold knee-high platform boots double as relatively comfortable shoes for a Halloween night and push me to nearly six feet in height.

Delilah spins me around. "Baby, we are so hitting the singles parties tonight!" She heads into my bedroom then twirls around. She's bouncing with energy. "Fix us some cocktails to drink while we get ready. I'm gonna get changed, and then we'll do each other's make-up."

The door closes behind her, and I go into the kitchen to see what kind of cocktail I can create. I shout so she can hear me from my bedroom, "Hey, what party are you planning on us going to? Anna said she and Jackson aren't going because you want to hit the singles scene?"

The door pops back open, and Delilah stands in her bra and panties in defensive mode. "They wanted to go to Chelsea. Every freaking place they want to go is in Chelsea."

"What's wrong with Chelsea?" I ask while pulling out the vodka from my freezer.

"Nothing's wrong with Chelsea. I live in fucking Chelsea. But get out of your bloody neighborhood once in a while. Come on now. Am I right?"

Delilah is in rare form tonight. Normally, I'm the one who's cussing like a sailor. "Have you been drinking?"

She twists her head and turns back to get dressed but doesn't close the door. "One cocktail while I was packing."

It's gonna be one of those nights. Halloween in the city. And it's a Friday night. It's gonna be a good one. The yellow refrigerator light reveals slim offerings. "How's vodka and lemonade? Or would you prefer vodka and OJ?"

"Vodka and lemonade works." Delilah walks into the den in a stunning Daenerys costume. The detail and quality material make me think it had to have cost hundreds of dollars.

"Wow. Gorgeous. It looks exactly like what she wore." She's wearing the infamous white dress Daenerys wore in *Game of Thrones*. She's holding the white wig with perfect braids. She gingerly sets the wig on my coffee table and pulls a stocking over her head to prep for the wig. I'm in awe of her costume.

My costume came from Halloween Spirit, and at the time, I thought I was splurging when I spent almost eighty dollars on it. I've had it since undergrad, and it has served me well. I love it because I don't have to deal with a wig, since my hair is close enough to Wonder Woman's.

I place a drink near Delilah while she struggles with her stray hair. I take a big swallow of my drink. The cold concoction quenches my dry, scratchy throat. "Where in Chelsea did Anna want to go?"

"The Ainsworth. Some martini and monster thing. That's fine and all, but doesn't a party billed as the largest Halloween singles party sound like more fun?"

I take another long swallow of my icy drink and think of Sam. It's not like we're exclusive. We've been on one date.

Even so, I have zero desire to meet anyone tonight. But that doesn't mean I can't be a great wingman for my lovely Mother of Dragons. "I read through a lot of the parties that are happening tonight. Seemed like some of the best were in Brooklyn."

Instantly, her palm aims skyward a few inches from my face in a stop sign signal. "I'm not going to Brooklyn. Way too far away."

I laugh. "I know. It's just there's a cool New Wave party in Greenpoint. The DJ is playing stuff from Echo & the Bunnymen, the Cure, the Smiths. Cool shit."

Delilah looks like a crazy person with hair sticking out from places all around her stocking cap. I walk over, make her sit, and take over preparing her hair for the wig. She peers up at me. "How old are you?"

"What? It was a phase. I love that shit."

She grabs her drink while I work away, tucking fly-aways under the thick stocking. I kind of know there's no point in trying, but deep down, I'd rather meet up with Anna than go to a singles party. So, I take one more stab at persuasion. "I know the party is billed as the biggest singles party, but it's in midtown. Doesn't that kind of make you nervous?"

Both hands fall to her hips in fists. "I've already bought tickets. Besides, rumor is the Chainsmokers may make a guest appearance."

"Okay, fine." I know determination when I see it. And I don't really care that much. "But, for the record, the Chainsmokers are not showing up to a midtown party." She smirks. She only made that band comment because I have Alexa playing the Chainsmokers right now. "Wait, a friend is meeting us. Does she need a ticket too?"

"Nope. I've got the two I bought for Anna and Jackson. They won't be using them. Here, let's text Chase and let him know we have an extra ticket." As she pecks a message off to Chase, she asks, "Who's this friend?"

"Someone I met on campus. She's pretty nice. I don't know if she'll actually meet us, but let me text her the address."

When I pick up my phone, I see a text from Sam and grin. We've been texting back and forth all week. Not too often, but he's sent me photos of San Fran a few times, and I've sent him zero snapshots of Manhattanville Coffee.

Delilah catches my grin. "Mr. Gorgeous sexting you?"

I roll my eyes. "No, he's just wishing me a Happy Halloween."

"What's he up to tonight?"

"He's in Texas visiting family."

"What's his costume?"

"No costume. He's with his parents."

Delilah's mouth drops. "How boring," she comments with heavy emphasis on *boring* while scrunching up her nose.

I ignore her reaction as I place bobby pins all along her skull cap. "He's in his mid-thirties. I'm guessing he's kind of outgrown the whole Halloween thing." In truth, at twenty-seven, I'd be happy staying in too. Or at the very least going to a more sophisticated gathering. A gathering where one can sit and drink like Anna will be attending tonight. Any location Delilah picks will mean standing room only. But, hey, only young once.

I turn the volume up, and we're singing along as we start our second round of drinks. After make-up is applied and we're ready to go, we lean together, trying for a good joint selfie. I've got a solid buzz going, and exhilaration pumps through me. I am in the mood to dance.

Right before we head out the door, I back up to my window so the city lights shine behind me and pass Delilah my phone. "Take some good pics of me. I want to send some to Sam."

She takes several then art directs them a bit to get better photos. My long legs look rather amazing, peeking out from my ultra-short blue Wonder Woman skirt, and my breasts are spilling out a bit from the top of my corset. With the eyeliner, my blue eyes pop, and combined with my dark hair spilling over the gold crown in soft waves, I have to say I look a bit like Wonder Woman. This is why I keep re-wearing this costume. Nothing at all to do with being too lazy to come up with another one.

I glance through the photos, pick the sexiest, and send to him. Before we've found a cab, I get a response.

Sam: Damn. I knew I should have come back today.

Then one more text.

Sam: Save that costume.

With a grin, I show his texts to Delilah and wiggle my eyebrows. "Guess he hasn't outgrown Halloween after all."

The cab drops us out in front of Croton Reservoir Tavern, and the line wraps around the corner of the block. It's a little after 10:00 p.m. The low tonight is forty-two degrees, and it's already pretty freaking cold. But since we're planning on drinking a lot, we opted for no coats. Didn't want to have to keep up with them or risk losing them.

Staring at that line, it's looking like that was a bad call. As we head toward the back of the line, I hear someone call my name and see Lindsey waving her arm frantically. "Hey! I went ahead and got a place in line. Come on."

She's about ten people from the entrance. I give her a giant hug, and she almost faceplants into my cleavage. I'm not used to being this tall. She's alone, so I ask her where her friends are. She says they wanted to hit a different party, but this one sounds more fun. Delilah's nodding in complete agreement. I can tell these two will be insta-friends.

Lindsey's hair is styled stick straight, the same as when I saw her last, but her make-up is wild. Expertly drawn black eye liner, making her dark eyes look almost evil as the tails go out to the edge. She's wearing a small silver sequin tube top that barely covers what must be D-cups. She has a matching sequin tube skirt, thigh highs, and dominatrix style fuck-me heels. She's a walking wet dream.

As I take her outfit in, I ask "So, what are you?" I can tell she's a sexy something, but I'm not so sure what the something is.

She gives an evil grin. "Sweet but Psycho."

Delilah shouts, "I love it!"

Once inside, we all walk straight for the bar. Lindsey squeezes into a vacant spot and shouts, "I've got first round." She's shouting because it's the only way we can hear her above the pounding techno beat. Blue lights flash through the pitch-black dark. The strobe lights illuminate bodies writhing on the packed dance floor.

A group of guys walk toward us, and I shelter next to Delilah, letting her carry on the entire conversation. Lindsey joins us, holding three large glasses. I drink what she gives me. It tastes kind of like a Coke but not quite as sweet. The heat from all the bodies has me slurping the entire cocktail through the straw, and after two or three slurps, only ice remains in my glass. I tap Lindsey's shoulder to tell her I'll get the next round and ask what to order.

Her tongue slides along her lower lip, and for one minute she looks like pure evil. It's like she's somehow personified her costume. Goosebumps run up and down my arms. "Long Island iced tea. But I have a tab started. Put it on my tab."

The lights flash. Bodies rub and press against me. It's a hedonistic whirl. Hard, firm, male abs. Men grind my ass, and I grind back, almost falling down a few times. At this point, I've had four or five of the Long Island iced teas. I'm not sure how much alcohol I've had, but I'm glad the dance floor is so packed. Someone always catches me if I lean too far.

Scantily clad women rock beside me. Lindsey comes up to me and grinds her hips against my ass. We both laugh and rub all over each other, attracting the attention of other men on the dance floor. My fingers glide along her bare, flat belly. Some of the guys we were talking to surround us, chanting and goading us on. Lindsey bites her lip seductively, and I grow more brazen and playfully caress her breasts.

She guides me off the dance floor and down a dark hall toward the bathroom. Her mouth collides with mine as she presses me against the wall, her thigh pressing against my crotch. I bend my legs to give her better access, and she reaches up my skirt. She's rubbing my clit while smashing me against the wall. I caress her breast while our tongues dance. She tugs at my top, and I drunkenly try to push it back up. The room sways, and far off lights blend.

Her top slides down. My thumb rubs over her nipple. She slides my panties aside, and I feel her fingers inside me while she expertly rubs my clit. My knees start to shake. I struggle to stand. One hand holds my top in place while the other latches on to Lindsey's shoulder for balance and to maintain some distance.

The moment ebbs and flows like a dream. Like I'll wake up, and it won't be real. This isn't what I want. I want to push away. I turn my head to the side so I can see the lights cascading through the dark hall. Lindsey's lips go to my neck. The Mother of Dragons storms down the black brick hallway.

Delilah yanks me away, and I close my eyes. My eyelids feel so heavy. Delilah and Lindsey are shouting, their voices barely rising above the blaring techno beat. When I open my eyes again, I see Lindsey has pulled her top back on. Damn. She has large, beautiful breasts with saucer-like nipples that taste delicious.

Delilah pulls me out on the dance floor, and I spin and spin and spin.

******

My head throbs, and my mouth is bone dry. I cautiously crack an eye open. My bedroom. A layer of sweat covers my body, and as I roll over, I'm met with the putrid smell of vomit. Death. I feel like death.

I am alone in my bed, and for that, I'm immensely grateful. I don't remember how I got home. I close my eyes and try to remember what happened. I remember dancing. Lights. Bodies. Then black.

Slowly, ever so slowly, I pull myself out of bed, stumble to the kitchen, and grab the orange juice. Thank the gods we drank lemonade last night instead of the OJ. I down a large cup and pour a second then fumble in a kitchen drawer that holds a shitload of random stuff and pull out a bottle of Advil. I pop two pills and drag myself back into bed.

I wake up again to the sound of an incessant vibration. I see my phone charging on my nightstand. It's lit up. Delilah's calling me.

I reach for the phone, answer, and hold it up to my ear. My head aches. Nausea overwhelms me.

"Olivia? Hello? Are you there?"

"Yes," I manage to croak.

"I'm at your door. I brought coffee and bagels."

The door feels like it's a mile away. When I get out of bed, I lower myself to my hands and knees and crawl to the door. For some reason, the nausea makes me want to remain closer to the floor. I'm still a little dizzy too. Maybe I'm still drunk?

I open the door, and Delilah stands there holding a white paper bag and a carrier that contains four drinks. She looks down at me where I sit sprawled on the floor.

"Damn, girl. I had a feeling you'd be hurting today, but I thought you'd be able to stand."

I look up at her but don't move. I'm wiped. I cannot move.

"I brought you some anti-nausea medicine, but I'm thinking we may need to stop by REVIV for an IV drip."

She steps over me and uses one of her legs to force mine out of the way so the door can close.

I crawl to the bathroom. The OJ I drank pours out into the toilet. Dee holds my hair back then rubs my shoulders as I continue to dry heave. The muscular contractions slow.

After handing me a toothbrush with toothpaste on it, she forces me to get dressed. "Come on, girl, let's go."

Less than an hour later, an IV full of saline solution has rehydrated me, and I'm chilled but starting to feel human. The nausea has subsided. The splitting head pain has subsided to a dull ache.

Delilah sits across from me sipping her coffee. All I really want to do is go home and crawl into bed and sleep. But that would be rude to my lifesaver, who traipsed all the way up to the upper east side to check on me mere hours after delivering me safely to my apartment. In the interest of being a good friend, I agree to head to a greasy spoon deli for breakfast.

I order cheesy eggs, bacon, and a biscuit. I normally don't eat biscuits, but they might absorb any remaining alcohol. I'm working with the theory that when a hangover is this bad, calories shouldn't be given any consideration.

The IV helped the physical ramifications of last night. It did nothing to ease the mortification or the unease of a black hole memory. I put my elbows on the table and rest my forehead on my palms. I don't look at Delilah but ask what must be asked. "Ah, I don't remember much from last night. How bad was I?"

Laughter rings across the table. "Oh, girlfriend. Oh, my, girlfriend."

I hide my face. "You know what? I don't wanna know. Don't tell me. Just...what the hell were we drinking?"

"You mean what were you drinking."

I look up, squint, and point at her. "No, we were all drinking the same thing."

She shakes her head.

I nod.

She's still shaking her head, so I speak the words out loud. "Yes, we all ordered the same thing."

She angles her head and clicks her tongue. "Nope, babe. You were drinking the Long Island iced teas like they were Diet Coke. Do you have any idea how much alcohol is in one of those? I had the first one Lindsey gave me then switched to beer. I always drink beer on marathon drinking nights. The chances of me getting shit-faced on beer are way slimmer." She taps her nose and gives me a thoughtful look. "You, my friend, may want to try a similar strategy, moving forward. If I hadn't been with you, there's no telling how many people you might have fucked last night."

"It was the straws." I groan, face down.

"Pardon?"

"The straws. You know you can't let me drink liquor drinks with straws." This is completely and totally her fault.

"Well, at least we got to see the Chainsmokers."

I lift my head and squint at her. I have no memory of any band. Last night is black. No memory other than lights and dancing, then black. Something about her face tells me she's trying to put one over on me. I slowly shake my head, but I'm definitely uncertain.

She laughs. "No, they didn't play. But you did miss the Killers. They played!" she says with enough energy that the gaggle of hair on the top of her head shifts back and forth. I stare at her. Then she laughs at her own joke and says, "Nah. Just messing with you."

I collapse my head on the greasy dinette table and groan. "Oh, god. I'm never drinking again."

Chapter 12

Olivia

Sunday morning, I walk out of my yoga class feeling like a new woman. I head to the corner Starbucks, and as I stand at the end of the line waiting for the barista to call "Olivia," I pull out my phone. Two missed calls from Sam. No voice message, but there's a text.

Sam: Can I take you to lunch?

I bite my lip and grin. I should spend the afternoon doing laundry, doing schoolwork, and getting ready for the week. But I can drop the laundry off at the wash and fold. And Monday, I don't go into my internship, so I can use my time tomorrow to get caught up on reading assignments.

Me: Yes.

Sam: Do you have a bike?

Me: Yes.

My bike's been in storage in the basement since before I left the country. I used to love riding through Central Park. Back when I worked at a midtown agency, I'd ride down Third Avenue to get to work. On a hot summer day, a bike was always preferable to standing on a stifling subway platform drenched in sweat. It's been a long time since I checked on my bike, and I hope the tires haven't rotted.

Sam: Can you be ready by 11?

I glance at my watch. That's in twenty minutes. Well, I guess if we're biking, then my hair back in a pony is fine. I hate how I look in a bike helmet, though. I'm most definitely not putting on my padded bike shorts. I consider my current outfit. Black, shape-enhancing Lululemon leggings and a loose fitting tank that hits at my waist. I'll need a sweatshirt, but this will work.

Me: Yep.

Sam: Meet you in front of your building.

Nerves and excitement have my insides turning over and over. It's the kind of nervousness that makes me hate dating, or at least dating guys I like. Suddenly, I'm glad he's being spontaneous, because I only have to deal with this borderline nauseating effect for a little while. It's a date, nothing more. This doesn't mean anything. It's not like anything is riding on this. No big multimillion-dollar account win. Other people aren't dependent on me. It's a day on the weekend. We're going to have fun, that's all.

I head down to my basement, unlock my bike, pump air into the tires, and then take it outside. He's on the sidewalk with his bike. Five minutes early. It takes longer than fifteen minutes to get to the upper east side from Chelsea by bike. He must have been in this area when he texted.

He's wearing bike shorts and a loose old t-shirt. The t-shirt is a triathlon race shirt from years ago. He's wearing bike shoes that snap into the pedals. One quick glance, and I'd guess he's riding a bike that cost about as much as a car. I don't really know my bikes, but I know my kind of bottom of the line Cannondale costs close to one thousand. I know from the guys in the bike shop that a person can spend a crazy amount of money, and glancing at his sleek bike, I'm guessing he easily spent over ten thousand dollars. Which means he's probably got an indestructible lock in the backpack he's wearing.

He runs his hand through his hair and grins as I notice his helmet hanging from one of the handlebars. Both dimples are on full, panty-dropping display as I head over to where he's standing.

"Hey." I feel like such a teenager as the butterflies twirl in my stomach.

He softly brushes his lips against mine, sending my heart racing into overdrive, and an airy lightheadedness washes over me. "Hey."

He moves around uncomfortably for a moment as he backs away, and my eyes go to his crotch as he pulls on the fabric. I readjust my bike seat to give him a moment and to find something to look at other than his tented shorts. Inside, I'm doing a little dance and screaming *he likes me!*

"If you're up for it, I thought we could ride around the park. We have lunch reservations at the Boat House. Then maybe we could go to my place. Hang out." He shifts on his feet and stares down at the concrete on the sidewalk. "Walk along the river before dinner."

I smile. "Sounds perfect."

He opens his mouth as if he's going to speak then closes it. He repeats the process once or twice, and I tilt my head questioningly. He breathes out loudly. "I don't want to be forward, but would you like to bring some clothes down? Maybe to change into after our ride or in case, you know, if you ended up staying over."

He almost whispers *staying over*, and I'm not positive I heard him correctly. Staying over on our second date feels a little too forward. Especially when he's already told me he wants to take it slow. And he's a publicized bachelor. He originally suggested we take it slow. No, I need to play this conservatively to earn his respect. I'd bet the Southern girls he grew up liking didn't put out on the second date.

I glance skyward. It's a chilly, cloudy, fall day. The high is gonna be in the low sixties, but I could get sweaty if we race through the park. A change of clothes if I'm staying through dinner isn't the worst idea. "I'll run up and get a change of clothes in case we get a bit competitive on the bike ride, but I'm not staying over on our second date."

He smiles so big that both of his dimples pop. Yep, I made the right call. He holds on to my bike while I run upstairs and grab a change of clothes and a backpack.

We take off, and once we're settled into the smooth, car-free circle in the park, we find a nice, easy pace alongside each other, stealing glances as we pedal along the six-mile loop. The leaves are a myriad of color, yellows, reds, and oranges, and they stand out against the backdrop of a sallow, overcast sky. Leaves scatter over the pavement, the sidewalk, and all along the grass and the wooded areas of Central Park. The unmistakable woodsy smell of fall is in the air.

He leads the way to the Boat House, and after we have locked our bikes, he sits down to change shoes. I'm just

112

wearing running shoes, as I chose to have pedals that allow regular shoes since I used to take my bike to work sometimes. He has the fancy pedals that require bike shoes to latch onto.

As he's putting on his shoes, he says, "You know, it's not really our second date."

"How do you figure?" It's rather cut and dry, unless he's counting the first night we had dinner at Anna's.

Still seated on the grass, he looks up at me and counts his fingers. "Anna and Jackson's." So, yeah, he's counting that. He continues. "McKittrick's, lunch today, this afternoon hanging out, and then dinner tonight." He's clicked off five fingers, and he's biting his bottom lip as he smirks, popping out that delectable right dimple. I tug off my sweatshirt because even though it's in the low sixties I am quite warm.

I wrap the sweatshirt sleeves around my waist, and he stands in front of me, watching my every move with his incredibly sexy smirk as he awaits my response. I roll my eyes. "Noted."

We're seated at an outdoor table right near the water. There are a few boats going across, and almost all consist of a pair, with one person rowing and one person sitting back and enjoying the ride. One white wooden boat holds two guys, another holds one girl and two guys, and another a guy and girl. At the table nearest to us, a girl with pink spiked hair and a couple of nose rings sits with a girl who looks completely conventional in a navy cardigan and braided hair. They're holding hands. It feels like we're on a movie set for a film titled *Love Is in the Air*.

Sam places his hand on mine and pulls my attention back to us. "Would you like to take a boat out after lunch?"

"Yeah, I definitely would. I'll row you."

"We'll see." He wrinkles his nose and gives me his boyish grin. "So, how was Halloween?"

I grimace. "Let's just say I don't remember all of it."

He lets go of my hand and leans back in his chair. He's still kind of smiling, but his demeanor has definitely shifted. "Come again? You were wearing a sexy as hell outfit, and you don't *remember* the whole night?"

I continue my dramatic grimace. There's no good response to that question.

"Do you know how many times I've looked at your text? That outfit is now your photo in your contact info on my phone. I've considered adding it as my screensaver, but I don't want any randoms to walk by and see you dressed like that."

His arguments are intensifying as he speaks. Oh, dear. I'm mortified by my behavior, so I struggle with how to explain. Sloppy drunk isn't my normal. "I know. I'm not proud. We were drinking these drinks called Long Island iced teas, and I was drinking out of a straw."

He bites his lip and kind of half-frowns, half-smiles. I can't tell what he's thinking. "I'm familiar with Long Island iced teas. Is that your drink of choice?"

"No. No," I say quickly. "Never had them before. One of my friends ordered them."

"How'd you get home?" His expression is pensive. The waitress starts to come by, and he waves her away.

"My friend Delilah. I don't think you've met her yet?" He shakes his head. "She apparently switched to beer. She got me home safe."

This seems to appease him, because he calls the waitress over and we order.

114

After we order, he taps his fingers on the table. I think he's amused, but again, it's a little hard to be certain. "How many men hit on you? That you remember?"

I think back to the photo I sent him of my outfit. Yeah, I can see why he hasn't let this drop. I went out to a singles party in Manhattan and got so wasted I blacked out. But nothing bad happened. Flashes of being pressed against a wall, groping Lindsey, come to mind. Delilah coming to my side then pulling me out to the dance floor.

He's waiting for my answer. "I didn't hook up with any men. I danced with several." We aren't exclusive. It's our second date. No matter how he chooses to count, it's our second date. This kind of does put a damper on that feeling of finding perfection in a coffee shop, though. Successful relationships don't begin with one of the partners in a dark hallway with a stranger. I squirm a bit in my seat. As if on cue, my phone, which is on the table facing upward, lights up. A text comes through.

Lindsey: Please don't feel weird. Still friends?

After reading the text, I glance up at Sam. I'm pretty sure he just read that text. Crap. This isn't the way to start a relationship. But fuck. I'm not going to lie. Lying is worse. I sigh. At first my arms are by my sides, but I cross them over me, a hand on each elbow to give myself a little comfort as I spill.

"I kissed a girl." Damn, I sound like a Katy Perry song. His eyes light up. "Actually, I'm fairly certain we made out. I only remember bits and pieces." I toy with my napkin and wish for a change in subject.

He cocks his head, and for the first time since we veered into this topic, I am positive he's fighting a smile. "A girl, you say?" I nod. He fingers his hair, and then both dimples appear. "That's fucking hot."

I don't move from my position with my arms crossed. I relax a bit, since it seems he's taking this well, but deep down, guilt wracks me. Not that it should. We aren't exclusive. I didn't do anything wrong. Stupid, yes. Stupid because I put myself in a dangerous situation.

Our food arrives, and we don't talk about it again for a bit. While we're waiting for the check, he bites his lip again and does that half-smile. It's a look I'm beginning to equate with him being amused by a question he's about to ask. "Are you bisexual?"

Oh, Jesus. I roll my eyes and huff. "No. Was I turned on? Yes. I think. But am I going to stop seeing you so I can hunt down a woman? No." I crumble my napkin and drop it onto my plate. "It was the first time I've done anything like that. It's a bit mortifying. I don't even remember how it started."

"I've been there." He rocks his head back and forth as if he's weighing his thoughts. "A long time ago, but I've been there. Meaning I've been that drunk. I'm from Texas," he adds while raising his eyebrows for emphasis.

He draws me to him so our knees touch as we sit facing each other. "I don't want to scare you with what I'm about to say. But I have to tell you that I like you. A lot. And I know we've only been out on a handful of dates. You may say two, I may say three or four." He grins. "But I don't share. If you and I are doing this, if we're dating, I don't want you to date anyone else."

The tips of his fingers along my wrist send tingling sensations all along my arms, and I have to fight the urge to crawl into his lap and play with his hair. "I don't want to see anyone else either. I wasn't looking for anyone on Halloween. I had planned to be Delilah's wingman." That plan didn't work out so well, given my inability to walk on my own probably served as a cockblock.

"And that's another thing. I know that's not you." I smile, loving that he's just getting to know me but sees me as a good person. That he expects I am a good person. He continues. "But, please, don't do that again. If you are going to drink cocktails loaded with multiple forms of alcohol in them—with a straw—then please do that with me so I can keep you safe."

Swoon. The idea that he wants to keep me safe, that he cares, it's like an aphrodisiac. We are in a public restaurant, and I don't care. I lean across the table and kiss him. Out of the corner of my eye, I notice a tourist with her iPhone snapping pictures. The Boat House in Central Park in fall. It's hard to get more picturesque or ideal than this.

We walk outside hand in hand as we meander over to the boat rentals. There's a wait, so we decide to just head back to his place.

As we're adjusting our bikes and he's snapping his shoes onto his pedals, he turns his head to me. "Now, just so we're clear, if you decide you're curious about women, I'm very open to a *ménage à trois*." His shit-eating grin has me rolling my eyes and fighting my own grin.

We bike down to the High Line, lock our bikes, and he swings my backpack over his shoulder as we climb the stairs to the walkway. Once a rail track, it fell out of use in 1980. In 2009, the strip transformed into what is now considered by many to be one of the most unique parks in Manhattan, if not the world. The path is lined with wildflowers, small trees, and tons of sculptures.

"So, you made out with a girl. Is that, like, kissing?"

I grin. "You're not going to let this drop."

"Hey, I'm a guy. Can't help but keep thinking about it. And, you know, be a little curious about your definition of making out."

I bite my lip. "We were in a hallway. Made out, in this case, is a bit more than kissing." My face heats.

"A bit more. What are we talking here? Boob action?"

I don't say anything.

He stops and stares at me and leans forward, a smirk plastered on his face. "Did you go down on her?"

"No!"

We continue walking. "Then what—"

"Do you really want to know?" I ask, interrupting him.

"Yeah, but I mean…"

I'm exasperated. This doesn't feel sexy to me. "She fingered me. I sucked on her breasts. I think? It's all really hazy. I'm not sure. Then Delilah arrived. That's what I remember. Happy now?"

He stops again and pulls me to him, his arms wrapping around me. He bites his lip and smirks. "I'm a guy. I had to ask. My imagination." He kisses me. He's been kissing me at random times this whole afternoon.

"But, you're not mad?"

"Oddly enough, no. If it was some guy you made out with, I'd be livid. Crazy jealous. I'd need some time to calm down. But, nah. Knowing it was a chick, I'm kinda turned on. That's a little backwards, huh?"

The clouds have lifted, and now we couldn't ask for a more gorgeous, blue sky, fall day. Where we are, we can see

118

the Hudson. The boats are far enough away that they have the appearance of large toys passing by. There's an empty bench facing the river, and Sam tugs me over to it then curls his arm around me, pulling me into his chest.

He kisses my forehead, and I sigh. Everything feels perfect. I can't imagine any other place I would rather be at this moment. Normally, when I feel like that, I'm with friends hanging out. I can't even remember the last time I felt like this with a guy—or, for that matter, if I ever felt this warmth and happiness when hanging out with someone. And to think I came close to possibly ruining this due to a drunken lapse in judgement.

I rest my head on his chest, and his arm wraps around my back, holding me tight. He shifts and angles my head up to him, and his brow wrinkles. "Everything all right?"

I lower my head back to his chest so I can feel the rhythm of his heart. "You know, if it had been you who hooked up on Halloween, I can't say I'd be as understanding as you're being. I think I'd be questioning your character. And yet, it doesn't seem to faze you."

He places a soft kiss on the top of my head. "Well, I've been there before. I've had drunken hook-ups. Lapses in judgement I'd give anything to undo. I'd be a hypocrite if I held it against you." He squeezes me until I shift to look up at him again. "And we weren't exclusive then. But we are now, right?"

I lick my lower lip and raise myself so I can kiss him. He holds me close and keeps our kisses socially acceptable. Kids are walking all along the boardwalk. Strollers are going by. This isn't the place for a public make-out session. There's a part of me that loves he's mindful of his surroundings and seems to be working at taking it slow. At least, for what is our third or fourth date, according to his count.

He props his legs up to rest against the railing, settling in and getting more comfortable. "Okay, tell me something that lets me get to know you better."

"What do you want to know?"

His brow wrinkles as he stares at a plane flying overhead. It looks like he's deep in thought. He takes his finger and taps the end of my nose. "I want to know how I got so lucky to meet you when you were single. How is a gorgeous, smart girl like yourself, this accomplished world traveler, a girl who could be a model if you wanted, how on earth are you single?"

I close one eye and look up at him, squinting a bit from the sun, trying to decide what to address first. "First, I appreciate the compliment, but I couldn't be a model. I'm unusual-looking, but that doesn't mean I could be a model."

"Are you kidding me? Those blue eyes and dark hair, olive skin? I can't get those eyes out of my mind. They remind me of the Caribbean Sea. Striking. Gorgeous. Those are words that come to mind. But you aren't a model because you love business. You've set about following the career path you've chosen, which makes you even sexier."

"I appreciate the compliments. I do. And, yes, I've always considered myself to be intelligent. And I've found my own success, but nothing compares to what you've done. What you've achieved." I absentmindedly trace the defined muscles of his chest as I mutter, "Compared to you, I'm basically a loser."

"Hey. No." He places his thumb below my chin and angles my head up once more, forcing me to look at him. "First, I'm almost ten years older than you. Second, I had a

120

good idea and was in the right place at the right time. If I was your age, my idea would have already been done, and who knows if I'd even be in business. Chances are I'd be a programmer working for someone else." He gazes out across the river. "So much in life is timing. I'm just one of the lucky sons of bitches in the absolute right place at the right time with a good idea. And the ability to code. But that brings me back to my question. What if when we met, you were dating someone? That would have been bad timing. Right?" His face contorts into a goofball expression as he emphasizes *bad timing*. I giggle. Damn. I'm so happy it's almost like I'm giddy. And that's so not me. "Tell me, beautiful, how did I get so lucky?"

I lean in for a soft kiss before answering. "I just got back from being overseas. You know, I went abroad after I broke up with my boyfriend."

"Yeah, so you said." He plays with my hair, twisting a piece of it through his fingers.

"I wasn't looking to meet someone when I was abroad. It was more about taking some time to be on my own. Explore the world. Prove myself capable. Make it on my own. I've dated a few losers. Time not dating anyone has been restorative."

"One ex cheated. Others too?"

I watch a ferry pass on the river as I reflect on my dismal dating history. Damien was the only one I considered moving in with and my only post-college relationship. Even so, it's disturbing that all three of my exes strayed. I turn to him, realizing I should be asking the same questions. "How are you single? When you walked into that coffee shop, I wasn't the only one drooling."

He grins. "Believe it or not, I don't date a lot. I know my mad dating skills might make you think otherwise." He wiggles his eyebrows. "But the last ten years have been insanely busy for me. When we were in start-up mode, it was insanity. Then we went public, and that was possibly even more manic. Only in the last couple of months have things calmed down. It's still busy as hell, mind you, but I have brilliant people working for me, and my role has evolved. Does that make sense?"

I think it all through, and then it hits me. "We really did both just have good timing, huh? One year earlier, or later, and it might not've been good timing."

He stands and helps me up and pulls me against him. "You know, many times I've thought of myself as one lucky SOB. But you might be the jackpot." He leans down and gives me another swoon-worthy deep kiss. It's tender and possessive. Inside, I'm buzzing.

"Would you rather go have a drink at my place or at Hudson Yards?"

A woman skates by on inline blades, holding her phone out and taking pics as she goes. I can't tell if she's taking photos of the river or taking selfies as she passes. So many people are milling about, it feels like every single person living in Manhattan is outside enjoying this last burst of warmth. I'd be happy to do anything with Sam, but there's a part of me that wants to have him all to myself, away from the world. "Let's go back to your place. I want to get to know you better."

Once again, his face lights up. As we leave, out of the corner of my eye, I see a man in a black suit with an earpiece. He looks familiar to me, and I turn my head to get another look. As I do so, I notice Sam give a quick nod in his direction. "Do you know him?"

He pulls me close to him and kisses my forehead. "Yeah. What do you say we stop by a deli to pick up some things to munch on? Grapes, cheese, and such? I have wine for us. And we'll order dinner."

I poke him in the ribs. "I thought you said you were cooking."

He responds with a rolling Texan accent and a cocky grin, "Darlin', that's how I cook. I'm a master of menus."

Sam lives in the XI building in West Chelsea. The building stands out as a feat in architecture, twisting upward on the west side of Manhattan. A glass and iron icon. I notice it every time I venture near the Hudson River. They advertised heavily for this building when it was under construction, promising unprecedented luxury. The lobby is a mixture of wood, marble, glass and refined metals. White marble lends an elegant ambience, not nearly as austere as I had imagined it would be. The towering ceilings and warm brass fixtures strike a balance between imposing and evocative.

Sam takes my hand, nodding a greeting at the doormen as we enter, and leads me to the elevator bank. He presses six on the panel and holds me close as others join us on the elevator. I had kind of expected he'd live in the penthouse.

In front of his door, Sam aligns his eyes in front of a slim black glass panel, and the door automatically opens.

"You have a retinal scanner to unlock your door?"

He holds the door open for me and answers, "I'm in tech."

"Huh."

"Technology's kind of my thing. Hence my Teslas." He grins. "I do love Tesla." He pulls me down a long hall. The marble floors resemble the ones in the lobby, but these are a more muted marble color. The hall opens to a living room lined with large windows. The marble transitions to light wood flooring. Floor to ceiling sliding doors on one end open onto an expansive furnished terrace.

"You have a terrace!" I exclaim. Anna and Jackson were the first people in my circle of friends to have a large terrace. Not a balcony, but a full terrace. As I approach the door, it automatically opens, kind of like the way they open at a store. I step through onto his terrace, which is about the size of my apartment. He has a seating area on one end and a table large enough to seat eight on the other side. In the center of his seating area is one of the concrete fire tables I've seen in the Restoration Hardware catalogs. The view is of the river.

"My mom found this place. There were other units in the building, but this was the only one available at the time with a terrace. I like being able to come outside."

I look around and notice there are no plants. From what I've seen, he favors a modern, clean aesthetic. So clean, in fact, that it feels a little unlived-in.

"Want me to show you around?"

"Yeah, I'd love that. Your place is beautiful. Stunning."

His hand hasn't let mine go the whole time, and his thumb rubs across my knuckles, sending shivers all along my spine. I circle the great room, taking in his home, aware of his hungry gaze as I do so. He opens his mouth to say something then closes it and leads me back inside.

"What? Were you going to say something?"

"Nothing. Nothing that wouldn't make me sound like the king of cheese." The sliding door closes automatically after we exit. He takes two steps to the side and points into another room. The pocket door is open. "Study." He lets me pass to get a better look. He gives me a quick moment to check it out. There's an attached bathroom at the end of his office. He tugs on my fingers to continue the tour.

He spins around and says, "Great room and kitchen." The kitchen is a modern masterpiece. The gray flat panel cabinet doors seamlessly coalesce with the style of the great room. He takes my hand and leads me down the stairs.

"Wow. I haven't been in many Manhattan apartments with two floors." Anna and Jackson also have two floors, but their stairs take you up to the terrace. All their indoor living spaces are on one floor.

"Yeah, you know, I like that it has two levels. Makes it feel more spacious."

"Spacious. It *is* spacious," I mutter as my fingers glide along the sleek ebony railing. My uncle has an enormous condominium in the city. Two floors in a building, the penthouse. He has his own private elevator. But my uncle is in a league of his own. My friends, well, we're more real. Sam, his place in XI, is not what I'd consider realistic for the majority of us.

As we get to the bottom of the steps, he points backward. "Laundry room and exit to elevator behind that door." He points toward an open door that looks down into a hall and adds, "Guest bedroom." Then he pulls me into another long room and says, "Master."

There's a wall of glass at the far end, a replica of upstairs but without the terrace. From his bedroom, you can see the murky brown of the Hudson, ships and ferries on the river, and the green of the Hudson Greenway and the activity along the running path.

A king-size bed with a gray headboard and nightstands line the opposing wall. The jet-black comforter stands out from the various shades of light grays throughout the room. The wide plank natural white pine floor gives the room an open, natural feel.

A series of black and white photographs in black frames line one wall. The photograph closest to me is of a black horse galloping across a field of tall grass. The photo reminds me of the cover art for the book *The Black Stallion*. The other images are black and white landscapes of open pastures and expansive trees.

Sam steps up behind me and pulls my back to his front. "Pictures from home." He spins me around to face him. His lips fall to mine, and finally, finally, I get the chance to freely rub my hands through his hair. He moans as his hands press up against my ass, pushing me against him. The curve of his hard erection presses against my needy core. He walks me backward until my legs hit the bed. He takes the bottom of my shirt and lifts it over my head. He stands back a bit, enough to look at me, standing there in my leggings and jog bra. As far as jog bras go, it's somewhat attractive. It pushes my breasts up, and the straps in the back crisscross in an interesting way. But still, it's a jog bra, and I'm kicking myself for not being better prepared for our first time together. I've been outside with him all day. I haven't even showered since yoga this morning.

He doesn't seem to mind. His assessing gaze takes on a look of hunger. Need. His fingers glide along my collarbone, down the middle of my chest. He caresses my breast, his thumb rubbing along my nipple. The sensation is mild

126

through the thick material, but it feels good. I want more. I finagle the loop under the light blue piece and pull it off. It's slightly awkward, and I'm sure anything but sexy, but he doesn't seem to notice. He helps me remove it and throws it across the room.

He looks at me like he could devour me. Though my hair is in a ponytail and I've been outside all day, his desire makes me feel sexy.

He swallows. "Does this mean…? I don't want to assume."

I rub his erection through his pants, in much the same way he felt my breasts through the jog bra. "I'm counting this as our fourth date."

He takes one step back and lightly caresses my breasts then pushes me back. His eyes darken as I bounce on the mattress. Within seconds, my shoes land on the floor. He grasps the top of my leggings and pulls down. They get stuck near my knees, and I sit up to help. I squirm and kick as I try to push them down. My cheeks blaze as I curse these stupid leggings now stuck around my blasted ankles. He cups my feet then slides the slick material over one foot then the other. I exhale. They are off. He smirks. I laugh out loud. Nothing at all graceful about that. From here on out, I need to wear skirts or dresses.

I sit up, leaning back on my elbows, then reach up to free my hair. It falls along my back. It's late afternoon, and bright light pours through the windows. The hungry look in his eye renews my confidence after the leggings fiasco.

"Damn, girl."

He removes his t-shirt as I lean forward to push his pants down. His ripped chest and abs are bronzed. He looks sunbaked, like someone who spent years working outside.

But the minor gradience of brighter white skin along his hips tells me he naturally has a darker skin tone, like me. I can see the outline of his erection through his black briefs.

I swallow, taking in the significant protruding form. I reach forward to rub along his length. He watches closely. I tighten my grip as I stroke through the fabric, and he angles his hips forward as he groans.

"Damn. That feels so good." He pushes me back on the bed then lies down beside me, kissing me passionately, his tongue swirling with mine, as I grind against him, seeking release from the increasing tension in my core. He sucks one nipple then moves to the other. He bites, and I gasp from the combination of pain and pleasure.

Daylight streams in, highlighting his defined quads and abdominals. For a moment, I'm self-conscious. I am naked on his bed, fully exposed and bare. I shift to close my legs and slide on my side, seeking a more modest position.

He clucks his tongue in a scolding way then slides lower and spreads my legs apart. "You are glistening. Is that for me?"

I whimper as his tongue slides in my entrance. I spread my legs slightly wider, opening for him. He finds my clit, circles it with the tip of his tongue, then sucks. He slips a finger inside and thrusts, finger-fucking me as his tongue ignites my sensitive bundle of nerves. I quiver as all the muscles in my core and through my thighs tighten. My orgasm ricochets through my body, forcing my toes to curl and my knees to rise. I'm spread out with him between my legs, and it strikes me as a touch embarrassing and improper, but I've been aching for him all day, my body an electrified orb from his frequent kisses and touches and sexy smiles and dimples.

He trails soft kisses along my thigh then up my stomach. He hovers around my breasts to suck and bite my nipples. As I slowly come back down to earth, I reach for him, my mouth claiming his, tasting myself on his lips. My hands explore the muscles of his back and then fall lower to grip and knead his firm ass. I push his briefs down as far as I can reach and use my feet to push them farther down his legs. He doesn't even bother with kicking them completely off.

He positions his erection over me, dipping his tip in then pulling back. Teasing me. He settles over me, sliding his tip in and out of my wetness as we both watch. My legs wrap around him, placing his erection in the middle of my wet folds. I lift my hips in invitation. My clit throbs. I ache to have him inside. His hips start to shift, and our hips move to create much needed friction, his erection pressing down on my mound. He kisses me deeply, and I revel in the taste of us mixed together. He hovers over me and hesitates, his eyes searching mine.

I think I know what he's questioning, and I offer, "It's okay. I'm on the pill."

He leans down and takes a nipple into his mouth and swirls his tongue. His right arm reaches out for the nearby bedside table drawer. He pulls out a condom, rips it open, and sheathes himself. In one sudden push, he's inside me. "God, you are so tight." My breath catches, and my body takes a moment to adjust to the intrusion. "You feel so good."

Then we are moving together, moaning, gliding. The headboard hits the back wall repeatedly as I wrap my legs around him. Each thrust forces the headboard to strike the wall, each blow sounding out a loud boom. I raise my hips to pull him in tighter, begging him for harder, for more, matching his pounding rhythm.

We move together in an erotic dance. It's as if I'm standing on a tall cliff, looking across an expanse of ocean, and then I jump. Arms forward, prepared to dive deep. I don't close my eyes. I keep them open. Watching our joining. In and out.

He shifts slightly, lifting my leg, adjusting our position so he's deeper. I'm so close, and then he rubs my clit, hard. I'm done, screaming out his name as he stalls and shudders. We both ride our climax, gripping each other, claiming each other.

He falls back on his back and pulls me to his side. He kisses my forehead and chuckles.

"Damn, girl. Just so you know. We are doing that again."

I kiss his neck and along his jaw. "Today?"

He laughs. "Hell, yes, today."

Eventually, Sam leads me to an enormous marble shower with two heads plus an overhead rainfall feature. Sam washes my hair then my entire body with an attentiveness I've never experienced before. He lavishes attention on each breast and bends down and twirls his tongue around each nipple, causing me to whimper. Then he braces me against the wall and his erection presses against my stomach. I can tell he's thinking about taking me against the shower wall, but he backs up two steps. He grips his hard cock and almost to himself says, "No condom."

I smile, tracing his pecs then farther down until my hand replaces his, taking a firm hold of his pulsing erection, teasing the crown with my thumb. "That's okay. I've got it covered." Then I fall to my knees and take him in my mouth as warm water runs down my back. I roll my tongue around the tip, tasting the salty precum while I massage his balls.

My tongue glides down his shaft along the veiny landscape. I take one of his testicles in my mouth and suck, slightly rolling the ball in my mouth. "Fuck!" he hisses.

Sam braces himself against the shower wall, as if he's having trouble standing. Bringing this gorgeous man to his knees becomes my mission. I sit farther up on my knees so I can take him in my mouth. I take him as deep as I can, using my tongue, my hands to stroke what I can't take. Ever so slightly, my teeth curve around his crown.

"Oh, hell, yes. Just like that." The sound of the shower intermingles with the sound of his heavy breaths. I massage his balls as I focus on taking him deeper and deeper. He groans, "Babe, I'm getting close. I'm going to come."

His hand rests on the back of my head, keeping me in place but never pushing. He groans, and his hips thrust. I take that as a sign to go deeper and suck more, using my hand to stroke the base and the tight balls below. His legs tremble; he groans and releases in my mouth. I swallow as much as I can, then I pull back and lick the cum dripping down his softening cock until he whimpers, then helps me up and pulls me flat against his chest and kisses me. Claiming. Possessive. He pulls back, his breathing labored.

"Thank you. That was mind-blowing."

I grin and he kisses me more. His finger slides inside as his thumb circles my clit, and my knees buckle. He continues the action as he sucks on my nipples. He places his thumb near my ass, circling the forbidden zone. I'm writhing against the shower wall, my knees shaking, completely exposed and open. I've never experienced intimacy like this. Of course, I've never dated anyone with a

131

shower that could accommodate this kind of activity so comfortably. He slips another finger in, moving in rhythm with his thumb against my clit. His fingers work me over like an instrument, working both holes. Forbidden. Erotic. I jerk forward, overcome as my muscles quiver. He holds me as my body trembles. "Has anyone been here?" His finger presses along my virgin hole as he kisses along my throat.

"No." I feel his finger enter me, and I step forward. "That's not for today."

He kisses the side of my mouth while his fingers remain firmly on my ass. "Good to know." Then, with tender care, he takes a washcloth and cleans all of me then allows me to return the favor. He continues to kiss me as we stand naked, clean, holding each other with the warm water pouring along our backs. Eventually, he nuzzles my ear and whispers, "Come on. Let's get dinner."

After drying off, he passes me one of his old Texas Longhorn t-shirts. It hits me mid-thigh. I braid my wet hair, looping the long, single braid around to my front.

He's put on a frayed, faded t-shirt that reads, "It Must Be User Error" in a computer font. Black dogs dot his boxers. He holds two pairs of white tube socks, and he tosses me a pair. "The floor can be kind of cold."

"I can go grab the socks I was wearing."

"Nope." He shakes his head.

I grin, looking up at him. He's pulled me close again, and I take the opportunity to run my fingers through his damp hair. He leans down to kiss me. "No?"

"Nope. I want you in my clothes. Let's go up, order some food, and enjoy a night in. How does that sound?"

"Perfect. It sounds perfect." Maybe it's all too perfect, but there's no reason to not enjoy the moment. Life's about the journey, not the destination. I'm walking down a trail I've never traveled. My heart races, and that familiar urge to run far away rises. But I'm done running. What's the worst thing that can happen? I've been hurt before. So what? I'm strong. Strong women keep moving forward. One foot in front of the other. Secure in the knowledge we can't lose everything, because we'll always have ourselves.

I'm strong. The last time my heart shattered, I grew stronger. Strong enough to face this. Whatever this is. This chance. This journey. This life. My life. I'm going to live a vibrant, full life. And to me, right now, that means taking chances. Jumping off proverbial cliffs.

******

The candescent fire casts a warm glow throughout the great room. Sam and I are snuggled together on his sofa beneath a thick indigo comforter he pulled off the guest bed.

He sips his wine as his fingers twist around my damp, wavy strands. "So, Ms. Grayson, tell me what it is you want from life."

"Hhmm. Digging deep, huh?"

"I want to get to know you. I want to know everything about you." His blue eyes penetrate me, his expression serious. Warmth spreads to my cheeks.

"What I want from life? That's the question?"

"Yes, ma'am." His right dimple appears, and I lean forward to press a kiss to it.

"I guess that's kind of what I'm trying to figure out. I want to be successful in my own right, not because of who my family is. And I want to be happy. I guess that kind of goes without saying, but I watched my parents dive into their careers, and that was fine. I'm not saying it wasn't, but they never seemed happy."

How many times had I sat down to dinner with my parents, and they barely said a word to each other? How many times had the question, "How was your day?" been answered with a brief, "Fine," and nothing more? No signs of happiness. There were times in my life I didn't know what happiness looked like, at least on grown-ups. But, for as long as I can remember, I've known what happiness doesn't look like.

Sam's fingers gently rub along my cheek, drawing me out of my rumination. "Serious thoughts?"

"Just thinking back on my parents. I don't think they were exactly happy. I want more than what they have."

"What do they have?"

I look up to the heavens with a loud exhale. "I don't know. A diligent pursuit of a life that doesn't make them happy? Perfect frown lines?" Sam's fingers play with mine while he studies me. His intense gaze makes me want to deflect his attention. "What about you? What do you want from life?"

Sam smiles and sips his wine, never taking his eyes off mine. "I want what my parents have. I want happiness. I want healthy, happy kids. Time outdoors beneath blue skies and star-encrusted nights."

"Sounds wonderful," I whisper.

"Oh, it will be," he responds as his hand tightens on mine. "I get the sense that you aren't very close to your parents." I raise my eyes to his. "Tell me about that."

"There's not much to tell. My parents weren't around much. They aren't bad people. I just think maybe they didn't want to be parents, or that a child was a low priority.

134

My uncle, he's kind of the patriarch of our family. He looks out for everyone. I don't think he thinks much of my parents. Over the years, there have been arguments when my mom would try to borrow money from my grandmother. Or maybe borrow's not the right word. Take. I don't know the details. They both work hard, but I get the impression they may spend above their means. For whatever reason, I always got the sense that my uncle didn't really approve of my parents. And I think, at some point, it started to become very important to me that he approve of me." This is the first time I've ever admitted this out loud, and tears blur my vision. I stare out the window, aiming to get my emotions under control.

"I can't imagine your uncle feels anything but admiration and love for you."

I do not want to start crying. As if he knows, his lips take mine, lightly at first, then deeply. My emotional turmoil dissipates as he pushes me back on the sofa, his body's weight cocooning me. The door buzzer sounds. Our food is here.

Sam and I are both unpacking the brown paper bags when he says, "You know, not only do I need a throw for this room, I could use a fur rug in front of that fire. Wouldn't it be nice to sit in front of the fire and eat and drink?"

I bite my lip, imagining a scenario in front of the fire on a fur throw, but my scenario doesn't involve food. "That would be nice."

After dinner, he leads me to the bedroom. He backs me up to the bed and pulls my t-shirt off and tosses it on the floor. I'm standing before him in my white silk thong. It's wafer thin and doesn't expose panty lines, so it's what I always wear when going to yoga class. It's kind of sexy, but not what I would have chosen for Sam.

His hands go to my breasts, fondling each one. "Damn, you are perfection." He kisses me. "These are perfection," he says as he massages my breasts, worshiping them. My pulse thrums in my core. He kisses me with a hunger that is starting to feel familiar. "Do you have any idea how beautiful you are? How perfect?" Soft kisses run along my throat and down to my breasts. "How perfect for me? These long legs, full breasts. You are my dream."

How could this gorgeous man be so into me? That's what blows my mind. This gorgeous man I saw in a coffee shop and thought I'd never see again. A fantasy. I remove his t-shirt and spend time exploring his muscular form. The dips and valleys. His perfect six-pack with a light dusting of hair that leads lower. Within minutes, we are both naked. The light in the room is dim. Outside, the sun has set, and city lights twinkle. For hours into the night, we explore each other's bodies, discover secrets, and moan each other's names.

In the morning, I stretch and become aware I'm alone in bed. Realization that I'm in Sam's apartment hits me. I check the time. I need to go back to my place and then head over to school. And my bike is here.

I'm out of bed and dressed when Sam walks in, hair wet from a recent shower and in a suit. "Good morning, beautiful," he says as he pulls me to him.

I push him back. I press my fingers to my lips as I mumble, "I haven't brushed my teeth yet. Do you have an extra toothbrush?"

He grins and leads me into his bathroom. "I might in the guest room. But why don't you use mine?"

"You don't mind?"

"I'm pretty sure we swapped body fluids last night. I'm good with it." He grins. I reach over and grab his toothbrush. I try, but I can't suppress the smile breaking out on my face.

I brush my teeth, then he grabs me and gives me a deep, vigorous morning kiss.

"I hate that I have an early morning meeting. Can I see you tonight?"

He's already walking back out, so I take it this means he has to go. And so do I. I follow him out. "You want to?"

"Yes, ma'am, I do." His southern twang sounds, making me giggle like a schoolgirl.

He peers over at me as if he's questioning my response. I'm aware that giggle is not my norm. But I'm happy. And he's laying on the southern charm. "Well, then, I'd love to see you later."

He holds me close while we wait for the elevator. "You know, if you still worked for me, I could see you every day at the office."

I wrinkle my nose. "It worked out for the best, don't you think? I'm not sure I want to be the intern banging the boss."

He laughs out loud, kisses me, then smacks my ass as I enter the elevator. "Banging? Is that what you call it?"

There's another man in the elevator, and I cannot believe he just said that in front of him. I am completely mortified, but I'm also having trouble not laughing out loud. I keep my head bowed to avoid looking at the stranger and hit the P button for parking when I realize Sam didn't.

"Why are you going to the basement?" he asks.

"My bike." The door opens, and the man walks out into the main lobby, a smirk on his face. Does this count as a walk of shame? Is an elevator ride of shame a thing?

Sam steps back in the elevator to ride down with me. We walk into the basement, and he takes me to a locked room and retrieves my bike for me.

He walks my bike back toward a door near the garage opening and nonchalantly asks, "So, you never answered me."

"What was the question?"

"What are you calling this?"

I grin, thinking back to the man in a suit who overheard our conversation. "Well, banging probably isn't the best word."

He stops and pulls me to him. "That, I agree with." He kisses me. Then slaps my ass. "Now, ride along. I want to watch that delicious bum of yours ride away in those skintight leggings."

I shake my head, hop on my bike, blow him a kiss, and push off.

Chapter 13

Sam

"Good morning, Mr. Duke."

Before I even sit down, Janet is handing me a steaming mug of coffee. She gives me my calendar and stands at my desk, pad of paper in hand, should she need to take notes.

I grin. Of course, I've been smiling like a quarterback who scored multiple touchdowns all morning. "Janet, have I told you recently what an amazing job you do?"

Startled eyes peer back at me from behind black-framed glasses. "Thank you, sir."

I chuckle. She's always so formal. Appropriate.

A soft tap on the frame of my office door sounds, making Janet turn to face the unscheduled intruder. If there is one thing that bothers her to no end, it's when someone tries to catch me for a few unscheduled minutes. Sometimes I think if I let her, she'd stand guard with a crop and whap anyone who tried to do what Bill is trying to do right now.

I sip my coffee and watch Bill and Janet face each other, settling back in my chair to enjoy the show.

"Mr. Withers, do you need to meet with Mr. Duke?"

Bill nods, looking to me and disregarding Janet. "Do you have a few minutes, Sam?"

Janet glances down at my schedule and answers for me. She's not one to be railroaded. "Staff meeting starts at nine a.m. He may need some time to prepare for it."

There was a time when I did need time to prepare for the weekly staff meeting. But now, it's more of a formality. The department heads have eight a.m. staff meetings with their teams. The heads come into my office at nine a.m. for an executive staff meeting, and we review any urgent issues or concerns.

Back when we were in start-up mode, Monday mornings were mission critical. Now, we are a better staffed, lucrative, well-oiled machine. It's not public yet, but I am going to be transitioning out of the CEO role for Esprit. I'll be leading up our yet to be named VC division, but I'll keep my seat on the board. Now, I sit in these meetings and listen.

"Jan, it's okay. He can come in."

She turns to me and nods.

"Everything looks good on the calendar today. Can you make sure I have something scheduled with Jason this week?"

"Yes, sir." she responds and heads out the door as Bill steps in and takes a chair in front of my desk. She closes the door as she leaves.

"Bill, how can I help you?"

He shifts in the chair so his shoulders and back are ramrod straight. I always find people's posture to be telling. I might think he's trying to oversee me. But a long time ago, I decided it's his military background coming out, and this is his natural disposition.

"Sir, I wanted to check in and see if the background report on Ms. Grayson was sufficient."

"Yeah. It was good. Didn't see any concerns. Did you?" I know damn well there are no concerns. She's financially secure. She's not someone who is targeting me because she saw me on some most wanted bachelor list. But I believe in making my employees feel their worth, and I know he thinks what he does is life-saving.

"No, sir." His gaze shifts to the ground then back to me. "May I ask, sir, are you planning to continue to see her?"

I pull my shoulders back and look him in the eye. "I am."

"Then, sir, I would like to encourage you to consider assigning security to watch her."

My grip tightens on my coffee mug. "We've been over this, Bill. That's not necessary."

"Sir, there are additional concerns."

"What concerns?" I bark out.

"We have had sightings of Ms. Ray. We suspect she has seen you with Ms. Grayson, and she may have taken an interest in Ms. Grayson."

I rub my hand through my hair and focus on my breathing. With my head back against my office chair and eyes closed, I ask, "Has she violated the restraining order?"

"No, sir. Not that we have observed."

I lift my head, lean forward, and glare at him. "Give me a rundown of the sightings."

"I don't have them with me, but I can send you a full report. Sir, I am suggesting a security detail for Ms. Grayson in an abundance of caution. That is all."

Damn. I huff. "I am not a celebrity figure. This is insane."

"Sir, in the Manhattan area, you are frequently cited as being one of the most desirable bachelors. The *Post* mentions when you eat out. There are bloggers who talk about where you are. Someone tweeted a photo of you yesterday at the Boat House."

"Are you kidding me?"

"No. Ms. Grayson was smiling in the photo. But the caption read 'Sam Duke Flavor of the Week?' It doesn't look like she staged it. Have you checked her Instagram account?"

I pause, torn between throwing him out of my office and hearing him out. "No."

"It's mainly food and places. No selfies. She doesn't fit the profile of someone seeking publicity." I nod, then he adds, "Even though she was smiling in the photo."

I run my hand through my hair, trying to regain a semblance of calm. I've had my fair share of women seeking social media fame, but that's not Olivia. I remind myself he's simply doing his job.

He continues. "The PR team is monitoring the situation."

The situation. My life is not a situation. I rap my fist on my desk. "None of that is dangerous. You mentioned a security detail?" I am losing my patience. Publicity issue or danger, Bill? Pick your fucking gun. The man constantly recycles the same arguments he made before the board when he recommended I live with security. I wouldn't be so against it, but it feels like fucking surveillance.

"No, tweets aren't dangerous, but we do believe Ms. Ray could be. As you know, stalkers are often unstable, and one out of two stalkers who make threats end up—"

"I am well aware. You have about two minutes before people are walking in that door. I don't need a recap of your spiel. What does this have to do with Olivia?"

"Sir, Ms. Ray is obsessed with you. She has to stay away from you because of the restraining order. It is not a stretch to believe she will now transfer her obsession and start stalking Ms. Grayson if she is seen regularly with you." The unspoken point he is making is that Olivia and I were seen all around Manhattan together on Sunday. The fact that this has been communicated to him via his security minions has my hands balling into fists. It's like living in a fucking fishbowl.

I am glaring at Bill when there is a knock on the door and Janet's head appears. "Mr. Duke, are you ready for the staff meeting?"

I continue to glare at Bill as I answer, "Yeah, send them in."

Collin, my partner at Esprit and one of my best friends, walks in first with others trailing behind him. He's carrying a file and his ever-present notebook. He heads over to the conference table that sits on the other side of my office.

Bill stands, acknowledging our meeting is over. In a low voice designed to keep our conversation private, he says, "Please, for Ms. Grayson's safety, consider it. That's all I'm asking."

Our meeting starts. My phone sits flat on the table before me. Collin starts off the meeting, and then others take over, giving project highlights. I want to take the meeting agenda that's sitting in front of me and rip it up and punch my fist into the wall.

A notification comes across my phone. An email from Withers. I pick up my phone and tap to open the email. There is a list of locations Ms. Ray has been seen at over the past two weeks with dates attached. As part of protocol, my security detail keeps an eye out for this woman. I do agree with Withers that she's unstable. As far as the danger she presents, I've never been afraid of her. I did find it unnerving to see her constantly located on park benches near any building I was in. She's definitely obsessed. But would she act on her obsession? Harm someone? I've never bought in to the theory she's dangerous. Of course, Withers's presentation to the board showed otherwise. He shared stalker case after stalker case where an obsession turned deadly.

The list provides bulleted locations and dates. McKittrick Hotel. Central Park. High Line. Manhattanville Coffee.

My hands turn cold as I read the Manhattanville Coffee bullet. The date isn't the one when I first saw Olivia. There are many dates listed that I have not been on the upper west side. She's been following Olivia, not me.

Collin touches my shoulder, and I snap back as if someone punched me. "Hey, are you okay?"

The others are walking out of my office. I focus on the wood grains running along the conference room table and think through what I need to do. "Yeah."

"Something seems off. Is something bothering you? Are you okay with this transition?"

I stare out the window. "Transition?" I am not following Collin's questions. I couldn't tell you one thing that was mentioned during our staff meeting.

"Yeah. If you aren't into the VC work you've been doing, we can pull you back into the business side. Don't feel like we've made any changes that can't be adjusted. I'm not trying to kick you out of the business." Concern radiates off Collin. I return to staring out the window. He's reading me wrong.

"It's not that." I rotate my seat to face him. "I started seeing someone."

Collin's head jerks back, and he squints. "Really? That's what this pissy mood is about? A woman?" he asks, sounding incredulous while he points at the conference room table.

"That crazy chick may be stalking her now." I watch his expression transition from incredulous to distressed. He gets it now. He pulls out one of the chairs closer to me and sits in it. "What are you gonna do?"

"I don't know, man. I don't know." I stare out the window. "It's so fucking ridiculous. But…Olivia. She's in grad school at Columbia. I can't ask her to put up with a security detail following her around. I don't wanna put her in danger, but…" I sigh, staring out the office window at the winter gray sky and mix of skyscrapers.

"Do you think she'd ever really do anything? You know, a lot of people with obsessions never act on it."

"She's been following Olivia."

"I mean act on it with violence. You know, do something bad. Hurt her. Do you think she's capable of hurting her?"

I lift my head and shake it. "I don't know. But how can I risk it?"

"Yeah, maybe you should keep your dating confined to Texas." I glare at him. He smirks. "You know, this all started when you got listed as one of the top ten most desirable bachelors. And that Ms. Manhattan blogger?"

I lift my eyebrows to signal he should continue.

"She keeps tabs on where you lunch, go out. That's kind of creepy. But she does it for, like, fifty men around the city. It's mixed in with all the gossip."

"How do you know this?"

"Lori tells me. She gets her weekly email and tells me if you're mentioned. Or if I am." He taps the table. "I think Lori really just checks that shit to keep tabs on me. She's been happier since I haven't been included on the bachelor lists recently. I think it makes her think everyone sees us as an item, and I'm off the market."

I rest my head on the back of the chair and stare at the ceiling. "Dude, you guys live together. You are off the market. At any rate, what are you suggesting? Have our PR team work to keep me off those lists?" This whole situation is ludicrous. "How many people read that shit?"

"I don't know. I've never looked into it. I'm gonna guess the blog readership is low. The *Post*?" He waffles his head back and forth like he's weighing possible answers. He has no idea. "Seems like trash to me."

I tap my fingers on the arm of my chair. "It doesn't matter. Most normal people wouldn't think twice about a bachelor list." Besides, I'm pretty sure Ms. Ray never used published media as her source for my whereabouts.

"What are you gonna do?"

"I don't know. I can't ask her to have a security detail. She's in grad school. No one wants some guy following them around on campus. At some point, classmates would pick up on it. I don't think she'd be in any danger. But can I risk it? On the other hand, I hate having security tailing me everywhere. I can't ask her to deal with that invasion."

He cocks his head as he studies me. "Well, I have to say, I can't remember the last time you wanted to date someone. Guess I always assumed you were doing all your dating back in Texas. But if you like her, you should date her. You've got the ability to keep her safe. If you have a real reason to think she's not safe, then listen to Withers. The man lives and breathes security. I'd bet that man is, like, assassin level. He's like James Bond. Use him. Don't let fear win."

I bite the corner of my lip thoughtfully before I respond. "I don't know. This one's too important to move forward on without thinking it through." Analyze and evaluate the risks. We built a company making well-thought-out strategic decisions.

Olivia flits through my mind. Her mesmerizing blues, thick, long brown hair, her smooth skin. Sweet, rich scent. Headstrong. Independent. She'd hate succumbing to security as much as I do.

I clench my fist. No, I can't ask her to give up her privacy. And I can't risk her safety. I don't see a good solution here. At least not a solution I like.

Chapter 14

Olivia

"Someone's looking happy." Paige grins at me from behind the counter as she hands over my mug of coffee, and I pay for it along with the banana and yogurt I grabbed from the refrigerator.

A subtle but noticeable burn radiates across my cheeks from the wide smile that's been plastered on my face all morning. I'm floating, and it doesn't shock me at all that my favorite barista notices.

As I gather my breakfast, I admit to my blue-haired friend, "Good weekend." Great, amazing, unforgettable weekend. But I'm pretty certain Paige doesn't want the details.

I settle down in my chair and pull out my calendar to get a grasp on all the stuff I have to get done today. Before I make any progress, *Take It Easy* sounds from within my backpack. Delilah. I'm like a bubble about to burst and can't get the phone answered fast enough.

"Hey!" I answer with so much enthusiasm I almost wince from how cheerleader-like I sound. Again, so not me.

Delilah doesn't miss a beat. "Tell. Me. Everything!"

I squeal. Literally squeal like a schoolgirl. "We spent pretty much all day yesterday together. He called me right after my yoga class."

"I knew when you blew us off for brunch that you'd spend the whole day with him. Did you stay at his place or yours last night?"

I hesitate for one second, then decide I've got to let it all go. "Delilah, he's amazing. Like earth-shattering, going to completely crush my heart, amazing. What am I doing?"

"What do you mean, what are you doing?" she screeches so loudly I hold the phone out from my ear an inch or two. "This is awesome. And it's so what you deserve."

"I don't know. I'm floating right now. Waiting for the bubble to pop. I don't want to sound negative. I don't. It's just, you know, can he really be this awesome?"

"Sweetheart, you deserve this. Enjoy it. No one is going to pop your bubble. And I'm going to be the best bridesmaid you could imagine!"

I laugh out loud at that, and the guy sitting across from me looks up from his laptop and adjusts his glasses. His perusal reminds me I'm sitting out in the open where everyone can hear my conversation. "I'm hanging up now."

I roll my eyes. Marriage. Leave it to Delilah to go there. I'll be happy if we make it through the week without me regretting this. I have a history of being attracted to jerks. And this guy is gorgeous, and I'm pretty sure there's a good chance he's a player. He said he's been focused on his business, but a guy that hot and successful? It wouldn't exactly be shocking to learn he's a one-night stand champion. That thought sobers me.

My stomach lurches as memories of that day resurface. Me walking deeper into the graphics studio, searching for Damien, my boyfriend. Most everyone had gone home for the day. I wanted to find him to see if he'd seen the real estate listing I'd sent him.

I walk toward the sound. Most monitors are dark, but purple lines zip across in screen saver mode on some. As I

149

walk around the corner of one large monitor, brown curly hair bobbing up and down comes into view. Everything goes into slow motion as I pass the monitor obscuring my view.

Damien's hands shoot up into the air as if I'm holding a gun. For a fleeting moment, I wish I was holding a gun. His eyes are wide, but he doesn't stop the woman bobbing up and down on his cock. One hand moves slowly down to her head, poised above it, as if he's thinking about stopping her but doesn't really want to.

A vise grips my chest, and the room blurs. I turn to leave, but then I visualize the apartment we almost signed a lease on last weekend. We didn't get it. Some other lucky, quicker applicants did. But if we'd gotten it, we would have signed a one-year lease together on an apartment I couldn't afford alone.

Anger mixes with shock. "What the fuck are you doing?"

The curly brown hair lifts at my voice and turns around then runs her tongue across her lips.

"It's not what you think. I promise," Damien says, drawing my attention upward, above his cock and the woman's head.

"Well, what the fuck is it?" I scream.

"Calm down. It's not a regular thing."

Curly brown hair sits on her butt, eyes darting between Damien and me before settling on me.

Damien tucks himself back into his pants as he says, "Olivia, calm down, and let's talk about this."

That's the last thing I hear him say. I head back out into the long hall that connects the studio with the account offices. All I want is to leave. I'm alone in the hall. He's not chasing me. He's not trying to catch up with me or talk to me. Tears blur my vision as I hurry out of the building.

Only one of our receptionists sits at the reception desk. The lights behind the desk are dimmed for close of business.

She looks up at me, and her lips contort a bit. Sympathy. She feels sorry for me. Somehow, she fucking knows. Stacy from reception knows I walked in on Damien cheating on me. From the look she's giving me, she's not surprised at all, but she feels sad for me because she knows I didn't know.

I hear Stacy call, "Olivia, everything okay?" as the elevator dings and the doors slide open.

I hate that sympathetic look. As a kid, I was always the last one picked up from school. Whoever had dismissal duty would stand with me, and parents would cast downward glances my way with their bottom lip pushed out a bit. Sometimes they'd offer something like, "Are you okay, sweetie?" For all things holy, I hate that look. Yes, Damien, Stacy from reception gave me that look because of you.

A chair sliding on the hardwood floor nearby pulls me out of my trance. I shake my head to clear the memory. For days, a slideshow ran through my head on repeat of her head. Damien's hands and his blasted "calm down." One call to my uncle, and I had a new job lined up, not only in a different company so I never had to see that bastard again, but a new country.

Damien texted twenty-nine times, mostly during the first week or two, sporadically since. I haven't responded once, but I haven't yet deleted them either. He had the gall to reach out to my mother and ask if he could meet her for lunch. If there's one thing I can count on her for, it's her lack of time. After showing him the hand, she texted me, annoyed my ex-boyfriend consumed any of her screen time.

I pull my calendar back out in front of me and attempt to focus on planning the week ahead. I move my undone tasks from the weekend into allocated time slots on this week's calendar. The somewhat mindless task helps me to focus, level the roller coaster of emotions flowing through me. Yes, historically, I've made some bad choices, but that doesn't mean Sam is a bad choice.

A shadow falls over my table. I glance up, and my mouth drops for a moment. Lindsey pulls the chair out and joins me.

"Hey, there. Do you mind if I join you for a minute?" She's holding a steaming cup of coffee, but it's a paper cup, the kind you can take out. I glance over and see Paige watching us before she turns back to the coffee machine.

Seeing Lindsey triggers flashbacks to Halloween night. Memories I'd kind of forgotten in my magical day yesterday. I stare at Lindsey, trying to decipher what she wants. We kissed. And did more. But it was a drunken haze. And now, here she sits.

She gives me a slight smile. "Are you okay? Can I sit here?"

Her repeated question makes me realize I never answered her. "Yeah, yeah, that's fine. How are you?" It's the first thing out of my mouth, and I blanch at the generic question.

"Hey, it's not going to be weird between us now, is it?" Her gaze darts from me, over to the coffee bar, and to several of the other folks sitting around us in the coffee shop. She doesn't look me in the eye.

Without thinking, I reach out and touch her arm in an attempt to placate her. "Hey, yeah, we're friends." I wait until her focus settles back to me, and I continue. "It was a crazy, drunken night. I mean, I don't even remember a lot

152

that happened." I lean back and wrap my fingers around my large coffee mug. "How'd you get home?"

She relaxes. Turns out she doesn't remember getting home either. We were both wasted. She spent Saturday on her sofa, completely hungover, just like me. We're sitting there discussing the insanity of Halloween night when a text comes through. I glance down to read it. My body temperature goes from room temperature to ice cold.

Sam: Hey, something has come up, and I've got to head to San Fran this week. Rain check for tonight. Talk later.

I read and re-read the text. "Hey, you okay?" I hear Lindsey ask, concern in her tone.

"Yeah. Yeah." I scratch my nails along my scalp before returning my attention back to Lindsey. "I met this guy, and now he's blowing me off." Maybe he's not, but the sinking feeling in my stomach says otherwise. I open my backpack and plop my phone into it. I do not need to respond and need to start focusing on school. My to-do list for today is massive.

"I doubt he's blowing you off."

"No, I'm pretty sure. Maybe not. Who knows? We'll see." I set my coffee on the table and resume filling out my calendar for the week.

A flirty smile crosses Lindsey's face. "Has he kissed you?"

I squint and cautiously respond, "Yeah."

She stands to leave and smiles down at me as she pushes the chair in. "Then, I promise. He's not blowing you off." With a grin, she tosses her hair over her shoulder and prances out, never looking back.

TRUST ME

Chapter 15

Sam

I head straight to the hostess stand at Jin Ramen, right past a line of people. Customers in line are now watching my interaction with the hostess to ensure I don't jump in front of them for a table. The hostess hasn't yet spoken to me, but I'm looking over her head anyway.

I see Jason sitting at a table toward the back of the restaurant and don't even bother to say a word to the hostess. I'm pulling a chair out from the table before Jason sees me.

"Hey, man. What's up?"

Jason shrugs in answer. He has no energy. I wish I could zap him or force feed him pills to make him return to his old self. I've seen him down before, but this doesn't make sense. His last PET scan results were good. Unless he hasn't told me the truth. I study him, not saying a word.

Finally, he notices. "What?" he asks.

"Your test results, they were good, right? You're in remission?" He's been given the NED determination before, meaning no evidence of disease. And it came back, so I know good results don't mean a guarantee. He'll be fighting cancer, in one way or another, for the rest of his life.

He huffs loudly and picks up the menu. "Yes, I told you. All good."

"Well, why are you so down? You look like someone died. I don't get it."

He flicks the menu on the table, annoyance radiating off him. "I'm fine. I'm fine, okay? Just settling back into my day-to-day, that's all."

I squint, considering his phrase, day-to-day. Does he not like his career? Is that what this is about?

"Anyway, I thought you wanted to talk about you. I'm sick of talking about me." He pauses and scowls at me. "Yes, talking about me is making me sick. I need to talk about, think about, someone other than me." He points at me. "Let's go. Tell me what's going on. I know something's up. Janet told me you needed to talk. Spill."

I flinch. "What did Janet say?" I haven't said word one to Janet.

"She said something's eating at you, and she's glad we're going out tonight. You know, she and I talk on the phone more than you and I do."

Yeah, Janet pretty much arranges my life. No surprise she's close to the players.

The waitress comes over, and we order. The moment she leaves, Jason taps the table and says, "Spill."

"Nothing to spill." He angles his head, and his expression tells me he's not buying what I'm selling. Fine. "Remember Olivia?" I run my hand through my hair and look out across the restaurant. "Well, we're seeing each other. It's only been a short while, but…" I rap my knuckles on the edge of the table, not sure where to go with this. "I've got to think it through."

"Think what through?"

"Do you remember the woman I had to get a restraining order against?"

Wrinkles form on his brow and around the corners of his eyes as he tries to connect the dots. "Yeah."

"Well, she's still around."

"Has she done anything?" He sits forward, arms on the table, alert.

"Nah. I didn't even know she was in the picture. I haven't seen her. But my security team, I guess they've been keeping an eye on her. They hadn't mentioned her to me in a long time, but it seems she's still…" I can't bear to admit out loud that some woman out there has an obsession with me. This whole situation has given me so much more empathy for actors. Or anyone in the public spotlight. Anyone whose privacy gets invaded so people can read about them. If my brothers knew I hired all this security for protection from a girl, they'd never stop ribbing me.

"But she hasn't approached you? Threatened you? Because, you know, if she threatens you, that's serious. Half of all stalkers who make threats end up acting out on it."

I gesture to stop him. "I'm fully aware of the stats." I glare at him to force him to drop it. "But I saw a list of the places where she's been spotted." I huff. "It looks like she's started following Olivia."

Jason starts to open his mouth to say something then closes it. I wait. "So, is it like transference? Like her obsession has transferred?" He stops and shakes his head as he thinks it all through then snaps his fingers. "No, she's obsessed with Olivia because it's the first person she's seen you date."

"Maybe. I don't know. My security team keeps an eye out for her, but they don't talk to her. We'd need a psychiatrist to understand what's going through her mind." And that's what made her scary to begin with. She refused to see someone. I offered to pay for a therapist. Her parents are

157

dead, and her ex-husband doesn't want anything to do with her. She's a loner.

Jason taps his index finger along his jaw as he absorbs what I've shared. "What does Olivia say about it?"

I shake my head. "Haven't told her."

Jason's facial expression shifts the moment the lightbulb goes off. "You're considering not dating her to avoid bringing her into this."

I open both my hands flat, flip them over, and study my palms. "Yeah. Bill wants me to hire security to trail her, but I don't want that for her. She's in grad school. It'd be unfair to her."

Jason sits back. "But you mentioned the security team is following your stalker. If she tried to do anything to Olivia, wouldn't they see?"

I jump up, grab his head, and pull him over so I can smack a giant kiss on his forehead.

Jason pushes me off and wipes at his forehead, smiling while saying, "Ew, man. Knock it off."

I get back in my seat. "I knew I could talk this through with you. That makes total sense. Why didn't I think of that? And why didn't Bill? I mean, we don't have anyone tailing her twenty-four-seven. Bill has someone who kind of knows her general vicinity. Maybe if she comes near me, they follow her. But I can have them adjust that. She might as well get tailed. At least, as long as they're discreet."

"Yeah, the stalker becomes the stalked," Jason says in an eerie tone while he wiggles his fingers.

"Interesting." I smile, thinking it all through. "This could work. I'll cover off on it with Bill, but this could work. Okay. So, we've worked out my situation. What's going on with you?"

"Nothing. You know, you still need to talk to Olivia. Tell her what's going on."

"You're right. She needs to know. Be aware. I hate taking any risk with her."

"Man, some risks are worth taking. You can't live your life in fear."

I study my friend. "Maybe that's some advice you should take to heart?"

He gazes out the window and quietly responds, "No. It's different for me. You've got a whole life in front of you. Make sure you live it." He turns to me, gives me the tiniest of upturned smiles, and sips his sake.

"You've got a full life to live too."

"Until it comes back."

"Shit. Is that what you've got yourself thinking? It's coming back?"

"There's a damn good chance it will. I just——"

"No, man. Even if it does come back, we'll kick it again. And it may not come back. You've got to get out there and live. None of us know when our last day is coming. It means we each have to get out there and live. Live as if it's our last."

He angles his head. "Says the man who was just debating not dating someone because of the risk from some crazy chick who likes to watch him from park benches."

"That's different. That's *her* safety," I argue. I stand firm on this. "You've got to put yourself out there. You can't live each day expecting a recurrence."

I can tell he's thinking about arguing with me, but instead digs into his food. I make a mental note to talk to Olivia and see if she has any ideas about people we could set Jason up with. Olivia. She thinks I'm still on a business trip, and I've been MIA. Not a great way to treat a woman. Maybe I can surprise her.

I turn back to Jason. "Did you ever get a chance to think any more about date ideas?"

Chapter 16

Olivia

"Hey, Olivia. What's up?" Lindsey plops down in the chair across from me. It's Thursday, early afternoon, and I've been plowing through reading assignments for the past two hours. It takes a few seconds for my vision to adjust when I look up from my laptop.

"Hey. Homework." I check my watch for the time out of habit. "About to head downtown for my internship. How about you?" I've seen Lindsey quite a bit this week. Sometimes on campus, but mostly here since we both love the same coffee shop.

"Same thing. Have an exam this afternoon. Stopped by for some energy. So, you never told me. How are things going with the guy? Tell me I was right. He wasn't blowing you off."

I sigh as I gather my things together. "Unfortunately, I was correct."

"Huh? No way!" Disbelief radiates off her. Frizzy pieces of hair stick out all around her head, giving her this crazed, rolled-out-of-bed appearance.

"Yeah. Crickets." He ghosted me. Yes, he's away on business, but it's Thursday, and I haven't heard a word since he waved goodbye Monday morning. If that's not a blow-off, I'm not sure what is. You don't have the kind of weekend we had and then go into radio silence. Unless you're a flavor of the week kind of guy, which, according to Delilah, he has that reputation.

Lindsey smiles and tosses her hip out to the side, getting comfortable in her stance. "I don't believe it. Wait and see. He'll be in touch."

"No. Trust me. I have this knack. It's a talent. Jerk magnet. Right here." Only he didn't seem like a jerk. He seemed so real. Not like a player. Damn me and my judgement.

"Well, is he not answering your calls and texts? I don't understand."

"Lindsey, I'm not calling him. We had a date on Sunday. It's Thursday. He hasn't called me."

"Oh, you're one of those girls."

"What does that mean?"

"You put it all on him. Wait for him to call."

"Well, yes. I'm not going to chase a guy. He canceled our date on Monday, and I haven't heard a word from him since."

"You should text him. Isn't he some super business guy? He's probably just been busy."

I roll my eyes. I've been feeding myself the *he's probably just busy* reasoning for days. That's bullshit. You make time for your priorities. It's not surprising that I'm low on his list. I've been low on other people's priority list my whole life.

I throw my backpack on my shoulder and stand. Lindsey jumps up and stands close to me. I take a step back, reclaiming my personal space. She places her hands on my shoulders, effectively holding me in place. "Listen to me. Trust me. Send him a text. Reach out. He'll appreciate it."

She looks like a train wreck. Smeared eyeliner. Eyebrow hair growing all outside the lines. Has she been going to raves all week? "Thanks for the advice, but that's not my style."

Still gripping my shoulders, her lips curl into a devious grin. "You could offer him a threesome. That would get him to call you."

I break away from her and head out the door. Her suggestive grin sends a bolt of nausea through me. It's time to drop this little joke. "Bye, Lindsey!" I shout as I head outside.

I'm wearing my prized, comfortable black Prada heels which were a gift from my grandmother, jeans, a white t-shirt, long necklace, and a blazer. It's my 'yep, I'm a hip intern' outfit. I need to drop off some research I completed for Esprit Corp and then walk the couple of blocks to get to the office.

My stomach somersaults as the elevator rises. I focus on breathing to quiet my nerves. He's still in San Francisco. I should not be nervous. I'll leave them with his admin and head right out.

Janet won't know he's blown me off. Maybe that's why my nerves are rumbling and I'm feeling on edge. If Janet does know he's ghosted me, I'll get that pity look. The look I hate. I do not want pity.

Yeah, I was aiming a little too high when I thought something could happen between Sam and me. But I don't need pity. We went out, like, twice. We are still in the perfectly acceptable blow-off stage.

I walk down the hall and see unmistakable surprise on Janet's face. Oh, yes, security didn't call up to let her know I was coming up. I'm on the vendor list now and told him I was dropping a package off, not meeting anyone. I give her a warm smile, aiming to set her at ease and get the hell out. I hold out the thick envelope. "Hi, Janet. I'm delivering research from Goldwater Brooke."

She returns my smile and takes the package. "If you wait a minute, Sam's about to finish a meeting. I'm sure he'd love to see you."

I draw in slow, steady breaths. So, not out of town. "How did his trip go?" I ask. Her confused expression tells me everything.

"What trip?"

That motherfucker. Wow. I mean, I knew he was blowing me off, but it didn't occur to me he lied about his business trip to get out of our date. I don't answer her but spin around and rush to the elevators. I'm reeling. I push the button to go down. As the elevator doors open, so does Sam's office door. He smiles when he sees me, then his face transitions to alarm when I glare back at him.

There are women who would smile and act like all is okay, but that's not who I am. It's not okay to act like you are completely into someone and then not call or text. I deserve more than that. Fine if I'm not his priority, but if he wanted to cancel our date Monday, he could have told me. Something like, "Hey, this is moving too fast. I need some time." That would have been acceptable. Not the emergency business trip lie. Motherfucker.

I'm a couple of blocks down on Broadway when I hear my name. I turn and see Sam speed-walking down the sidewalk.

I turn back and sprint toward my destination. Tears sting my eyes. I do not need this. He wanted to ghost me. The least he could do is let me leave without confronting me.

I almost fall backward when he grabs my backpack and pulls hard. I spin, ready to fight. "What the fuck are you doing?" I shout. The street vendor selling nuts peers over at us. We've got an audience. Good. *Let's go, asshole.*

164

He steps back, arms out in a defensive gesture. "Hey, Olivia." Concern etches his face. "What's wrong?"

Is he fucking kidding me? "You lied to me." Thank the gods I actually know he lied to me about his trip. Telling him I'm pissed he didn't call would make me sound weak.

He angles his head and squints, and wrinkles form on his brow. "About the trip?"

"Yes, about the trip!" What else has he lied to me about? "If you didn't want to go on a date with me on Monday, you could have just said so. You didn't have to lie to me."

"No, look. I can explain."

"I'm sure you can." I turn and charge toward my internship. I don't need explanations. A lie is a lie. I'm just glad I saw through his whole act before I fell for him.

He rushes along beside me. He grabs my arm, but I snatch it away and yell, "Do. Not. Touch. Me!"

Matching my stride, he keeps up with me along the sidewalk.

"Stop for one minute. Just one minute." His tone is just shy of demanding.

We are approaching the entrance to Goldwater Brooke. If I run inside, he will likely follow me, and I'll either have to listen to him or risk making a scene. Or I can give him a minute outside. Ensure no one I work with sees us. I stop and step to the side near the building. I hold out my index finger. "One minute. One."

"Okay. Damn, spitfire." He grins.

"Forty-five seconds."

"I thought you were in danger, and I needed some time to think through what to do. Risk assessment. I should have called you, but I wasn't sure I could see you without putting you at risk."

165

"What?" I've dated some losers before, but this story has to take the cake. At least the fucker didn't tell me to calm down.

"Can I explain?"

I look at my wrist, more for dramatic effect than to actually learn the time. "I am due for my internship in five minutes."

"That works."

I roll my hand in a silent gesture for him to begin while glaring at him.

"I'm not quite sure how to start."

I huff. I don't have time for this. Excuses. Male excuses.

"I'm gonna blurt it out. No sugar coating. There's a woman who became obsessed with me. Almost two years ago. I have a restraining order against her. I have security following me because of her." He turns and looks down the sidewalk and stretches out his arm. He's pointing at a man in a black suit standing at the intersection farthest from us. He nods at Sam.

I am familiar with the need for security. My uncle has hired security before for events. He's never had security for himself, but I know at one point he considered it for his wife and kids. My aunt vetoed it.

I study Sam. My anger starts to subside, but I still don't see how any of this explains this week. Is this woman a danger? To him? "Is she dangerous?"

"I don't know. I don't think so. She has an obsessive personality. She stalked me for around two years, to the point she lost her job. She's antisocial. Delusional. I don't know if she would ever turn to violence, but it's a risk my company mitigates by hiring security for me."

"What does this have to do with you lying to me about going on a business trip?"

"Bill believes she has started following you."

"What?"

"I found out Monday, and my first reaction was to put some distance between us. I don't want to put you in danger."

"Let me see if I understand this. You think this woman might be a danger to me. Because of you?"

He slowly nods.

"And so you don't want to see me because you don't want to put me in danger?"

"Well, that's what I was thinking. But then my buddy Jason and I were talking, and we came up with a different plan."

"Go on." If he's making it up, it's an outlandish excuse. Creative. I'll give him that.

"Yes. I'm gonna hire security to follow her. I don't want security trailing you. I hate knowing some guy is always watching me. Hate my loss of privacy. You're in grad school. I don't want to invade your life." He reaches out and caresses my face. "I want you to be untouched by this. I don't think she's dangerous, but I can't risk you getting hurt. Can you get that?"

"Yes." He's making sense. His touch soothes me. My muscles relax, and the anger that had been about to violently explode within me dissipates. He pulls me close, wrapping his arms around me.

His story replays in my mind. I don't want to be the whiny girl. But I have to ask. "Well, I get not wanting to be seen with me while you figured this out. But why didn't you call me? Or text?"

He bites his lower lip before answering. "I wanted to. So much. At first, I didn't see how I could still see you, but I didn't want to tell you that or tell you what was going on. I didn't want to scare you. I thought not talking to you was the best plan until I figured it out."

"When did you figure it out?"

"Last night."

"It's almost the end of day Thursday." Now I'm whining, but I've spent the whole week thinking he was ghosting me. I went from being in the clouds to the pits.

"Yeah, well, I wanted to clear my plan with Bill."

"Who's Bill?"

"Our head of security. You've met him." Oh, yeah, I remember the interrogation. Mr. Gun Holster. "I also thought that given I've been MIA, a little surprise might be needed to win you back over."

"A little surprise?"

"Can you miss class tomorrow?"

"Not my morning classes." I could miss class. Tomorrow, I happen to know my professor is out and the TA will essentially be reading notes that will be emailed out. But I'm reeling from what he's told me. I'm not willing to cancel my plans to make time for him. I need space to think it through. Evaluate. I can't trust my emotions on this.

"What time tomorrow can I pick you up?"

"Pick me up?"

"I want to take you away this weekend."

"Where?"

"A surprise."

He leans down and kisses me. My barriers break. Those blue orbs mesmerize me, and I find myself wanting to dive in.

"Okay." It's just a weekend.

"And what about tonight? Can I take you out to dinner?"

Alarm bells go off. My muscles tense. No. I can't let him think I'm readily available. If I hadn't caught him in his lie, would he even be asking me out for tonight? No. Going away for a weekend is enough. "No. I need to study." Now who's lying?

He studies me. Then he backs me up against the wall and kisses me as if I'm his long-lost love. "Are you sure about that?"

"Yes." *No.* I walk backward, away from him. I'm not going to let him change my mind on this. I need time to figure this out without a flurry of emotions twisting reason.

"Tomorrow. I'll pick you up at your apartment. Noon?"

I nod then wave goodbye as I enter the building. A sense of frustration rises that I didn't stand up to him. That I agreed to a weekend away. I tell myself I'll evaluate it all this evening, when I'm calmer. If I don't feel good about it, I'll text him and cancel. If he can text and cancel, so can I.

Chapter 17

Olivia

This unexpected trip out of town has me scrambling to wash laundry and missing my Friday morning classes. Now, with laundry done, I'm standing here looking at my clean clothes with no idea what to pack and less than an hour before he picks me up. He told me to pack comfortable, warm clothes. Therefore, he's not flying me off to an island. It could be Paris or almost anywhere in Europe. November calls for warm clothes in many European locations. Of course, it could be Chicago or San Francisco. He goes to San Francisco all the time, and he did mention he has one business meeting to attend. The temptation to cancel rises. Avoiding this whole colossal time suck would be smart and a much more relaxing way to slip into the weekend.

Three dresses, four pairs of jeans of varying shades of blue, a lingerie mishmash pile, several sleeveless silk tops, mini-skirts, long skirts, and long sleeve tops crowd my bed and chair, and boots, sandals, fuck-me heels, running shoes, and platform options litter the floor. The jumble of clothes, my attempt at finding suitable outfits to pack, reminds me of my childhood room. My mom snapping, "Clean that room." When I was sixteen, I'd had a similar clothes fiasco when trying to pick out my outfit for my first date, suffering from a world of indecisiveness.

"What's going on?" Mom stands in my doorway, striking her toe on the hardwood, a light tap emphasizing the slight jerks of the pointed heel.

Tim will be here in twenty minutes, and I have no idea what to wear. My first date. Ever. With a senior. Every outfit looks too young, too sophomoric, too nowhere-in-his-league.

"I thought you were going out tonight?" Anger saturates her words.

I finger a white blouse I'd been considering wearing. "I am. What do you think of this with jeans?" I'd already had it on once but worried it might be too plain.

She stares at the blouse for one quick second then rolls her eyes, annoyance radiating through her frown. "It'll do. I need you gone in thirty minutes. I have a friend coming over." She spins away, sending a flurry of platinum blonde hair fluttering behind her shoulder. As she charges down the hall, she bellows, "And clean that room!" Of course she has a friend coming over. My father is out of town. By the time Tim arrives, my cheeks are red and splotchy, but I am no longer crying.

I hear a knock on my door and freeze. Sam wouldn't show up early, would he? I'm nowhere near ready. The knocking gets louder. Loud enough to be heard by my neighbors. I rush to the door and swing it open.

Delilah tosses her arms in the air and half shouts, "Surprise! I'm here to help."

I should tell her that she's being silly, she shouldn't be using her lunch break to come up to the upper east side and help me. But there's another part of me that feels immediate relief that I have someone to run my packing decisions by.

171

That part wins out, and my arms wrap around my friend, so extraordinarily grateful.

"Thank you so much. I'm second-guessing everything." I grab her hand and pull her back to my bedroom. The room looks a bit like someone opened my closet and threw everything out on the bed and across my chairs. "This is insane. I rock at packing. Like, I could teach classes on effective packing. And look at this." I stomp my foot as frustration overwhelms me. This is not me. *Why am I letting this guy get me so worked up?*

Delilah exudes calmness and control. "We'll get it done. Take me through the outfits you've packed so far. And you don't know where you're going, but he says to pack warm clothes, right?"

I nod. I don't think I've ever seen this side of Delilah. She's all business. She taps her cheek with her index finger as she speaks. "No ski trip, wrong time of year. He'd tell you if you needed bathing suits. I'd bet he's taking you to a city, so let's plan for that. Gotta be flexible in case you're going to some remote location where you never leave the cabin."

She makes a few adjustments to what I've set aside. In less than twenty minutes, I'm zipping up my suitcase, shoulders back, standing tall. I've packed interchangeable pieces, mostly prepared for a casual weekend, but ready for a restaurant scene too. I've even packed running clothes. Thanks to my friend, I've got this.

"You are the best. The absolute best." I hug her to make sure she understands how much this means to me. I didn't ask her to show up and help. In fact, she offered, and I told her not to bother. She heard the panic in my voice, I guess, because she disregarded everything I said and showed up in my time of need. Not many people in my life do that for me.

"Yeah, you and Anna are saying that this weekend. You two are gonna owe me. I've just gotta figure out how I'm gonna get payback." She grins.

"Anna? Is everything okay?"

"Dog sitting. It's me and Chewie all weekend. Jackson's taking her away this weekend too."

"He is? Where?"

"Surprise. Just like you with Sam. You are two lucky bitches. You have romantic men. What do I have? Enough bizarre dates to publish a dating memoir." She taps her nose. "Maybe I should pitch that? Isn't that what nonfiction writers do? Pitch their idea before writing it?"

"I don't know. You could Google it," I say as I ponder the possibility that Jackson and Sam got together and planned this weekend. It would be fun, but I'm kind of hoping for a weekend alone with him. Maybe he's not ready for a weekend away with just us? It is kind of a daunting step. And just last night I was debating even going.

Delilah tugs on my hair as we're heading out of the elevator with me wheeling my well-worn black carry-on behind me. "Hey, you okay?"

I shake my head to clear it as we step out into the lobby. "Yeah. You made me wonder if Sam and Jackson might have gotten together to plan something. It's kind of coincidental we're going away the same weekend, right?"

"No, I don't think so. Jackson and Anna seem to go away at least one weekend a month. They usually go places they can take the dog, though. But still, given they're both workaholics, they like to escape together." She bounces a bit on her toes. "Yeah, I guess it's possible. You said Sam and Jackson are friends, right?"

"Yep. They work together a lot too." I haven't been a part of the meetings, but I've done a ton of prep work for Jackson for various projects they are working on. Investments and acquisitions they are exploring. Jackson's even been considering leaving his firm to start something up with Sam. Jackson has shared a lot about it. Sam hasn't mentioned it at all.

Delilah squeezes my shoulder. "Look, even if you are meeting up with them, it doesn't mean anything. Don't second-guess. Enjoy. Women can second-guess the shit out of a new relationship. Create so much anxiety they miss the magic of falling in love." She wags her finger at me. "Do not do that. You enjoy. Enjoy each moment. Be in the moment. Not in your head."

I can't help but smile at my golden friend. A romantic optimist. I pull her in for another hug as Sam walks through the door.

"Hello, there." He's smiling big enough that both his dimples are showing. He bends and presses his lips to mine then turns to Delilah, extending his hand. "Hi. I'm Sam."

Delilah places her hands over her heart. "Hi, there. I'm Delilah. And aren't you just a bundle of goodness." She tosses an approving smile my way as they shake.

Sam takes my luggage handle in one hand and reaches for my hand with his other. "I've heard a lot about you, Delilah. Glad to finally meet you."

"Same here." Delilah grins. "Well, I have to get back to work. You two have fun." She speeds out of the lobby and right before opening the doors turns and says, "Olivia, in the moment!" She blows a kiss and walks out the door.

Sam squints from the sunlight through the glass and I expect a question about her parting comment, but instead, he squeezes my hand and asks, "Ready? Car's outside."

Chapter 18

Sam

"Where are we going?" Olivia asks with an eager smile the moment the car turns right onto 82nd Street.

I lean over to secure her hand in mine and reach my left index finger over to tap her nose. "That's a surprise." I wiggle my eyebrows and grin. I've never done anything like this before. Of course, I've never dated someone I wanted to whisk away.

She shifts slightly to watch the city whiz by. I imagine she's wondering where we're headed. Given we are flying out of Teterboro, New Jersey, she's gonna have a hard time guessing what we're doing. I feel like a kid who is hiding in an awesome place with the knowledge the seeker is going to be hunting for a long, long time. "I like Delilah." I say.

Olivia's wearing a sweater dress that hugs her curves and tall suede boots. The same tall boots she wore on our second date. Well, our first date solo. Her dark, glossy hair and large sunglasses make her look a bit like an actress. Effortless elegance. She turns to me and flashes her brilliant white smile. "She's the best. It was really kind of her to come up on her lunch break to help me."

"Help you with what?"

She glances down to the floor, sort of timid, and mutters, "Nothing."

I'm not at all sure it's nothing, and I angle my head, trying to decide if I should push harder.

She tilts her head to the side and then, as if she's admitting an embarrassing secret, "I wasn't sure what to pack. I was nervous."

A huge smile breaks out on my face. "You were nervous to be with me?"

"Well, yeah. We've just started, you know, and I don't know where we're going."

I tug her hand. "We've just started what?"

"I don't know what. Whatever it is we're doing."

"Dating. We are dating. I want to hear you say it."

The corners of her lips lift into a smile. "Dating. We *just started* dating."

I unbuckle my seatbelt and slide closer to her and give her a long, slow kiss. She must use some sort of rosemary mint shampoo. It smells fresh and inviting, and I hope she never switches to another kind. A soft whimper escapes her as we kiss. My hand slides up her thigh. My erection is hard and uncomfortable in the confines of my jeans, and I can't help but wonder if she might entertain joining the mile-high club.

I slide back into my seat, putting space between us while still holding her hand. There's no divider in a Tesla, and I don't need to make Wes feel uncomfortable. I trace her knuckles with soft kisses. "As ego flattering as it is for you to be nervous about what you wear around me, let me tell you. There is no need to be nervous."

She smiles as she shifts in her seat, and her sweater dress rises higher, exposing more of her shapely thighs. Yes, she might be willing to join the mile-high club.

Traffic is light, given the time of day, and we make it to the small airport quickly. The car turns, and we pass the blue and white sign that reads "Airport Teterboro."

She immediately asks, "We're flying somewhere?"

"Yep. Guess where." I can't hold back my boyish grin because surprises are fun.

She shifts to look out the window, watching carefully as if she's trying to figure out which plane is ours. She's doing what I'd do without missing a beat. She's sizing up the jets, planning to use the size of the plane as a clue. As we drive around to the back of the airport, there are several jets lined up for takeoff. One of the jets bears an Esprit logo, but from this angle, it's not visible.

She wrinkles her nose in indecision, a cute little thing I've noticed she does. "Paris?" she asks, hesitant.

I laugh. "Paris? Wouldn't that be a little too expected?"

She grins. "Okay. Let me guess continent, and when I get that right, we'll go to country and then I'll work from there."

"Okay. And I'll toss in a hint. You've never been there. Or at least it wasn't on your list."

She gives me a look that says, 'I seriously doubt that.' And she could be right. It wasn't in her list of locations she told me she visited, but that doesn't mean she gave me her life's full list. Now I'm a little nervous. I want to take her somewhere she's never been before. A first for her with me. Of course, I planned this around a business trip, instead of aiming for a remote destination.

"Europe?"

"Nope."

"North America"

"Yep."

She squints and wrinkles her nose. So cute. "Now you've got me stumped. I'm pretty sure we're going to a city, and I've been to the big ones." She mutters, almost to herself, "Maybe it's not a city."

The car stops by our jet, and we step out. Our flight attendant greets us and asks, "You do both have your passports, correct, sir?"

Olivia turns to me. "Canada?"

"Yep." I'm smirking at her as we follow the flight attendant into the jet and Wes collects our luggage.

"Montreal?" she asks, sounding unsure.

I lean down and loudly smack a kiss on her lips. "Winner, winner, chicken dinner. How'd you guess?" There are a lot of places in Canada we could go.

"Well, because of all the cities in Canada that I could think of that I hadn't been to, Montreal sounds the most romantic."

"I thought so too. You haven't been there, right?"

"No, I haven't."

I want to fist bump someone. *Yes*.

We get seated. I have a business meeting this afternoon, so we're taking the Esprit jet. The jet features two seats on each row facing each other, with a walnut table between the seats. The table can slide away if it's not needed. It's a good configuration for business discussions or to get work done.

This is a business trip, but it's also a two birds with one stone kind of event for me. And I have no intention of taking my laptop out, because on this flight, I'm focused on Olivia.

The flight attendant offers to bring us something to drink. She mentions she'll be serving lunch after takeoff and then heads to the front to sit in an area for the crew. Glancing around the cabin, it hits me we don't have complete privacy. I make a mental note to look at other jet options for the future. With Olivia by my side, the mile-high club now resides as a recent addition to my life's wish list.

The attendant delivers Prosecco for Olivia and Wild Turkey on ice for me. We've pulled out the table between us, a smooth walnut piece wide enough to accommodate two laptops. No, I'm not sure I like this jet configuration at all.

Olivia buckles her seatbelt and pointedly watches me until I also buckle mine. "So, tell me more about this stalker person. I have more questions."

"I'm sure you do." I lean back and rest my arms on the armrests. "Shoot."

"How did it happen?" she asks, concern etched on the outset of caring blue eyes. Her long hair drapes over her shoulder, curving around her breast. I force myself to return my gaze to her face. She taps her fingers on the armrest as she awaits my answer.

We do need to have this conversation. By dating me, she's placing herself in some degree of danger. I'll do what I can to mitigate it, and while I like my plan, she should be aware. "You mean how did the obsession start?"

"Yes." She leans forward and wraps her fingers around the stemless wine glass.

"I wish I knew. When we went public, our PR team was out doing everything they could to get press. It's a big part of going public. We hired an agency that specialized in investor relations. Tried to get lots of press leading up to IPO day."

She tilts her head and crosses her legs. "My background is in advertising, you know? I'm familiar with the PR world."

Of course she is. She could be running a division of an ad agency in Europe right now if she hadn't turned down a job offer. "Well, one small angle," I say, placing my thumb and index finger close together, "was to push the fact that the two founders are bachelors. We were in our early thirties. It was easy to get some of that press and buzz, and I didn't think much of it. A photographer came out, took some photos of Collin and me one afternoon, and that was it. The vast majority of people don't care at all what a CEO looks like. But then we had a successful IPO." I stare out the window at the bright sunlight, not sure how to explain. "Things started to change. At some point in that whole press phase is when it all started."

"What do you mean by 'things started to change'?"

"Well, it's not just this one woman, right? Suddenly, I'm a CEO at a public company worth close to a billion dollars. My assistant's overwhelmed with charity invitations. I walk in a room, and, yeah, to some degree it's business. People know deals can be made fast if you start with the CEO. Which is fine, right? I built my business by seeking out the right people too. But then, after the IPO, shit became real. People started telling me my kids will need security because they're a kidnap risk. Now, every time I'm on a date, my brother is telling me to be sure to 'wrap it up' because someone might want to trap me." She giggles, and I grip the armrest. It's crazy and sounds funny, but it's not so funny when you're living it. It's not so funny when it actually happened.

"Did it feel like it happened overnight?"

"Yes and no. For the most part, it's all fine." I pause, thinking about how to best explain it. "It's a bizarre sort of celebrity. The vast majority of people have no idea who I am. The financial freedom I gained has taken away a bit of the trusting person I used to be. Want to be. And that part, I'm not really okay with."

Our lunch is served, and we take a moment to get our food set up. Once we are alone again, Olivia cocks her head and asks, "The IPO led to a form of fame?"

"Yes." I sip my drink as a touch of turbulence has us both sitting straighter in our seats. The plane levels out, and I continue. "But the thing is, actors, they seek out fame. When they're struggling to make it, some part of them wants that fame. Me? I'm a geek. A coder. A business guy. A ranch hand. I didn't ask for fame. And for the most part, I don't have it. The only people into me are into my bank account. Not how I look in a photo or the character I played in a movie."

She chews on the corner of her lip. I want to bite that full lower cherry-red lip. She smiles at me and hesitates. Her hesitation tells me she's second-guessing what she's about to say. I bump her foot with mine and gesture for her to say whatever it is she's holding back. "Are you sure it's not because of how you look in a photograph? Because, I didn't know who you were at all, and I couldn't stop looking at you in that coffee shop."

This woman is genuine and real. She's sophisticated, but not so hoity-toity that she'll hold back from saying what she's thinking. Back in the coffee shop, I'd immediately thought she knew who I was. But, in reality, she'd simply been a girl checking out a guy in a coffee shop. I sip my drink and notice the light reflecting off her diamond earrings. "You know, before the IPO, I never questioned a woman's intentions. If she approached me in a bar, I'd move forward if I had an interest. Now, I always wonder."

"When did you realize you had a stalker?"

I run my hand through my hair, thinking back. "It took a while. At first, I thought it was in my head. It was a

182

coincidence that this woman was on a bench outside my work and outside my—well, at the time, it was a hotel. Then she somehow got my cell phone number. The frequency of hang-ups and texts started disrupting my ability to work. I mentioned it to Bill. He had my cell changed. Wanted to put security on me. Started sharing stats on stalkers. She broke into my hotel room and was waiting for me one night. I opened the door, and she was lying on the bed in only lingerie. I backed right out and went down to the lobby. Police came. Bill took over." There's more to the story, but I've shared enough. I pull up the photos I asked Bill to send to me and pass my phone to her.

She takes the phone from me and flips through the photos. "I can't tell much with the toboggan and scarves. She looks like she's wearing layers. Is she homeless?"

"No. She has an apartment. You're right. Those photos are recent, and it hasn't been that cold. Maybe it's a symptom of her mental illness? Her husband left her. She doesn't have anyone in her life. I haven't seen her in person in ages. She used to be more put together."

She passes the phone back to me. I glance through the photos again. They were taken on the street recently. She's wearing enormous sunglasses, her signature incognito look. Her clothes are ratty. So different from her streamlined, professional look from years ago.

Olivia thoughtfully toys with her wine glass, swirling the light golden liquid, then changes direction with her questions. "Well, now you have security. And the security keeps you safe from her?"

Frustration rises with her question, and I clinch my fist. I'm not a weakling. Regardless of what the board believes, I can keep myself safe. "I suppose. Some days it drives me nuts. Mostly when Bill makes a comment that lets me know his team has been reporting back to him. That he knows every single thing I do. That I've lost a degree of privacy. But Bill is head of Esprit security. It's not like he's trying to be invasive. His goal is to keep me safe. Can't fault him for that. And another way of looking at it is if someone stole my laptop, the amount of damage they could do to our company could be monumental. Not that anyone would, but as the stakes rise, the risks do too."

She reaches out and takes my hand. Squeezes it. Her touch soothes my frustration. As a rule, I try not to think too much about how my life has changed. Try to focus on the business like I always have and corral the bullshit away from my day-to-day. Talking about it kind of reminds me of the negatives, but those blue eyes. Her touch. There's an energy current between us that draws me to her. Her touch simultaneously invigorates and relaxes. It's a powerful, heady combination.

We drop the subject for the remainder of the flight. Our driver meets us on the tarmac and delivers us to the Ritz-Carlton, my favorite hotel in Montreal. Elizabeth Taylor stayed here with one of her husbands. There's an eight-foot portrait of her in the lobby to commemorate her visit.

After checking in, I lead her to the spa. I've got a meeting I need to attend, so I've planned an afternoon of pampering for her. I hope she enjoys it. It's the kind of thing my dad would do for my mom. She always seemed to enjoy it.

Once I get this meeting out of the way, it's me and my girl for the rest of the weekend. My conscience tears at me, reminding me I haven't told her everything. But I've told her enough. There's no need to get her paranoid and burden her with the bullshit. It's all under control.

TRUST ME

Chapter 19

Olivia

The Ritz-Carlton is one of my preferred hotel chains, and I'm impressed with Sam's pick. I love the Ritz bedding. The crisp Frette linens and thick comforters are a step above. Sam checks in while I look around the lobby of the Ritz-Carlton Montreal. I pause to study two glamourous, oversized paintings coated in glitter. One's of Elizabeth Taylor, the other of Marilyn Monroe.

Sam arrives at my side and guides me to the elevator. He hits the spa level, and I give him a questioning look but don't say anything as there are others in the elevator.

The elevator opens at the Spa St. James, and aroma surrounds me. I'm a total spa girl. Sam leads me over to the reception desk. The woman behind the desk smiles and immediately greets him. "Mr. Duke, good to see you again. We have everything prepared for your guest's afternoon at the spa."

He kisses my forehead and in a quiet, private voice, instructs me to enjoy my afternoon. "Pick any treatment you like. I'll be back as soon as my meeting is done, and then I'm yours for the rest of the weekend."

I bite back a bit of annoyance at not being allowed to attend the business meeting and remind myself that being presented as his lawyer's intern would make for an awkward introduction. Sam hands me a menu of services, and I read through the many pages after he departs. I always have difficulty deciding between facials and massages. I'm leaning toward the advanced facial with oxygen blast. Glowing skin would be good at dinner tonight. Then I see the maple sugar massage, and I'm sold. Two-hundred-minute massage with a hot stone treatment. Done and done.

I'm whisked away to change into a robe. After my heavenly massage, I'm delivered to a relaxation room with lounge chairs in front of a fire wall. I wrap myself in a plush blanket and drift in and out of sleep.

Bridgette arrives to take me to wash and dry my hair and offers to do my make-up too. Now, this, I like. I don't think I've ever been so pampered before. It's like a dream. After having my hair blown out and a light make-up application completed, I dress.

With my luxurious pampering and preparation complete, Bridgette escorts me to my room. She beams as she opens the door, full of pride for the suite. The room is impressive. The fireplace blazes in the living room. She leads the way to a bedroom with a king-size bed and an adjacent luxurious white marble bathroom. She points out the amenities of the suite as we walk through. The heated floor in the bathroom and the Japanese toilet, with customized options, including heating and cooling the toilet seat, stand out.

A gorgeous black cocktail dress lies on the bed, and below it, Christian Louboutin black stilettos and a smooth leather clutch to match. Either Sam has good taste, or he has an assistant who does. My money's on Janet. The tags are still on the dress, and a note provides a number to call if anything doesn't fit or isn't to my liking.

After dressing in my new outfit, I stand before the floor-length mirror in the master bedroom and breathe to revel in the moment. I've dated men—or, rather, twenty-something men with money before. Never has anyone given me such a magical weekend away or made me feel like a treasured princess.

The gorgeous dress fits perfectly, as do the shoes. Shoes I know I shouldn't accept but have no intention of returning. I never splurge on shoes like these, and I have to wonder why. They fit so much better, and the quality of the leather is readily apparent. I twirl in front of the bathroom's full-length mirror. The professional hair, make-up, and clothes combine to create a magazine-worthy image. No wonder models and actresses always look so damn good.

Delilah's words drift through my mind. Live in the moment. Be. We each have one life. This is one magical moment in my journey. Enjoy. With one last glance in the mirror, I depart to find my prince.

In the lobby, I spot Sam sitting at the bar of the restaurant, the Maison Boulud. I'm a fan of his day-to-day casual look, but his form-fitting crisp black tux blows casual swagger away. I know the moment he sees me. Both dimples pop, and his blue eyes blaze as they hungrily devour me.

He steps forward to greet me and places a possessive hand on my lower back as he leads me into the restaurant. Ever the gentleman, he pulls out my chair and waits until I'm seated before approaching his own chair. A stunning lateral electric fireplace flanks our table. The weather outside has turned chilly, and there's a possibility of snow later tonight. The amber fire removes any chill from the air.

As soon as we sit, a waiter approaches and pours Dom Perignon into the two champagne flutes on our table. Sam lifts his glass. "To exploring together."

We clink glasses. After I take a sip, I can't help but respond, "But Montreal is not new to you."

"I've been here a few times. Several years ago, there was an AI company I wanted to buy, but Google beat me to it."

"Is that why you're here now? There's another company you want to buy?"

He answers with a quick nod as he tilts his glass, watching the bubbles ascend. The golden liquid glimmers in the firelight. "Yes. But I know you don't want to talk about that. How was your time in the spa?"

I sit straighter in my chair and uncross my legs. *He did not just try to treat me like my brain does not matter, did he?* "I'd actually like to know about the company. There's a good chance if you move forward, you'll be bringing it to our team and I'll be doing the research." His gaze levels on me. "Right?" My Louboutins tap the floor between us as I await his response.

He sets the glass down and places both elbows on the table. "You're right. I guess I'm used to people finding my businesses boring. I tend to talk around it."

"I don't find your business boring."

This brings a half-grin to his face. "You're working with me on some potential investment or acquisition deals. That's a more interesting angle. You have to remember, my company is back-end for financial services. Over the years, even my parents have had difficulty talking to me about my business."

"Well, I'm not like the other women you date. While I appreciate spa time, I'd like to hear about your meeting."

He rubs his jaw then leans back. "No, Olivia, I have to agree with you. You are not like anyone else I've dated. But what you fail to realize is I don't date very often."

I narrow my eyes as I attempt to ascertain his veracity. He smirks at me, and I call it. "Bullshit."

He chuckles. "Seriously. I dated around before Esprit took off, but not much after. And by the time the load lightened, I didn't like the idea of making *Page Six* with a date. I've had some dates in San Fran, but no one I wanted to see more than once."

"So, this whole thing," I whirl my finger around the restaurant, "isn't your status quo?"

He captures my hand and nips my finger then kisses it. "No, not at all. I've never done this before. Today, I pulled some of the cards from my dad's playbook."

"Your dad's playbook? Isn't he still with your mom?"

He grins. "He is. And they've been happily married for almost forty years. And you wanna know why?" He doesn't wait for me to guess. "Because he has a playbook. He romances her and lets her know every day how much he loves her. Adores her." My heart beats erratically as he kisses the back of my hand, his dusk-blue eyes locked on mine.

He then releases me, shifts in his seat, and reverts to business Sam. "You said you wanted to know about my meeting."

I cross my legs again and lift my glass. "Yes."

"It's a company called Croesus Finansoft. They create financial software. Have some talented programmers. It's an interesting company to either invest in or acquire." Throughout dinner, he tells me about the company and how it might align with Esprit. His passion for business shines through, and I'm fascinated, impressed by the potential in the deal, but even more so by his mind. He's brilliant, and he discusses the nuances of the potential deal in an enlightening and informative way without ever coming across as condescending. He toys with my fingers as he talks,

and our legs brush below the table, each touch quietly
stoking the embers, preparing me for our night ahead.

Chapter 20

Sam

After dinner, with her hand secure in mine, we head up to our suite. This woman didn't just listen to me all through dinner. She participated in the conversation. Made suggestions. Asked questions. She could hold her own at any business meeting. The only women in my past who held their own in business conversations weren't at all desirable to me. I can think of many in my company. Intelligent but no spark.

Olivia is unlike any other woman I've met. Inquisitive. Intelligent. Perceptive. Sophisticated. It's clear she's been hurt in the past, and every part of me wants to protect her so she's never hurt again.

I open the door to our suite and stand to let her pass. The fire lights the room. I survey the room, deciding on my plan. A modern uncomfortable-looking sofa overlooks the fireplace. The surrounding white chairs are for a single person. While I sit there debating my next step, she takes charge.

Olivia saunters through the bedroom door and pauses, close to the threshold. With her back to me, she slides the zipper down the back of the dress. As I register what she's doing, she lets the entire dress fall off her slim shoulders and slip to the floor. I swallow, hard, frozen in place. She stands in the doorway wearing only a black silk thong and sky-high fuck-me heels. She tosses her hair as she turns to the side to face me, displaying her full, round, gorgeous tits. She beckons me with her finger to come. My cock fills to full mast.

She steps out of her dress and continues to the bed, where I catch up with her, her back to me. My hands rest on her hips then slide up her sides to her breasts. Heavy in my hands, I knead them, twisting her nipple. I release one of her breasts and slide down to her panties, sliding underneath to rub her clit. As I apply pressure, I pull her to me, my cock cradled in her ass. She leans her head back against my shoulder, and I kiss her while fingering her. She's so wet. Ready.

I want to go slow, but I can't. I need her. Now. I turn her and push her onto the bed. I start taking off my clothes as quickly as I can without looking like a frantic teen. I throw each piece on the ground, kicking off my shoes and pants and socks until I'm completely naked in front of her. She's still wearing her heels and thong. I slide her thong down her long, smooth legs and consider the heels but decide to leave them.

She's sitting on the edge of the bed, and I fall to my knees, spread her legs, and taste what's mine. She's sweet, delicious, and wet. All her little moans and whimpers are driving me crazy. I dip my fingers deep inside while my tongue circles her clit until I hit the mark and her muscles tighten on my fingers and convulse.

As her orgasm takes over, her body jolts forward and she cries out. She fingers my hair, alternating between pulling and pushing. Like it's too much and she can't decide if she wants to pull me away or make me continue. My cock pulses, painfully hard, and I grip it and stroke.

I kiss along her stomach, sliding along her as I lift her to set her further on the bed. Her legs are still open, and her pussy glistens. I can't wait. In one stroke, I slide in, and it feels like home. Where I want to be every single day. I could never get enough of her. Of this woman.

Her muscles quiver around me, aftershocks from the orgasm I just gave her. She wraps her legs around me, the sharp heels digging into the back of my thighs. I don't care if she punctures holes in me with those things. Right now, I need her, and I drive into her. Hard. Claiming. Mine.

No one has ever felt this good. This right. I'm lost in the moment. Holding out, determined to give her one more orgasm before I follow. I'm so close. I want her to come. My thumb presses against her clit, right above where we're joined. I watch our movement. My cock sliding in and out. The pressure builds around the base of my spine. I'm close. I press her clit, around and around. She whimpers. "That's right, baby." Her eyes meet mine. Then we both watch our union.

Her back arches, and she gasps, "Right. There." She detonates. Her muscles clamp down and quiver. I groan as my release pulses through me, pouring into her, her muscles tightening around me and coaxing me.

I collapse on her then kiss her neck and her breast. "Damn. You. Are. Amazing." Still inside her, I place soft kisses all along her tender neck. Then I kiss her. A passionate kiss. A kiss that says what I'm not ready to say out loud.

As I pull out, a chill crosses my skin and goosebumps rise on my arms. I forgot the condom. The champagne, the wine, the moment. Fuck. I lie by her side and stroke her hair. "I'm sorry. I didn't use a condom. I just...fuck. I didn't think."

Jesus. I'm not a kid. I'm not new to the dating game. I know better than to do that without a conversation first. Shit. What if she's not on birth control? But didn't she tell me she's on the pill? I hold my breath, looking at her, waiting for her to say something.

She presses a kiss to my lips. I pull her naked body closer to mine and bend to take a nipple with my lips. I'm still waiting for her to respond, but I can't help myself. Her dark nipples are large, round perfection. Her fingers run through my hair then along the outline of my ear. She tugs my hair and I release her nipple, looking up.

She smiles a soft, coy smile. "It's okay. I'm on the pill. Clean." I breathe a sigh of relief. Although too many women have mistakes on the pill. A part of me believes she'd never have a mistake on purpose, but damn if my brother's warnings don't haunt me. I've seen the real-life stats on the pill, and they aren't good. Of course, no condom feels mighty damn good too.

She strokes my chest, lightly plays with the smattering of chest hair, soothing my concern and warming my skin. Her fingers caress the curves along my chest, and then she explores lower. She continues the same caress on my half-erect cock. Blood pours to my dick, readying for round two, as she coaxes and strokes me. And that's the last time I think about the stats on the birth control pill.

Chapter 21

Olivia

The drapes completely cover the windows, but sunlight breaks along the edges. A golden haze bathes one wall of the otherwise dark bedroom. The day beckons, but lying here together, the last thing I want is to break this bliss. Sam's fingers run along my body as my leg drapes lazily over his. He slows to a rest on my hip and squeezes. "We need to talk."

Whoa. I'm not sure the phrase *we need to talk* ever ends well. I roll away from him and reach out for his crumpled dress shirt lying on the floor. I slip it on and head to the bathroom to brush my teeth. "Give me a minute," I mumble as I pull the bathroom door closed.

The last guy who said those words to me was my college boyfriend. I suppose his approach far exceeded the one Damien chose. I'm over him now, but thinking about that day still pisses me off.

After brushing my teeth, I replace Sam's shirt with one of the plush white cotton Ritz robes hanging on the wall. Whatever he wants to talk about, it'll be okay. And even if it's not, we've had an unforgettable weekend so far.

I open the bathroom door to face Sam. He's propped the pillows back against the headboard and appears to be reading email on his phone. He glances up then pats the bed, signaling for me to join him. "I ordered room service. Coffee. Juice. We can get whatever you want for breakfast. I was thinking if you're interested, we could head out for a run then have a real breakfast later. Brunch. Whatever you want."

I slide onto the bed beside him and lean against the headboard facing him. "That sounds good to me."

He continues reading email as he offers, "You don't have to go for a run if you don't want. I'd like to get my run in. But you don't have to come with."

My phone buzzes beside me, and I glance over. Delilah is calling me, but I choose to ignore it. The phone is on silent, so it vibrates on the table. Instead of answering, I shift to face the firing squad head on. "You said we should talk?"

Sam's hand lands on mine, and he holds it, like I'm in a hospital bed and he wants to comfort me. My breathing stalls, and my fist wraps around the thick comforter.

He sets his phone down on his leg. "Last night, we didn't use protection, or I didn't." He sucks on his lower lip and looks like he's bracing for a swift punch.

I breathe out air I didn't even know I was holding in. "I remember. I'm good about taking the pill."

He scratches his head. "The thing is, I shouldn't have done it. I mean, it felt amazing. But have you ever looked at the reliability of the pill?"

I shake my head while sucking on my lower lip. I've been on the pill since I was sixteen and haven't had a conversation with a doctor about it since. My periods can be irregular and heavy. I went on the pill to regulate my periods and would never consider going off it.

He continues. "It's not good. I know so many women who swear they never missed a pill and got pregnant."

I squint my eyes at him, half teasing. "How many kids do you have?"

That makes him crack a slight grin but doesn't clear the seriousness in his expression. "None. And I want to keep it that way. At least until it's planned."

Now I know where he's going with this. "You want us to still use a condom?"

"Well, no. I'd rather not. Could we look at other options?" He angles his head and squints, an expression I'm starting to recognize as his method of softening a request.

"Like what?"

"An IUD. It's the most effective birth control. Or there are shots too. Effective options that are not prone to user error."

I know little about an IUD other than Anna has one. I do know I like the regulation a pill provides. But I've been on the pill for over ten years. I'm probably due to talk to my doctor about birth control options. "I'll talk to my doctor, okay? But I'm good about taking my pill. I never ever miss."

He leans his head back and gazes out the window, still holding my hand. "Yeah, but have you ever asked yourself, if there was such a thing as a man pill, would you trust me to take that pill?"

"What?"

He turns to face me. "I don't want you to take this the wrong way. But let's say it's not even me. If you're dating some guy, and he tells you 'I'm on the pill. You can trust me. I'll never miss a pill. You're safe from accidentally becoming a mom.' Well, would you jump in and say okay?"

I think about it. Would I open myself up to pregnancy? Trust my partner to take the pill? Maybe not, but another thought comes to mind. "You do know, the only way to be absolutely certain to not get pregnant is to not have sex?"

"Oh, I know." He holds his hands up in a defensive gesture. "And, look, if we were to have an accident, I don't want you to get the wrong idea. I'm not some jerk who's going to run away. I'm all in. I'd be there for you and our baby." He stops and kind of angles his head back and forth as if he's weighing what to say next. "It's just I believe in mitigating risk. I think we can both agree that right now isn't a good time in our relationship to have a surprise baby."

I get what he's saying. It's not the most romantic of conversations, but we are adults having sex. It's a conversation we should have. Researching birth control options makes sense.

He squeezes my hand. "Hey, I've never felt like this with anyone else. For the first time in my life, I feel like…well, I feel like this could be it. You could be it for me, so don't take this conversation the wrong way. I want us to work out. I am all in. I just want it to work out in the best way. For us to have kids when we want them and we're ready for them."

I don't have words to respond to all that he has shared, so I do the next best thing. I kiss him. My kiss tells him I'm all in too. I can't say the words out loud yet. I can't express my hope out loud yet. But my body can communicate. Connect.

I climb onto Sam, straddling his lap. I push the sheet down that separates us. Sam unloops the sash on my robe and slides it off my shoulders. I rub myself across his very hard cock. As I slide across him, my slick folds coating him, his tip teasing my clit, we both moan, the sensation ecstasy. Our kiss deepens, and he flips me over and in one thrust fills me. He glides in easily. Possessing me. Owning me. All of me.

My hips arch up, and he plunges deeper. My body quivers.

"You feel so good. So tight." His words ignite. We move in tandem. Taking each other. Giving. Taking and giving as we bring each other to the edge.

"That's it, baby." His fingers slide between us, over my clit, and he finds the rhythm he's oh-so-good at. "Come. Now," he demands. And I do. My orgasm rips through my body. He pauses, watching as I curl forward, calling out his name.

"God, you're so beautiful." Then he thrusts and joins me. He pulses his release as my muscles spasm from my own powerful orgasm.

We hold each other for several minutes. Quiet. Our heartbeats mingle. My emotions swirl. I'm freefalling. I close my eyes and breathe him in. The scent of our sex fills the air. I kiss him, tasting his salty sweat. I live in the moment as we hold on to each other.

A low whir sound continues on and off. I glance around the bedroom, searching for the source. The whir continues. My phone light casts a glow around the night table. I stretch and reach for it. I see it's Delilah right as it goes to voicemail.

A light layer of perspiration remains on our skin, and he holds me tight. He moves my hair out of the way to place soft morning kisses all along my neck.

The phone vibrates again, and Sam groans, pushing up from the bed, away from me. "You better get that," he says as he steps into the bathroom.

I pick up the phone, tap it, and send a quick text saying I can't speak and asking what's up. Then I notice she's called four times this morning. Shit. Maybe I should call her.

The bathroom door opens, and Sam's standing with a towel wrapped around his waist. "I'm gonna go for that run. You up for joining me?"

"Run walk?" I ask. He holds his thumb up in the air to give his consent. "After coffee arrives, we can head out. Sound good?" After I agree, he slides the bathroom door closed.

As I watch him close the door, the phone in my hand vibrates with the arrival of a text.

Delilah: Help me! Chewie is sick. Super sick. Call me!

I roll my eyes. What does she want me to do? What do I know about dogs?

Me: Take her to the vet.

Delilah: Which vet?

Me: Didn't Anna give you the info before she left?

I've dog sat for Anna before. She always leaves the vet's number. I drop the phone and pull out clothes to get dressed. I'm putting on my running shoes when my phone rings. This time I answer.

I don't even say hello. "I can't do anything. I'm in Canada. You need to take her to the vet."

Delilah screeches in response. "Anna loves this dog, and I think I killed it. Why the fuck did she ask me to watch her freaking dog! I can't even keep plants alive! I hire someone to fucking water my plants."

This thought gives me pause. "You hire someone to water your plants?"

"Pay the fuck attention! Her dog is dying. I killed it!"

"What did you do?" Sam exits the bathroom and stands in the middle of the room watching me, listening.

"I left the food open. The dog ate the whole fucking bag. The whole bag, Olivia!"

"But Anna keeps the food in a canister. The lid snaps shut. How—"

"I didn't carry the blooming canister to my house. The dog won't stop dry heaving. She's really sick."

"Calm down. You need the vet."

Sam sits beside me now, his brow wrinkled. He whispers, "What's wrong?"

I set the phone a little away from my head and update him. "Delilah's dog sitting for Chewie, Anna and Jackson's dog. He ate the whole bag of dog food."

Sam's brow relaxes like this is no big deal at all. "The dog's going to be fine. She just needs to take her to the vet."

I pull the phone back up to my ear. "Did you hear that?"

"I'm already at the vet! She looked at me like I'm a moron. I'm half expecting animal protective services to come and arrest me any minute now. So, if I call you again, pick up the fucking phone because it means I need you to bail me out of jail."

"You aren't going to jail." I shrug. "These things happen." I don't really know if these things happen, but it seems reasonable and like a good thing to say. Sam's response makes me think he's seen this kind of thing happen before. He's outdoorsy.

I hear Delilah sigh. "They should have asked Chase. He's a better human than me."

"Oh, please. Do not say that. Chewie is going to be okay."

Sam massages the back of my shoulder as if he thinks he needs to calm me down. Some noises come through the line, and it sounds like someone is speaking to her.

After a minute or two, Delilah returns to the phone. "I'm being allowed back now to see Chewie. I swear this woman hates me. I can't read Anna's handwriting. I can't read the vet's name. Her regular vet may not even be working this weekend. If I call you, return. My. Call." Then I hear a dial tone.

Sam smirks. "Just for the record. When we adopt a dog, we're hiring a professional dog sitter."

Our coffee arrives via room service. Sam pours us both coffee while I rummage through the suitcase for a pullover. Once I've found something suitable for our upcoming outing, I join Sam at the small table where he's set us up with coffee, fruit, and croissants.

He squeezes my knee. "So, the condom thing may not work out. Now that we've gone without, I can't seem to stop to put a condom on." We both grin, and a warmth rises along my cheeks. "But will you talk to your doctor? Then let's talk about the best birth control options? I mean, I'm not wrong for it to be a joint discussion, am I?"

"No. Not at all. You're the first guy I've dated who has shown this much interest. But it's a good thing." I sip my coffee and give him an affirming smile. I should research options. Especially since he doesn't trust the pill.

After leaving the hotel, we walk the few blocks to the park, then start running the steep stone stairs. We receive more than a few glares and strange looks from the walkers as we glide right by.

Parc du Mont-Royal, referred to as "Mont Royal," towers over Montreal. The temperature hovers above freezing, but the skies are a crisp blue. On the horizon, clouds are moving in, and the air has a smell that says the forecast for snow might be accurate. The view of the Montreal skyline from the overlook draws tourists and residents alike. Sam and I are no different, and we head straight to the edge.

"Stand against the railing," Sam says.

I hesitate. Cheesy tourist photos aren't my thing. But he's already backed away from me and has his phone out, so I pose for him, my back to the city, both hands on the railing, and smile.

A fellow tourist offers to take a photo of us both. Sam stands behind me, both arms circling my waist, and we smile. As I'm asking him to send me the photo, his phone rings.

Sam answers the phone, and I hold onto the railing as I gaze over the city. It's a gorgeous view. I'd like to come back here when snow blankets the park and tobogganing and snowshoeing are options.

"Wait, tell me again what happened." Sam sounds concerned. He comes to stand beside me, looping one arm around my shoulder. "Okay. I got that. But why do you think it's an emergency?"

I can't help wondering who Sam is talking to. He's not using his business voice, which has a distinct tone to it.

"So, go knock on his door." Now he sounds exasperated. "Ollie, I'm in Montreal. What exactly do you want me to do? I saw him last week. He seemed okay." There's a pause, then Sam adds, "I mean, he seemed like he has been for a while. I told you I'm concerned. I am. I'm just not understanding the urgency."

A minute or two passes while Sam listens. The person he is speaking to seems to be getting louder, because I can hear the voice coming through the line. I can't make out exactly what he's saying.

"Ollie, I'll tell you what. Go to lunch with Mom and Dad. Talk to them. If you all want to talk to Jason tomorrow, I'm in. I'll make it back."

Hearing that, I look up at Sam, and he winces apologetically. After he hangs up, I turn and pull him against me. "What was that about?"

Sam rubs his hand through his hair, concern etched on his face. "My buddy Jason. Ollie's concerned. He's not wrong. I've been concerned too, but I tend to think Ollie's jumping to conclusions. Freaking out when there's a reasonable explanation."

"What does your brother think?"

Sam sighs, leads me away from the overlook, toward a hiking path he wanted us to take. "He believes he's suicidal."

I stop. "Sam, if you need to, let's go back."

Sam leads me forward, shaking his head. "I don't think he's suicidal, but I will grant you, I don't want to be wrong on this." He pauses. "You actually know him."

"I do?"

"He's your accounting professor."

"Dr. Longevite?"

"Yeah. Have you ever noticed anything? Does he seem, I don't know, normal in your classes?"

I mentally review my encounters with him. I meet weekly with the guy, but he's my professor. We don't chit chat. "I'm not sure the question to ask is whether he seems normal.

People suffering from depression often seem normal and can function." I suck on my lip, thinking through what I know about depression, a limited knowledge sourced from random articles and from a friend who started taking meds in college. "What did your brother say? What concerned him enough to call you?"

"He blew him off. Won't answer his door. Not answering his phone."

It's the weekend. That could just be a single guy tuning out the world. A depressed person wanting to sleep in. I remember how antisocial I was after Damien. How many weekends I'd spend never leaving the apartment. Time alone allows us to heal. "Did something happen?"

Sam squints, either at me or from the sun. "You mean, like, did someone die?"

"Or did someone break up with him?"

"You know, I don't know. I see him a couple of times a week. But he's struggled with cancer for almost fifteen years. Non-Hodgkin's lymphoma. But he got confirmation it's in remission, so you'd think he'd be happy. He's had partial remission before, but now it's considered complete remission. Which is huge." Sam's staring off into the trees as we walk, lost in his own thoughts.

"Do you think maybe someone he's close to didn't get good news? If he's been in and out of treatment for so long, do you think someone he knows isn't faring as well?"

"You might be on to something. I know he did have a good friend who passed away years ago, and he took it hard. I went to the funeral with him. He's still close to that guy's fiancée. In fact, she's his best friend. He could've become close to other patients." He picks up the pace, and leaves crunch under our feet as we walk. "You know, maybe I haven't been asking the right questions."

"What does Ollie want to do?"

"He wants us to meet Jason for lunch tomorrow. That is, if he can get a response from Jason. If not, I think he's going to break into his apartment tonight. He's considering calling the cops."

"Does he think he's suicidal?"

"Yeah. I don't know if he's...I don't know."

I stop and force Sam to face me. "Look, your brother is in town. If he's this worried, you should be there. You're worried too." Sam opens his mouth to say something, and I speak louder so he won't interrupt. "Let's go back. We can come here again."

"Are you sure?" His glove gently brushes along my cheek.

"Yeah, I'm sure."

Sam pulls me close and gives me a slow, soft kiss. A kiss that says *thank you*.

"I was going to take you to Quebec City tonight. The Christmas market opened, and holiday decorations are out."

I press up on my toes and place a soft peck on his moist lips. "Next time."

He grabs my hand, and we continue our hike. "You know what I love about you saying that?"

"What?"

"You sound confident there will be a next time. I want my girlfriend to be confident. In us." He tightens the hold on my hand. "Now, even if we go back today, you'll still spend the weekend with me, right?"

"I'd love to."

"Good. You can meet my parents tomorrow. And brother."

"You want me to meet your family?" My muscles tense.

"Yeah. I haven't had a girlfriend in ages. They're gonna love you. Just like I do."

My legs stop moving as I absorb this offhand remark. My heart beats erratically, and my breath quickens as if we were out running and not hiking.

When he sees I've stopped walking, he smirks and returns to me. He drops a kiss on the tip of my nose as he pulls me close. "Yes. I love you. You don't have to say it back. But I want you to know how I feel. I want you to know I'm all in. I know this seems fast. Maybe too fast. But it's kind of who I am. Be all in or get all out. There is no halfway with me. And with you, I can't slow it down. I tried. There's no point. I've fallen in love with you."

His admission sends heat through my chest. My skin tingles. I should say it back. It would make for a better moment. But it's a leap I'm not quite willing to make. My chest tightens. I do love him. Love everything about him. He's kind, smart, caring, a family guy. In so many ways, he's better than anything I could dream up. But there's no way I know everything about him yet. We're still so new. I'm still learning who he is. I've been with other men far longer before I learned their true colors.

When I gaze back at him, I'm lost in his blues. They're a shade darker than the clear sky behind him. This wonderful guy loves me. I'm not going to say it yet. The unruly nerves in my stomach tell me it's not time. One day, I will tell him. When I'm ready. When there's no chance it's just heightened emotions from a romantic weekend getaway.

We walk for a while in silence. I don't say anything, and he doesn't press. Tourists and joggers walk along the park paths. The trees are barren, but the ground is still covered with leaves. A small stream to the side of the path flows, but pieces of ice form on the edge. Soon, the stream will fall under a hard freeze. The park shall become a winter wonderland. I track the ice formations along the stream as we walk.

Sam's voice breaks the silence. "Don't your parents live in New York?"

I answer cautiously, fearing where he may be going with this line of questioning. "Yeah."

"So, when am I going to meet them?"

"They aren't around much, but we'll see. Sometime, I'm sure."

Sam stops and pushes me up against a tree. His gloves slip up the sides of the pullover I'm wearing and lightly tease my bare skin, tickling me. The tickling makes me squirm and involuntarily snort a laugh.

"Sometime? Sometime?" he repeats, a large dimple bearing smile on his face.

"Sometime!" I shriek as I try to break away from the tickling. I can't stand to be tickled.

He roughly grabs me, arms circling around me, and kisses me, an intense, not really appropriate for a public setting kiss. Within minutes, I forget all about the risk of tickles. Forget what we're talking about. My nerves calm, and a different scintillating tension builds.

Still holding me close, he breaks the kiss and steps away, creating space I don't want between us and leaving me breathless. "Meeting the parents, that's a next step. Got it?" He then loudly slaps my Lycra-covered butt and tugs me along the rest of the hiking trail.

Chapter 22

Sam

Olivia and I land in New Jersey around 5:00 p.m. on Saturday. One phone call to my assistant, and our private plane was ready and waiting on the tarmac for an afternoon departure. Flexible, on demand travel arrangements might be the one thing I love most about having enough money to do anything I like.

As I open my apartment door, Olivia by my side, my phone rings. It's Ollie.

I answer while holding the door open for Olivia. "Hey, we just got back. Was about to call you."

Olivia strolls in ahead of me and stops in front of the large window overlooking the Hudson. The sun has started to set, casting golden shades of yellow all along the horizon. I walk up behind her but keep my distance, watching her, memorizing her curves.

"Thanks for coming back, man. I'm heading over to his place now. Want to meet me?" Ollie asks.

"What are you gonna do?"

"I reached the super. He's gonna let me into the apartment." That's good. Somehow, having the super let us in feels less intrusive than involving cops. Ollie's probably overreacting. Chances are, Jason is fine. Has his cell off. But I'd never forgive myself if I'm wrong and Ollie's right.

After I hang up, I slide my phone into my jeans pocket. I wrap my arms around Olivia, pulling her back against me. I lean down and breathe her in. She calms me. Holding her settles me. She fills a void in my life I hadn't quite recognized. I slide her hair out of the way and place a kiss below her earlobe, a place I've discovered she loves to be kissed. A quiet moan escapes. No part of me wants to leave her.

"Are you going to be okay here?" I know she will but want to ask.

She turns in my arms and tilts her head up. Kisses my chin, then my lips. "I'm gonna be fine. Go on. Some of my textbooks are on Kindle. I'll catch up on reading."

"And you'll be here when I'm back." It's a question, but I make it a statement.

I kiss her again then force myself to leave.

When I get out of the car in front of Jason's apartment, I see Ollie talking to a guy in jeans and a black t-shirt. Ollie waves me over and introduces me to Scott, Jason's building supervisor. It turns out he lives in the building, so it's easy enough for him to let us in.

Jason lives in a fourth-floor walk-up. Scott pushes the door open and stands in the doorway as we walk around, calling out Jason's name. Everything looks in order. His bed's unmade. His cell phone rests on the bedside table, charging, so that explains why he hasn't answered it.

I leave the bedroom and turn to check out the kitchen. The fridge hasn't been cleaned in a while, judging by greasy spills on the shelves, but it's mostly empty. I spin around the kitchen while Ollie pulls open drawers in the credenza below the TV.

The place looks like a single guy's apartment. It's not spotless, but there's nothing to indicate he's depressed. Of course, I'm not sure what I'm supposed to be looking for. I know Ollie's biggest fear was that Jason was in here and had hurt himself, and that's not the case. Jason's nowhere to be found.

I'm about to suggest we leave when I hear Jason's voice talking to Scott. "Scott? What's going on?" He sounds confused, and I'm sure he is.

Ollie shouts, "Jason! There you are. What the fuck? Why haven't you returned any of my calls?"

Jason steps into his apartment and stands facing Ollie, his back to me.

"Returned your…? What the fuck are you doing in my apartment?" Jason grunts. I've never heard him sound so pissed off.

I can tell from Ollie's reaction that Jason's anger has him off guard. "Man, I've been trying to reach you for days. You wouldn't answer your door last night. Or today. I was worried, okay?" Ollie says defensively.

Jason rubs his forehead then points to the door. "Get the fuck out."

Ollie takes a step forward. "Man. It's not like you to not return my calls. I got scared. Okay?"

Jason lifts his head. "I'm not an invalid. What the fuck did you think? Get out. Go." He sounds broken. His hands are balled into fists, and his cheeks are blazing crimson.

I walk around the kitchen island to head out. It's clear Jason doesn't want us here. He's okay. I don't know what's going on, but he doesn't seem to be in the frame of mind to have a heart to heart.

My movement catches Jason's attention, and he turns. His eyes glisten. "You too? You're supposed to be in…" He stops speaking and glares at me. "You know what? I don't even want to know. Both of you, get the fuck out of my apartment. Now."

Jason walks down the hall to his bedroom and slams the door.

Scott mutters something I don't catch, but it's clear from the way he's holding the door he's expecting us to leave. Head down, Ollie walks out into the hall. I follow, and Scott closes the door behind us.

Scott shakes his head with a somber expression. "Don't ask me to do that again."

****

I push my apartment door open and kick off my boots by the door. Olivia appears at the end of the hallway. She leans against the wall, studying me. "How'd it go?"

It feels damn good to have her here, waiting for me. I wrap my arms around her and pull her to me. Like a salve to a burn, she provides instant relief. "I know something's wrong, but Jason's not up for talking about it." Bright blue eyes take me in, and I inhale, breathing in her scent. It's a combination of mint and floral I'm becoming addicted to.

"Do you think he's suicidal? That's what Ollie was worried about, right?"

"Yeah, I guess. I agree with Ollie that something's not right. He probably does need some sort of therapist, but no, I don't think he's suicidal. It's not that serious."

"What made you think it might be that serious?"

"Not me. Ollie. Something happened with one of his friends back in high school. I'd gone off to college, so I didn't live it. I agree Jason's going through some heavy stuff right now. I'm not sure it's depression, though." I squint, peering over Olivia's head at the gas fireplace she's turned on. Jason's okay, but I still have a sinking feeling something's not right.

I tilt Olivia's head up to me. "Hey, thanks for being willing to adjust our plans." I place a soft kiss on her lips. "Thanks for being here." Her being here, greeting me when I come in the door, it feels right.

She leads me to one of the bar stools near my kitchen island. "I have a casserole in the oven and made us a salad. I also have some cheese and crackers we can munch on while we wait for the casserole."

She's poured two glasses of wine and leans over the island to hand me mine. Then she turns to put together the cheese plate. She's at ease in my kitchen. Barefoot, in jeans, and a form-fitting black sweater that hits right at her waist. Her dark hair sways as she moves around.

I feel torn, because I want everything right now. I want to take her on the kitchen counter. I want to watch her fix our dinner in my kitchen, but I want it to be our kitchen. I want to sit and talk with her over wine. How quick is too fast? How long do we have to date before I can ask her to move in with me? Because at that moment, I know. This is it for me. I want her by my side for good.

Chapter 23

Olivia

Sam's hand cocoons mine as we walk along 20th Street to meet his parents. He can't seem to stop touching me, and I love it.

The gold lettering on the Cookshop window catches my eye. As we approach, Sam pulls me to him and kisses me. At first, it's a soft kiss, but it builds until our tongues dance, and I forget we're standing on a sidewalk. "What was that for?" I ask, a full smile on my face.

"To thank you for meeting my family. And to remind you that you have nothing to be nervous about." He places another quick kiss on my lips, then my forehead, then leads me into the warm restaurant.

The combination of yellow walls and plants create a warm ambience. We could be in someone's kitchen instead of a packed restaurant. Potted rosemary plants line an entire half wall.

We're not even to the hostess stand before a woman with shoulder length blonde hair has Sam wrapped in her arms. She kisses his cheeks and beams up at him with a warm smile. Then she turns and pulls me in for an all-encompassing hug. My arms fall by my side, frozen.

"Mom, meet Olivia." He's grinning as watches his mom engulf me. I lift my arms to sort of hug her back because she still hasn't let me go.

Once she sets me free, she stands back and appraises me. I feel a bit like a dog at the Westminster dog show. "It is so nice to meet you, Olivia. When Sam said he's dating someone, well…" She trails off as she grabs my hand and pulls me back to the table.

"Sam and Ollie, this is Olivia."

An older gentleman that looks a lot like Sam, with less hair, sits in the corner and holds his hand out.

"It's nice to meet you, Mr. Duke," I say as we shake hands.

Ollie, a taller, thinner version of Sam, grins while I meet the eldest Mr. Duke.

"Call me Sam, dear. And my wife, you can call her Patty."

"Well, it's nice to meet you both."

Ollie slides out of the booth and bends down to give me a welcoming embrace. Out of the corner of my eye, I see Sam tap Ollie on the shoulder. "Enough. Get your own girlfriend."

Everyone at the table laughs as I slide into the booth. Ollie takes the chair that's up against the table, and Sam slides in next to me.

Ollie kicks the chair back a bit, so the two front legs are in the air. A part of me wants to tell him not to do that, that it's dangerous because he could fall backward, but I refrain. Patty's at the table. She can play mom if she wishes.

"Girlfriend, huh? When was the last time I heard those words come out of your mouth?" Ollie asks, grinning ear to ear.

Sam wraps a protective arm around my shoulder. "Lay off." He leans over, pretending to be whispering in my ear as he loudly confides in me, "This guy over here's just jealous. He's always got a girl, and I never do. He's feeling a little sore the tables have turned."

A chair leg scrapes the floor, and Sam lets out a quick "Ow" while he swats at Ollie. Both of them laugh loudly, causing the diners nearest us to look over at the commotion.

Patty admonishes them with a stern, "Boys, stop that, now. We are in a restaurant." She sounds serious, but she's wearing a beautiful smile, and her blue eyes shine. Hers are the same dusky-blue as Sam's.

After we order, Patty sips her coffee then asks, "What's going on with Jason?"

Ollie and Sam stare at each other for a minute. Sam speaks up. "Not much to say. Something's wrong, for sure. But he's not ready to talk about it."

"Well, I think I know what it is." Patty sets her coffee down, her gaze flitting between her sons.

Sam angles his head and asks, "What do you think it is, Mom?" He sounds somewhat amused, like he's expecting her to tell him something that's going to humor him. I want to pinch him and tell him to take his mother seriously.

She doesn't seem to notice his smirk or attitude. "I think he's got a broken heart." Ollie laughs out loud at this, and I notice that Sam Sr. rolls his eyes but remains silent. She continues. "No, mark my words, I'm right about this."

Sam huffs. "Well, he's more than a mite pissed at us right now. Given we broke into his house yesterday, can't say I blame him. I'm guessing it'll take some time before he opens up to us if that's it."

Sam Sr. leans over and kisses his wife's head. "Always a romantic."

Patty disregards him. She turns her attention to me. "Honey, tell me about yourself. We don't need to be hashing out what's going on with the boys. I want to get to know you."

217

She reminds me a bit of the actress who played June on *Leave It To Beaver*. Or at least the way I imagine that character would behave had I ever watched an episode. She's direct, warm, and kind. I have no idea what to say to her, though. Everyone at the table watches me. I decide to go with the kind of introduction I'd give in a new class in business school. "I'm from Connecticut, and I'm currently attending Columbia's business school."

"Oh," she responds enthusiastically. "Are you in undergrad or grad?"

"Jesus, Mom, if you want to know her age, just ask her." He's smirking as he pulls me closer to him in the booth so our legs touch.

She smiles at him. Then gives me a timid smile, like yes, she does want to know my age, but doesn't think she should actually ask me that question. I half laugh at both her being uncomfortable about asking me and her curiosity. "I'm twenty-seven. I'm pursuing my MBA. I had a career in advertising, and I'm using the program to change, or alter, my career path." My explanation is a bit formal, but it's the easiest and most efficient, and for heaven's sake, meeting the family is a bit like a job interview.

She beams a smile at Sam. "Intelligent and beautiful. You've done well, Sam."

He laughs out loud, as does Ollie. I kind of want to shrink below the table as I once again feel like a show pony.

Ollie says, "Don't worry, Olivia. That's about the worst of the evaluation you're gonna get. I've been working on training her for years."

Patty opens her mouth and slaps his knee. "You have not been training me. I'm not doing anything. I'm just trying to tell Sam that I approve. He's always been very picky, and I think he's done well selecting her. I like her."

Ollie's eyebrows raise almost up to his hairline. "Jeez, Mom. She's not a piece of fruit." All three men laugh.

I catch Patty's eye. "It's okay. I understand what you're trying to say. Thank you." Sam leans over and kisses my forehead.

Ollie taps the table and with a wide smile says, "Okay. It's time we segue into funny Sam stories."

Sam guffaws. "There are no funny stories about me. All the funny stories are about you."

"That's not true! You got in trouble some. Maybe not as much as me, but some," Ollie retorts.

I'm grinning now. "Oh, share some stories, Ollie."

He rubs his chin as if he's trying to decide which family story to share. "Well, there was this one time, he got in so much trouble. I wanted him to take me to Taco Bell. I was a little stoned. Needed me some Taco Bell. He completely refused to take me."

Sam breaks in. "How is that me getting in trouble?"

"Because I had to steal Mom's car to get to Taco Bell! I was grounded for months."

Sam turns to me. "Do you hear this? He's stoned at fifteen and blames me when he gets in trouble. That's what I lived with my whole life."

Ollie has a huge smile on his face. "I'm just saying. A good brother would've pulled an assist and taken my ass to Taco Bell!" Ollie shakes his head. "Not this guy here. He may be right. He's always been a studious do-gooder. Always the parent pleaser."

Sam Sr. clears his throat. "Would have done you wonders if you'd watched and learned."

Patty turns a mock angry face to Ollie and playfully pops his head with her palm. "Your brother is not the reason you got in trouble, young man."

Everyone laughs. The warmth and love between this family can't be missed. They continue to laugh and joke with each other as they reminisce. It's a camaraderie I've never experienced in my life. I don't have one memory of my family ever sitting around a table, happy, joking, and laughing. Even my meals with my uncle are serious and more akin to a business dinner. I settle back into the booth, held tight next to Sam, and soak in the love.

After brunch, we stand on the sidewalk saying our goodbyes. Sam's parents are returning to Texas this afternoon. They don't say it, but I suspect they flew here this weekend in case Jason needed them. Ollie's going to be staying in town for the rest of the week. Right now, he's heading to meet some friends at a sports bar to watch the Longhorns game.

Patty pulls me aside away from the men and holds both my hands. "Now, listen, I want you to know. I like you. But if you bring my boy home to Texas, I'll love you." Before I can respond, Sam has his arm around her shoulders, and he's pulling her away.

"Mom, you're gonna love her no matter where we choose to live." He winks at me, and his smile's so deep, both dimples show. My stomach flips and flutters. Damn. He has no idea what he is doing to me. I can't believe he just said that to his mom.

His mom winks at me. It's the same wink Sam just gave me. Guess I know where he got it from.

As Sam turns to give his dad a hug, his mom grabs my hand. She dramatically mouths "Texas" then gives Sam an

220

innocent look when he turns around. I don't think I've ever felt more welcomed in my whole life.

I can't help but wonder if they are like this with all his girlfriends. It's hard to believe the tabloids have it all wrong and he doesn't date a lot, but I can buy he might not bring many women around his family. As much as I like his family, and as good as it feels to spend time with Sam, I cannot let this go to my head. Our relationship is new. Newness means uncertainty. I've been down this path before. Almost moved in with someone. There are no guarantees in relationships. This much I know.

******

Saturday morning, I push the door to Balthazar open. The restaurant is packed, and a couple of people stand waiting in front of the hostess stand. I brush past the crowd to find my crew. It's been two weeks since we've had a girls' brunch. I've been immersed in new boyfriend world, but I've missed my girls. As I slide around the dark wood hostess stand, Delilah jumps up, energetically waving.

Anna greets me with her customary, "Hey, you!" and pulls me into a hug. "We are dying to hear about your surprise weekend!"

Lindsey mumbles something I can't hear. She's twirling the olives in her Bloody Mary with an annoyed expression. I grimace, guilt hitting me. She texted me several times, asking to meet up. But I've been kind of in my own little bubble. I've stayed at Sam's every night since we returned from Montreal. Sam acts like I've moved in, but I haven't.

I sit. The girls have already ordered my standard Champagne Pick Me Up. As I sip it, all three of my

221

girlfriends stare me down, awaiting details with glee. I take a larger swallow, not sure where to start.

Anna breaks in. "So, how was Montreal?"

"Good."

Delilah squeals and tucks both hands under her chin and waits for more.

I wrinkle my nose. Somehow, saying all this out loud makes it real and makes me nervous. I can't shake the feeling that it's all going to fall apart. It's been too perfect. *Live in the moment* is my mantra getting me through my days right now. A life without risks isn't living. I breathe deeply and share.

"It was awesome," I blurt. "So romantic. I met his family. And they're incredible. Kind, funny, and warm. He asked for a copy of my keys. And he gave me his codes, and I'm on his list at his apartment. And we've spent every night together since we got back."

I pause, letting my rush of information sink in. Three smiles beam around the table.

"It's too much isn't it? Too fast?"

"No!" Anna squeals. I roll my eyes. Anna wasn't like this before Jackson. Now she's this romance reading believer in love. It's kind of a one-eighty from the girl I bonded with in undergrad.

Delilah reaches out and places her hand on mine, a huge grin on her face. "I think that maybe, sometimes, when it's meant to be, it all moves forward quickly. Because, you know, it feels right. Does it feel right?"

I pause, thinking through it all. We've had sex in almost every room in his apartment and mine. But it's not just sex. It's how he looks at me, holds my hand, checks in on me during the day. He makes me feel like I'm his everything. I know I'm not, but when he's with me, he's not on his phone. He's present. Engaged. Into me. "Yeah, it feels right. But too good?" I squint as I say this, bracing for the cascade of contradictions to come from across the table.

Delilah squeezes my hand then picks up her drink. "Not too good. This is it for you. I can feel it. Let's toast to true love."

We toast, and I look to Delilah and Anna. "How's Chewie? I've been such a bad friend." Out of the corner of my eye, I see Lindsey roll her eyes.

Anna laughs. "Chewie is fine. And it seems our blondie here now has her own feel-good story to share."

"Yeah?" I ask, focusing my attention on Delilah.

She smiles. "Yeah. Chewie's vet asked me out!" She's beaming.

"I thought you said it was a woman?" I ask.

"Nope." She turns her head right and left. "That was his vet tech. Royal bitch. But the actual vet. Very nice. We've been going out. He has a daughter. I've met her. He's this incredibly hot single dad."

"Wow." I'm stupefied. That's not Delilah's MO to date the same guy. Kids too. That's a different level of seriousness.

The waitress comes, and we all place our orders.

Lindsey tilts her head, and the moment there's a lull in conversation, she breaks in. "So, I still want to hear more about Olivia's new guy. Delilah's been keeping me updated on her guy." There's obvious innuendo there in her statement. She continues. "It sounds serious, Olivia. Key exchange and all. Do you think you're going to be moving in with him?"

"No." I toy with the napkin on my lap as I stare across the packed restaurant to the window.

"Has he said anything about it?"

I halfway glare back at her. The question strikes me as intrusive. Because she's a new friend? Because she's touching on a sensitive topic? Anna and Delilah both take sips of their drinks at the same time.

I know I shouldn't be defensive, so I answer. "He's hinted at it a few times." Delilah grabs my hand and grins at me. Anna smiles behind her glass. "Anyway," I continue, "his birthday is coming up, so that's something else to stress about. Shortly followed by Christmas. I hate having to figure out the right gift when a relationship is new."

"I can ask Jackson if he has any ideas. He and Sam are spending a fair amount of time at the office together," Anna offers. "But I totally get it. Jackson and I aren't new, but I still stress at gift time."

Delilah sits there tapping her chin, as if she's running through a mental list of new boyfriend gifts. Lindsey shocks the table when she offers, "If you plan a threesome, it would blow his mind."

She's staring at my breasts. I'm wearing a flannel top that's unbuttoned enough to show a little cleavage. The shirt shifted a bit to reveal the skin almost up to my low-cut bra. I set about straightening my shirt. Delilah knows what happened between Lindsey and me, but Anna doesn't. I haven't given that night much thought since Sam's return. But there's something about the way she's gazing at me that brings back the memory of her mouth on my nipple in the hall. Uneasiness penetrates my psyche.

"Well, would you be open to that?" she asks, and then bites her lip, releasing it in a slow, taunting way.

Underneath the table I cross my legs. To lighten the situation, I scrunch my nose and say, "I'm not sure we're there yet. Or that I'll ever be there." But I am firm. She needs to know I'm not game.

Anna bites her straw, oblivious to any tension at the table. Her eyes pop as she says, "You know, I read this book where the girlfriend invited a friend over as a birthday surprise. You should borrow that book." Anna taps my arm to get my attention. "Really, so hot." She looks up at the ceiling as if she's trying to think through the details. "I mean, there were extenuating circumstances. Her friend was a prostitute, but super hot. They had been dating for a while, if I remember right." She tilts her head, still thinking it through. "Maybe not. I think that's how she ended up doing it. She was going to do like a double girl on him blow job kind of birthday present. Then it kind of became more." She jumps a bit in her chair. "Oh, I know! Her friend had her blindfolded. She was going down on her when he walked in. That's it! Best freaking series! *The Blindfold Club*. You gotta read it."

Delilah laughs out loud. "Damn, Anna. No wonder you get so into your books. I'm gonna start coming to you when I want a book to read. Screw my grandmother's Goodreads picks."

I laugh, any discomfort forgotten, thanks to my friends, and excuse myself to go to the restroom.

As I'm washing my hands, Lindsey enters. She bends to peer under the stalls. One other person is in one of the two stalls. I give Lindsey a slight smile and turn to pull down a paper towel.

She walks up behind me and cups my ass and squeezes as she says, "Think about it. I'd be thrilled to be your unicorn."

Before I can think of a response, she's slipped into the vacant stall. I hurry to exit.

When I approach our table, Anna and Delilah are standing, ready to leave.

"You want to hang out this afternoon?" Anna asks. "It sounds like the boys have already made plans for us to have dinner together tonight." She holds out her phone so I can see a text chain between her and Jackson.

"I'd really love that." I turn to Delilah to see if she's going to join us.

Lindsey hasn't returned yet. I'm not aiming to be the mean girl, but I'd love some time to talk to my friends about the vibes I'm getting from Lindsey. Maybe I should have a talk with her, but this is new territory for me. Or it's kind of new territory. If she was a guy I'd hooked up with right before I started dating someone new, I'd know more about how to handle it. It's not different because she's a woman. But it's different since I want her to be my friend. I wouldn't invite a random dude hook-up to girls' brunch. But she keeps pushing. And I'm beginning to question the friendship potential.

Delilah wraps a scarf around her neck and leans in to give me a hug. "You two have fun. I've got a full day of date prep ahead of me."

"Pampering and such?"

"Nope. Nap. But blow-out later. Have to do something a little special." She grins.

"So, you like him, huh?" I ask as I nudge her shoulder.

"Yeah. For now. You know I'm gonna go back to New Orleans." She grins and wiggles her fingers in a goodbye motion to someone behind me as she heads out. I turn to see who she's waving to. It's Lindsey.

Lindsey walks up and asks, "What are you ladies up to this afternoon?"

I answer first. "Not much. What about you?" Anna glances my way but continues buttoning her coat.

Lindsey leads us out of the restaurant without answering. When we step outside, she gives us each a hug. When she hugs me, she pulls me close and whispers in my ear, "Just think about it. You'd blow his mind." I step back and stare at the sidewalk, feeling awkward and uncomfortable, and wave goodbye.

Anna and I turn to head west on Spring Street while Lindsey crosses the street and ducks into a deli.

"That's weird."

"What's weird?" Anna asks.

"We just ate brunch, yet she just went into a deli."

Anna grabs my arm so we are walking arm in arm down the street. "Maybe she remembered she needs something? Like tampons. Who knows." Anna sounds chipper and cavalier. I know I'm being petty. Probably overly critical because I'm feeling uncomfortable around her, and I shouldn't be. What happened between us was nothing. A drunken mistake, nothing more.

Anna continues rambling as we walk. "You know, actually, I may need to stop to grab some tampons." I cut my eye to her. "But we'll go closer to my apartment."

"You need to tell me what you guys did when Jackson surprised you. I didn't even get a chance to ask you." I've been in the clouds. Floating. But behind on both school and my internship project. When I'm at the coffee shop, I force myself to work through my checklist and leave my phone in my bag.

We walk side by side as Anna tells me about their trip to Mohonk Mountainhouse. I've heard about the spa there, but it sounds like it wasn't so much the place as time together that made it a special getaway.

When we approach Anna's apartment, she pulls me into the deli on the corner. She stands staring at the tampon selection. There are only, like, three brands to choose from. As she's standing there, I look in my handbag to see how many I have. I have a small bag I keep tampons in, and I throw it in whatever handbag I'm using. I open it up and see it's still full.

This week was my off week on the pill. Did I even start? I know I'm supposed to start a new pack tomorrow.

I'm pretty sure I did start. It was light, though. On Wednesday, I did bleed. I used a tampon. But then by Thursday, it was gone. I'm biting my nails while trying to remember exactly how many tampons I did use this week, when Anna squeezes my arm.

"Hey, you. Are you okay?"

I snap my pocketbook shut. "Yeah, I'm fine. I only had my period for, like, one day this week. Is that normal?" My periods have always been so screwed up. Could this be a side effect of being on the pill for too long? I need to schedule that appointment with my doctor.

Anna doesn't say a word. She takes one step farther down the aisle and picks up a pregnancy test box.

"Oh, no. I definitely had my period. I'm not. Put that back," I say.

She continues walking to the register. "Nope. There's no reason to wonder and drive yourself crazy. We'll go back to my place, you'll pee on a stick, and you won't go nuts waiting for your next cycle."

"What? No. That's not what I was wondering. I'm not scared."

Anna isn't listening to me. She pays for her purchases and walks out. I follow her.

"Anna, seriously, you just wasted that money. I'm not worried about that. I definitely started."

Anna doesn't say anything. She keeps walking while holding her small brown paper bag. Once we're in the elevator, she turns to me. "It's possible to spot when pregnant. It can be mistaken as a very light period. Pee on the damn stick. The earlier you find out if you're pregnant, the better off you are."

"Fuck me," I mutter in exasperation. I know I'm not pregnant. This is ridiculous. But Anna's a bit of a birth control zealot. She's been hounding me ever since college to get an IUD because she thinks the real-life stats on the pill suck. Which, come to think of it, didn't Sam say the same thing?

We walk into Anna's apartment, and I follow her into the den. Jackson's sitting back on his sofa, a laptop in his lap. A muted basketball game plays on the TV.

"Hey, Jackson." I say as Anna thrusts a three-pack pregnancy test box into my hand. Jackson's eyes go wide, and he immediately turns back to the game and his computer. Smooth. Thanks for that, Anna. That's not awkward at all.

"I'm not pregnant," I say, loud enough that Jackson will hear.

"Go pee," Anna demands. "Want me to come with you?" I don't answer. She's not listening to me, so why should I respond? She huffs and pulls me down the hall into her bedroom.

She opens the box and pulls out a white metallic plastic envelope then thrusts it into my hand. "Go. Open this. Pee on it. Then come out, and we'll sit on the bed and chat." She gives me a big smile that shows her well-aligned teeth.

I know I'm not pregnant, but I know Anna. She's not going to let this go. And who am I kidding? I will feel better with negative proof now that Anna has placed this absurd notion in my head.

One thing she said rings true. If I were, god forbid, pregnant, more time to think through options is better than no time. Sam and I could afford a kid, but this so isn't the right time. We've been dating for less than two months. I'm in business school, for crying out loud.

There's a soft knock, and Anna pushes the door open. I place the cap back on the stick I peed on and set it on the counter. I wash my hands. I'm calm. But there's something about peeing on a stick. All sorts of "what would I do" kinds of thoughts are running through my head.

Anna grabs a hand towel and the handheld side of the stick and walks out of the bathroom. I follow her and watch her set out the towel, the stick, and the instructions on the corner of the bed. Then she leaps onto the bed and crawls back toward the pillows.

"Come join me. Let's catch up." She sounds eager and happy and not at all like a friend who forced me to take a pregnancy test.

I hesitate but do end up joining her on the bed. "Whose side am I on?" I ask.

"Huh?"

"Am I on your pillows or Jackson's?"

She kind of giggles. I'm glad she can giggle while my test results are on the end of the bed percolating. "You're on Jackson's side. So, no farting or anything."

I don't say anything. My mind kind of goes blank.

"Hey, you know whatever happens, I'm here for you, right?"

A numbness sort of runs through my chest. I force myself to look at her instead of studying the navy and gray pattern on the comforter. "I know that. And, actually, if this were to happen, I think for the first time I'm with someone who would be a good dad. It's just…it's too early, you know?"

Anna nods.

"He told me he's all in. I've fallen harder for Sam than for anyone. Ever. But this isn't…" I shake my head. I can't continue speaking. I'm thinking back to him wanting to keep using condoms, to me saying the pill was okay. A heavy weight lands on my chest.

I gaze down at the end of the bed. I can't see the result on the stick from where I'm sitting, but it looks like a pink line has formed. I should lean down there to look at the results, but I'm frozen in place.

Anna crawls down to the end of the bed. She picks up the stick, and I hold my breath.

She flips her hair over her shoulder and gives me an enormous, genuine grin. "Not pregnant."

Oxygen whooshes back into my lungs, and I tilt my head back. "Thank fucking god!" I shout. The relief is enormous. Then a thought comes over me. "You bitch. I told you I wasn't pregnant, and you just scared the fucking piss out of me!"

I'm grinning at her because I'm not really angry, and I can't stop smiling because—Hello! Not pregnant! But damn

Anna and her hyped-up, totally on the ball approach to all things birth related.

Before she can react, I've pulled her to me and climbed on top of her, tickling the absolute crap out of her. She's squirming like crazy and laughing and screaming, "Stop! Stop!" because she's having trouble breathing, but I have no mercy. I haven't done anything like this since we lived in a dorm room together, but I'm not giving up. Not only am I tickling her, but I get it in my head that she deserves a good old fashioned wedgie. Knowing Anna, she's wearing a thong, so it's going to be easy to do and painful.

We're both laughing, and she knows what I'm trying to do, so she starts shouting louder screaming, "Help! Help!" as I try to reach around to grab the elastic.

The bedroom door swings open. Jackson's standing there, amusement written all over his face, taking us in. Anna and I are both breathless, but I stop tickling her, surprised by the intrusion. Then, over Jackson's shoulder, I see Sam.

A bead of sweat drips down my forehead, and I wipe it away while still straddling Anna. "Hey, there. What are you doing here?"

With a smile, Sam wedges past Jackson into the room. At first, he's watching us, and I half expect him to jump on the bed and join in. Then he glances to the end of the room at the same time I become aware of the pregnancy test crap on the end of the bed. On reflex, I grab a pillow from behind me and throw it over everything lying at the end of the bed.

I know I'm too late and momentarily stop breathing, waiting for his reaction.

"Hell. Fucking. No. We don't need to use a condom, huh?"

The muscles in his jaw flex. He pulls his arm back as if he's going to punch the wall.

Confusion sets on Jackson's face. Sam pushes past him as he exits the bedroom. Then I hear him shout, "Fuck!"

I'm reeling. Anna lifts her belly and pushes up on her elbows. In a whisper, she says, "Go tell him there's nothing to worry about."

I move to get off her. She pushes me forward, and I speed up, following him. I catch up to him in the den. Sam has his arm pressed to the window frame, his back to me. Anger radiates off him.

"I'm not pregnant. You don't need to worry." My voice cracks. Emotions are pouring through me right now. Fear. Guilt. Anger.

He turns to glare at me. "No? I don't need to worry? You told me you were on the pill."

"I am on the pill!"

He turns to face me full-on. Rage colors his face. I take a step back. This is a side of Sam I've never seen. "On the pill, huh? So, I pop by and you happen to be taking a pregnancy test. What happened? Did you conveniently forget to take your pill one morning? It's been two weeks. And you're already buying pregnancy tests? Hoping for eighteen years of child support checks?"

I gasp. "Is that what you think? You think I'd do that to you? Willingly? For money?"

He rubs a hand over his face then through his hair. He mutters, "You wouldn't be the first."

I study him. That's what he thinks of me. This is his version of all in. Fuck. What a nightmare it would have been if I'd been pregnant.

Tears well up, blurring my vision, and I turn to walk down the hall. He grabs my arm. "Wait."

I spin around, ready to spew venom. I've dated some real losers, but none of them have ever accused me of trying to trap them. "No, Sam. This is good."

He puts both hands into his jeans pockets and takes a step back, eyes cast to the ground. He's ready for me to slay him, and oh…my anger is rising, and slay, I will.

"This is good. It's good I found out what you think of me this early on in the relationship." He jerks his head up, shaking it. Before he can speak, I continue. "And it's good I know what 'all in' means to you. Because maybe your head is too far up your ass to get this, but any time you have sex, there is a risk of pregnancy. Any. Time. And you know what? This!" I point at him and wave back and forth between us. "This isn't what I want to be in if I ever do have an accident."

I turn and storm down the hall, pausing to snatch my coat off the rack as I rush out the door.

I repeatedly push the elevator button. Then I notice the stairwell door at the end of the hall and speed through it.

Once outside on the sidewalk, I spin around, unsure where to go, then head to the river. It's cold outside, but I need air.

It's only after I cross the street and turn the corner to head west that it occurs to me. He didn't follow me.

"Hell. Fucking. No. We don't need to use a condom, huh?" His words play on repeat in my head. The anger. Vitriol. Borderline hate.

What would have happened had I been pregnant? Would that hate have been turned toward our child? If I chose to have it?

I don't have an issue with women choosing abortion. There are a million reasons a woman could choose to have an abortion. Children are an enormous responsibility and expense. Would I choose an abortion? On one hand, I can afford a child. A child wouldn't put me over the brink into poverty. Unfortunately, even from a career perspective, I don't have the passion for my career right now. I'm not in high school, or in a degree program that prevents me from taking time off.

But would I bring a child into the world knowing one parent hated it simply for being alive? Probably not. I know the pain of being unwanted. My parents didn't want me. They only kept me so my grandmother wouldn't write my mom out of her will. No, if I ever have a child, that child will be loved. Fully loved. Not half-assed, in an obligatory way.

A bench by the river sits vacant, and I crash onto it. I place my elbows on my knees and my face in my hands. I cry. Completely bawl. Snot runs out of my nose, and I use my coat sleeve to wipe it away. He didn't even chase after me. He let me go. The rejection slices. I rock back and forth on that bench, crying, my arms around myself, until I have no more tears.

I'm not sure how long I spend on that promenade watching the sky change color as the sun falls to the west, casting oranges, pinks, and purples along the skyline and reflecting on the river. After the sun sets, the river turns black, with city lights twinkling in a mixture of small and wide white orbs. A black crow perches on a nearby tree limb. The air turns colder, and bundled pedestrians with scarves and gloves speed-walk by. My bare, frozen hands ache from the raw cold.

When I rise from the bench, I decide this is the end for Sam and me. A child isn't something I am craving right now, but I can't be with someone who can't handle it if life doesn't go according to plan. I can't be with someone who makes abortion look like the best option.

On the cab ride home, I dig into my coat pocket for my phone, expecting some texts from Anna. She has to be worried after witnessing that shitshow. A part of me doesn't want to look at the phone, because I know if he hasn't texted me, it'll feel like another knife wound. But I need my friend. I survived Damien almost completely on my own. Sam, though. The pain ripping through me is brutal.

My tender, ice cold fingers dig deeper into each coat pocket, hunting for my phone. Then I open my pocketbook. The small tampon bag brings fresh tears. I rifle through the rest of the stuff, my apartment keys, small bag for make-up, subway map, some receipts. No phone.

Chapter 24

Sam

"What the hell do you mean you can't find her?"

Withers's calm, slow voice on the line ramps up my frustration. "Sir, there are millions of people in this city. You have her phone. She's not at her apartment. I do have someone accessing street feeds, but it's going to take some time."

I run my hand through my hair and pace. Dammit. Three minutes passed, at most, before I was running after her. I thought for sure my elevator was just behind hers. She vanished. I called her, and Anna answered the phone.

The glint of her apartment key catches my eye. It's sitting on a small plate on my dresser. "Keep searching for her. I'm going up to her apartment to wait."

"That's a good idea, sir. I have a security person outside her apartment building scouting for her. I think that's where we are most likely going to find her."

"Yep."

I go to hang up, and Bill's voice sounds out. "Sir, at this point in time, there is no indication you should be concerned." I nod and hang up without saying a word. He has no idea. I should be very concerned. I acted like an ass, and I know it.

The doorman greets me with a wave. He's on the phone, calling someone who has a visitor. I stride past him to the elevator bank. I hold my breath as I use the Schlage key to turn the knob. The apartment is dark, lit only by streetlight cascading through a window. I don't bother to turn any lights on. I alternate between pulling at my hair and punching the futon cushion. My phone sits on the coffee table, dark except for occasional electronic lights when a news alert comes through or a text. No updates from Withers.

The knob eventually turns, and I brace myself. She walks in, flicks on the light, and hangs her coat up. She stops in her tracks when she sees me. Her cheeks are red, swollen, and wet. "What are you doing here?" she asks, her tone a mixture of surprise and anger.

"I couldn't find you. You left your phone at Anna's." I point to her phone that rests beside mine on the coffee table. "I looked everywhere. Knew you'd eventually come back here."

She closes her eyes and sucks in her bottom lip. "You need to leave." She points her index finger, opens her eyes, and repeats herself. "You let me know how you feel. You need to leave now. Leave your key too."

She wipes at tears as she heads to her bedroom, dismissing me. I follow her, and before she can close the door on me, touch her shoulder. "Please stop." I try to guide her to turn and face me, but she won't budge. "Please listen to me. I did not handle that situation well." I hear her sniffling. Her tears hit me like shrapnel. "Please listen to me. Then, if you want me to leave, I'll go."

She wipes her face and twists away from me. She drops into the single chair in her den and angles her swollen face up to me.

This is my chance. "Look, for most of my adult life, I've been warned to watch out for women trying to trap me. Based on my net worth and income, the child support check

238

alone would be enough for most women to not have to work."

She raises her hand like a student in class. "I get it. I understand." She's staring at my feet.

"No. You don't."

She leans back in the chair and closes her eyes. I wait for her to open them, but she keeps them closed as she says, "Go on. Say what you need to say. I've cried a lot today, so if you don't mind, I'm going to close my eyes while you speak." She rolls her hand in the air to indicate I should continue.

"Over the years, I've been approached by a lot of women. A lot of women interested in money. I regularly make the list of most eligible Manhattan bachelors. Every time I see my brother, he can't help but remind me I should wrap it up. My financial advisors and lawyers have all told me to be cautious. After years of that, a certain level of paranoia sets in. For Christ's sake, I had a woman claim her baby was mine. As if I wouldn't require a paternity test. When I saw that pregnancy test on the bed, I panicked. You and Anna were laughing. Happy. It was a gut reaction."

Her eyes remain closed. My heart rate increases, and I clench my fists.

"When I calmed down, I thought about it. I knew you'd never be the kind of person to trap me. I tried to run after you, but I couldn't find you. Where'd you go?"

Her eyes remain closed, her head angled up to the ceiling. "Is that it?"

"What?"

"Is that what you needed to say?"

"Yes. Do you understand?"

Eyes still closed, she sits completely still. "I understand. Have a good life, Sam."

Fuck that. I drop to my knees in front of her and place my hands over hers on her lap.

She opens her tear-filled, red eyes. "You need to leave now."

I tighten my grip on her. "I am so sorry I hurt you. But please know, it was a gut reaction. An emotional reaction. I don't really think you'd try to trap me."

Her head bobs forward slightly, and she sniffles. "I appreciate that. It's good to know. You can leave now."

Damn it. She is like a wall. She's not hearing me. "That's it? You can't forgive me? You need to understand, Jackson was acting weird when I first walked in. It put me on edge. Then we heard you laughing, and I walked in thinking you guys were doing something silly, but I saw that box, and you tried to cover it up."

She closes her eyes again. "I know what you saw, Sam. But you see, here's the thing. When two people have sex, there's always a chance of a pregnancy. Always. And I don't want to be with someone who has the reaction you had to an unplanned pregnancy." Her words pummel me, and I fall back onto the floor, willing her to look at me. "You need to leave now. We've both said what we need to say. Goodbye, Sam."

Fuck. She won't open her eyes. I stand and in slow, measured steps make my way to the door. This is such bullshit. Yes, I was wrong. But, she's wrong now too. If she'd given me five minutes, I would have gotten my shit together.

I turn and charge toward her and hold on to the sides of her chair as I lower my face inches above hers. "No. What we have is a good thing. A great thing. I love you. I. Love.

You. I haven't ever felt this way about any woman. I want you to move in with me. I want to wake up next to you, go to sleep next to you. I want to talk about business ideas with you. I want to go on runs with you, explore the world with you by my side. One day, have kids with you. And this screw-up…" I wait and drop my hands to hers and squeeze until she opens to me. "Yes. This screw-up is big. And I'm so damn sorry. I lost my mind. Just for a moment. It was a reaction. And, yes, it was fucked up. But you know, I just had to calm down enough for my instinct to slow down and my head to take over. When I couldn't find you, I returned to Jackson's. I walked in the room and picked up the stick. I held it and looked at the results. And you know what?"

She angles her head, questioning, some semblance of life returning.

"I felt disappointment. A part of me wanted to see two lines, not just one. Liv, kids are part of the life I want with you. And if it happened today, I'd be okay with it. More than okay with it. I'd be fucking thrilled. I love you so much. I do."

She snaps, "Could have fooled me."

I lean over, slide my arm under her legs and my other arm behind her, lift her, and sit in the chair, placing her on my lap. I breathe her in and hold her close. For a moment, she's stiff like a board. With an exhale, she relaxes into me and rests her head on my chest below my chin.

"I will make this up to you. One day, I'll be the husband you deserve."

She lifts her head and pushes away from me as fresh tears glide down. "You need to slow down."

I tilt her chin up and kiss her. Softly at first. She relaxes against me once more, and our kiss becomes deeper and tender. "Hey, I told you, I go after what I want. I'm not going to let you go. I'm gonna screw up at times. But what we have is real. We'll work through it."

She lays her head back down on my chest. "I don't know. I need to think it through." She exhales loudly. "Let me sleep. I can think through everything tomorrow."

I can live with that. I stand, lifting her with me, and carry her into her bedroom. I lay her down on her side of the bed and gently remove her shoes, her jeans, and sweater. She has a t-shirt on beneath the sweater, and I leave that on and pull the comforter around her, tucking her in. I strum my lips across her forehead and whisper, "Sleep."

I'm not letting her go. No way. I walk around to the other side of the bed, kick off my boots, and slide off my jeans and climb into bed behind her and wrap myself around her sleeping form.

******

Sun shines through Olivia's bedroom window early, as I never closed the blinds last night. I pull her close and breathe in her scent, the smell of her lavender shampoo calming me. I shudder to think how close I came to losing her. All due to my kneejerk reaction to seeing that test on the bed. Damn my brother and his repeated "wrap it up" comments. My financial advisors. Security. All those warnings got to me more than I realized. And I fucking hate it.

I kiss the back of her head. At some point yesterday, Bill suggested planting a tracking device on her moving forward. For once, that damn crazy Navy SEAL might be on to something. Tempting. But, no. I wouldn't do that to her. If

242

she had a car, I'd put a tracking device on it. I have one on all my cars. Admittedly, from a theft perspective. But I draw the line on personal tracking devices. We don't live in South America where kidnapping of expats is a real issue. But damn if not knowing where she was yesterday didn't drive me out of my mind.

My morning wood presses against her ass, and as she shifts in bed, she rubs me, teasing my dick into a painfully engorged state. I don't want to let her go, but I know after what we went through yesterday, we need to talk this morning. She doesn't need me to molest her before she's woken up.

I force myself to slide back, trying not to rock the bed, so as not to wake her. There's about a foot of distance between us when she grabs my cock, and I stop breathing in shock. Her back is still to me, but she's reaching behind her, stroking the outline of my cock, then her hand slips into my boxers and she continues to stroke.

Holy shit. So unexpected. She's gripping hard, just the way I like it. I groan. "Baby, I'm…I don't think you understand how hard I am right now."

She tosses her hair back as she turns to see me and lets me go. Ah, fuck. I miss her hand. But right now, I've gotta veto my dick's desire. She gives a seductive smile and doesn't say a word. Lifts the t-shirt she's wearing and pulls it over her head, unsnaps her bra, then slides her panties down her legs.

I can barely swallow. She's the most gorgeous woman I've ever laid eyes on. Her dark nipples are erect, and I reach out to massage her breast, twisting the taut nipple.

She pushes my boxers and the comforter down the bed. Then she straddles me. Slides over me, capturing my cock between her lips, coating me with her juices. Her breasts bounce. Sexy as fuck. She uses her body to massage and tease my erection, using my tip to press against her clit.

I swallow, watching her. "Does this…? Are we…?"

Without slowing the movement of her hips, toying with my erection, she whispers, "We're good. You ever pull that again, and we aren't." She pauses, hovering her dripping wet pussy over my tip. "Got it?"

"Yes." I gasp. "Fuck, yes."

Her hips rock back and forth over my erection, and she slides in enough to use my cock as pressure against her clit. I'm spellbound as she brings herself to orgasm, teasing herself across me, placing pressure and heat against my enormously sensitized tip. As she lifts her head back to come, I can't take it anymore and flip her over and drive myself in.

She's tight, and her muscles quake from the orgasm she's still experiencing. I won't last long. She feels incredible. Tight, warm, wet, perfect for me. "God, you feel good."

I start to pound her as her legs wrap around me, her nails along my back. I'm so close. I reach down and massage above her entrance, circling her sensitive clit. She arches forward, screaming my name, and I pour myself into her.

I collapse onto her, holding her tight as I catch my breath. I kiss behind her ear, down her neck, then position us so I can take a nipple in my mouth and twirl my tongue around it. I glance up from my position, place a soft kiss between her breasts, and smile. "That might be the best good morning ever."

I slide out of her and squeeze her ass, keeping her tight against me. She sort of giggles and runs her fingers through my hair. "Maybe mine too. That felt amazing."

"Amazing, huh?" I kiss her lips. "I'll take amazing." She kisses along my neck then sighs and leans over me to check out the time on the alarm clock. "Time to get moving. Want to shower with me?"

"Hell, yes." She grins and starts to get off the bed, but I pull her back to me. "Hey, we're really okay? You forgive me for being a jackass?"

Her deep blue eyes gaze upon me as she plays with my hair. The way she looks at me, I can see her love. She hasn't said it, but right then, I know. She loves me too. We are going to be fine.

"Yeah. We're good. I understand what happened. And, after a long night of sleeping in your arms, I'm over it. Past experiences color our reactions. I get it. And I guess I just decided sometime between last night and this morning that I'm not ready to give up on us." She places a soft peck on my lips then hops off the bed, walking toward the bathroom while baring her shapely derriere. "It's a work day. We've got to get moving."

I get out of bed and stalk toward her. "And then I'm going to feed you."

"Feed me?"

I squeeze her butt cheek as she turns on the shower and holds a finger under the streaming water to check the temperature. "Yep. What time is your first class?"

"Nine a.m."

"Let's shower quickly, then. I want to take you to the diner. I didn't eat dinner last night, and I could eat a whole cow."

We take turns washing each other in her bathtub shower. I take special care to clean her all over. I need to remove any doubts she may be having about me. Or about us. She said she's not willing to give up on us. Well, that's good. Because I'm not going to let her.

While she's drying her hair, I strum through my messages and see a text from Bill from last night.

Bill: I know you are back at her place and she's returned safely. We should talk about finding an apartment for security in her building if you think this might happen on a regular basis. Night shift not particularly fond of spending the entire night on a bench.

I groan. Damn the twenty-four-hour detail. They have an apartment in my building, so the night shift can stay nearby. They have monitors on my hallway and can be one flight up within minutes. We have three eight-hour shifts for my security. I didn't request this. When I signed on for a full security detail with Bill's firm, I read the contract but didn't fully comprehend the impact. A few board members tell me all this hooplah's normal and expected for a CEO of a public company with a death threat.

I run my hand through my hair. I won't respond right away. I'll talk to Bill about this later. On some level, I can agree a security contract for Olivia might make sense, but I don't believe she's in real danger. We've been staying at my place. Hell, I want her to move in with me. Then my security night detail can work from the comfort of the security apartment. Bill hasn't mentioned Ms. Ray recently. I text him to ask her whereabouts. Security needs to be watching her. She's the wild card, not us.

Olivia walks out of her bedroom. Her hair is still damp and hangs in thick, dark waves around her shoulders. She's wearing jeans and a chunky blue sweater that highlights the curve of her hips. She sidles up to me, weaves her fingers into the loops on my jeans, and pulls me close. I hold her tight and vow to do whatever I need to do to keep her with me for the long haul. She is mine.

Chapter 25

Olivia

Blissful coffee aroma envelops me the moment I open the door to Manhattanville Coffee. It's almost eleven a.m. but there's still a line at the counter. I float over to it. I'm on a high. A fabulous sex high. An everything-is-going-awesome-with-my-boyfriend high.

What a difference twenty-four hours can make. I've gone from deciding we are over to accepting he had a kneejerk reaction that doesn't define him or us. When I woke this morning, I lay there, thinking it all through. And I decided, aside from his initial reaction, I've never been happier with another guy, and I'm not ready to give up on us. Quite the opposite, actually. I want to see where this goes, because, while it's scary to admit it, I can see a future with him.

The kiss he gave me while holding me close said so much. He loves me. I've had guys look at me with sexual interest before. But the way his aqua blues latch on to me, it's different. I sense more love from him than I ever felt from my parents. Well, my dad, sometimes, at small windows of time showed an interest in his little girl. He may have looked at me with that kind of love. Before he and my mom had nothing to say to each other. Before being in the same room with the two of them grew painful.

Paige sees me standing in line and calls, "Hey, girl. You want your normal?" The couple in front of me glance my way, and I smile politely at them while answering Paige. "Yep. Thanks. How was your weekend?" Her blue hair is now streaked with white. Part of me wants to tell her Cloroxing does bad things to hair, but I refrain from giving her the parental kind of lecture.

"Great, actually. Didn't have to pull a double shift. How was your weekend?"

I'm about to respond when someone bumps into me from behind, and I turn on reflex.

"Hey, there, girlie. How was *your* weekend?" Lindsey asks.

I turn back to Paige, but she's facing away from me and is flipping levers on the large coffee machine. She didn't even wait for my response. I don't respond to Lindsey immediately but gather my mug and breakfast plate and head over to my normal table.

I keep staring at the counter, waiting to catch Paige's eye. Something feels off. When she finally turns around and looks our way, I nod and smile at her from my table. She gives a quick nod in acknowledgement then turns to another customer.

Lindsey flips the extra chair at my table around and sits on it backward, facing me. I notice she doesn't have coffee.

"How are you?" I ask. I keep glancing at Paige, since she seems uncharacteristically cold. Lindsey doesn't answer me. She stares as I pull out notebooks and get myself set up to work.

"What's up?" I ask.

"I'd like to ask you the same thing. I texted you yesterday and got crickets. What's going on?" There's an edge to her tone.

"I'm sorry, Lindsey. Yesterday, I left my phone at Anna's and didn't get it back until evening. Then, when I got it back, I didn't even look at it."

"Hmmm. That's all you're going to share?" There's an accusatory tone that I don't quite comprehend. Yeah, there is more to the story, but it's not like she knows that. I sip my coffee, and my foot taps out my growing frustration with Lindsey and her inexplicable attitude.

"What did you text me? Everything okay?"

I pull out my phone and plop it on the table. Looking at the message app, I see I've missed several texts, mainly from Anna, but also from Delilah and Lindsey. Did Anna send out an SOS when I left her apartment yesterday? I'm eager to thumb through my messages, but Lindsey's annoyed stance keeps me from doing something so blatantly rude. I take my coffee mug in both hands and turn to give her my full attention and alleviate the temptation to read texts.

"Are we friends? Or are we not friends?" She grits out the words, shoulders back, dark frizzy hair uncombed and wild.

"We're friends, Lindsey. I'm sorry. I'm not the best at checking my texts now that I'm not working full-time. I spent years glued to a phone, and I'm kind of enjoying this break from it."

She studies me and shifts in her chair. "Okay. I get that. But I care about you, and I want you to tell me what's going on. Where you are and stuff. I feel like you are shutting me out."

"I'm not shutting you out," I respond. But at the same time, I do know I'm keeping her at a distance. She's not as close to me as Delilah and Anna. She's someone I see on campus and go out with every now and then. That's how I see her, but the emotion roiling off her makes me question her perspective.

"Do you ever think about us?" she asks as if she can hear my thoughts.

"What do you mean?" I counter, cautious and uncertain I want to have this conversation.

"About the night we made out. Because I think of it. I know you have a boyfriend, but my offer, I want you to know it still stands."

I swallow. Oh, dear. She sees me like a potential girlfriend or something. I need to handle her the way I'd handle a guy I hooked up with but don't plan on dating. "Look, that night was fun, but I'm with Sam now. And I think I love him." I take her hand for emphasis, to try to warm the air between us. "I know I love him."

"Are you going to move in with him?"

"What? No, we're not at that stage yet. I can't imagine we'd take that step for a while. This is all new."

Her head angles downward, sending her black hair forward and creating a curtain around her upper body. I wait for her to respond. I'll be patient. And I'll keep her at a distance for a while. Like I'd do with a guy I hooked up with but wasn't interested in.

After a few moments, she lifts her head. "So, he's your boyfriend?"

I bite my lip and nod.

"Has he told you he loves you?"

It might lack sensitivity, but I can't hold back my smile. "Yeah, he did."

She stands from her chair and pushes it back under the table. "That's good. I'm happy for you."

She starts walking away, and I call out to her, "Hey, I'll see you around, okay?"

She flips her hair over her shoulder and says, "Probably not too much. But I'll see you." Then she turns and leaves.

What the hell does that mean? I may have misheard her. There's a healthy hum of noise in the coffee shop this morning. I blow out air and pick up my phone.

I have a couple of texts from Anna. It seems she knew I'd left my phone when I was out of touch that afternoon. The texts were sent later in the evening.

Anna: Hey, you, just checking in. Hope all is okay. Want you to know that Sam did a 180 after you left. He knows he fucked up. He loves you, hon. Give him a chance to explain.

Anna: Just checking in. Hope all is okay.

And one from Delilah with her signature, short "Call me!" and a flower emoji.

Before I have a chance to respond to any texts, my phone rings. It's Sam.

"Hey, there." He can't see me, but I know I have a flirtatious smile on my face. I can feel it.

"Hi. I need you to pack up your stuff and come to my office." The tone of his voice is all work Sam. No hint of the man I was holding and kissing earlier this morning comes through the line. But I still want to play a bit.

"Am I getting called down to the office for a midmorning quickie? Or is there such a thing as a mor—"

"Olivia. I have a car sitting outside for you. Two of my security guys are there. One is watching you as we speak." Desperation mixes with the commanding tone. He's not joking. This has nothing to do with sex.

I glance up, and sure enough, there's a man with a dark suit standing at the window. Staring directly at me. My heartrate speeds up, and my hands grow cold. "What's going on?"

"I'll tell you when you get here. Please. Pack up, get in the car, and stay with security. If anything happens, do not leave them."

"You're scaring me. Can you just—"

"Olivia. Get in the car. I'll explain. In person." Frustration seeps through his tone.

My calendar is open, and I glimpse my lengthy to-do list. Damn. I do not have time for this today. I shake my head. I'll catch up this evening. We can order in, and he can do work while I catch up on missing my morning work session.

I drop my mug and plate up by the bar, and Paige greets me with a warm smile. "Leaving already?"

I pull my heavy backpack up on my shoulder and nod. Paige passes change over to a customer, and I wave goodbye.

A black Range Rover sits directly outside the coffee shop, and as I push open the heavy wooden door, I notice the two men in suits standing by the waiting vehicle. One man holds open the car door, while the other stands on the sidewalk. He's the one who had been watching me through the window. He's sort of watching me but also scanning the street.

I slide onto the back seat, and the guy closing the door for me then gets in the driver's seat. The other guy walks around and gets into the front passenger seat.

He shifts to turn and face me. "We're taking you to Esprit Headquarters."

"Can you tell me what's going on?"

"No, ma'am. Mr. Duke will meet us when we arrive. He'll explain."

I pull out my phone and send a quick text to Sam. "In transit."

What the hell could be going on? A frightening thought occurs to me, and I slide forward on the black leather seat so I can see the man's face when I ask my question. "Is Sam okay? Did something happen to him?"

"He's safe, ma'am. We're here to make sure you're safe too." His deep voice, buzzed haircut, and no-nonsense attitude remind me of military movies. Or spy movies. Movies with guns.

"Are you in the military?"

He keeps his head facing forward, constantly scanning the sidewalks as we pass. It's a little unnerving. This whole experience is unnerving.

"I'm no longer active, ma'am." I hear a distinctive southern accent.

When we pull up to Esprit headquarters, Sam and Bill Withers are standing on the sidewalk waiting for us.

Sam opens the car door and pulls me close to him the moment I stand. He kisses my forehead, takes my backpack, then leads me into his building. We don't say a word in the elevator. Bill follows and joins us. There seems to be some unspoken request to maintain silence.

Sam leads us into his office as my frustration rises. "What's going on?"

Sam runs his hand through his hair and walks to the small conference table in his office. He pulls out a chair and signals for me to sit. "Do you remember the stalker I mentioned?"

"Yeah."

"Well, she's stalking you. We'd suspected it, like I told you, but this morning, we saw her sitting at your table. You seem to know her."

"I do?"

Sam slides a large black and white photo of Lindsey across the table to me.

"Lindsey?" The photo shows her on a sidewalk in her black leather motorcycle jacket. There has to be a mistake. She's a student at Columbia. She doesn't look like the woman in the photos he showed me.

"Her name is Tiffany Lindsey Ray. She's been stalking me for almost two years. How long have you known her?"

I try to remember. Did I meet her before or after I started dating Sam? I don't remember. Wait, I do. I tap the desk with my fingers. "I met her right before Halloween." At school. I remember the moment in the hall. I bumped into her. "But when I met her, you and I barely knew each other. We'd had dinner at Anna and Jackson's, that was it."

Sam rubs his chin. "Damn. She must have seen me kiss you goodnight out on the street that night."

"One kiss and she decides to meet me?" Skepticism fills me. None of this makes sense. "She's a grad student."

"She's not stable. And she does not attend Columbia." He taps the table. "At first, Ray was only an annoyance. Now, the fact that she's followed you, made contact with you, lied about who she is to you…" He paces to the window and back to the table. "It's not good."

"I don't understand. This seems too crazy for someone who saw you on a list. If Lindsey is your stalker, she's gone through a lot of trouble to get to know me. Did you two date? Is she an ex?"

Sam cuts his eye at me. "Not really."

"What does that mean?"

"We hooked up once. In a bar. She couldn't let it go."

I remember how Lindsey and I hooked up. Was she having trouble letting that go? "So, you've had sex with her?"

"Once. Years ago. Not my finest moment. But yes, that might have kicked off her obsession."

"You think?" Annoyance and jealousy rise within me, but the rational side of my brain tells me it's not warranted or deserved. It's not like he cheated on me.

He places both palms firmly on the table and stares me down. "Look, it doesn't matter how it started. She's not emotionally stable. Hasn't been for years. Doesn't have a support network. She might be harmless. But this is scary behavior."

Bill speaks up. "The point is, we don't know what her intentions are. I have recommended to Sam that we place a full security detail on you."

"What does that mean?" I have to spin my chair to see Bill, as he's standing behind me. I had forgotten he was even in the room with us.

"Twenty-four-seven security. We'll get an apartment in your building, preferably on your floor, so security won't need to be in your apartment. We can monitor feeds. We'll have someone discreetly follow you at all times."

Sam won't meet my eye. He's staring at the table. I know he fought his own security detail. I'm not in a public company, though. Lindsey does kind of freak me out, but I don't think she's actually dangerous. Odd. But not dangerous. I shake my head, slowly at first, then quickly as I make up my mind. "No. I don't want a detail. My uncle is worth about as much as this guy," I point at Sam, "and he doesn't have that kind of protection. I don't think Lindsey would hurt me. She's never threatened me. Not once." It does cross my mind that Sam doesn't know she's Ms. Halloween, but sharing that with him may weaken my argument.

Bill glares at me. "We don't know what she's capable of. She's made threats against Sam. Told him if she can't have him, no one can. She is a threat to you."

Sam still won't look at me. He's leaving me to fight this out with Bill. Great. Fine. I can take Bill Withers on. I straighten my back and sit taller. "Maybe. But what you are asking feels extreme." I pause then direct my question to Sam. "How did you know she was in Manhattanville Coffee with me?"

Bill answers. "I have a security team that keeps an eye on her. You know this. But we didn't know you know her. She's interacting with you, which raises the risk level. And she's smart. She's been good at losing her tails. We need to increase security to keep you safe."

The idea of her following me around does give me pause. She's an odd bird, sure. Clingy. And she hasn't been honest with me about who she is. But I can't stomach having a suit follow me everywhere. These men even carry guns, and I do not like guns. "I don't want security around me on campus. It's not needed."

"Ms. Grayson, one out of two stalkers who make a threat eventually takes action on that threat. Are those odds you want to gamble with?" he asks as if he's talking to a petulant child.

Sam finally lifts his head. "Look, Liv, I get where you're coming from. I fought a security detail tooth and nail." He glances over to Bill then leans closer to me. "I hate, and I mean hate, the idea that being close to me puts you in danger. I hate that my wealth puts me in the public eye and makes me a target. If I was a good guy, I wouldn't date you to ensure you weren't at risk." He stops for a moment and takes my hands. "But, Liv, I love you. I can't imagine not having you in my life. Maybe that makes me selfish." He looks down, biting his lip.

I squeeze his hands. "Hey, look at me. I want to be in your life. I do. I love you too." Both his dimples break through as a relieved smile spills across his face. He leans forward a few more inches and lightly presses his lips to mine. I press on. "I want to be in your life. I just don't think this is necessary. My gut tells me she's not a real risk. Maybe a nuisance. And, yeah, it's creepy thinking she's out there watching me, or us. But she's been stalking you for two years, and she hasn't actually hurt you. And how much does a full security detail even cost?"

Sam immediately responds in a curt, clipped tone. "The issue is not money."

Of course it's not. He has more money than he could ever spend. "No, the issue is excess. It's not necessary. And it's privacy and freedom."

Bill speaks up. "Our security prides itself on being discreet. Have you ever known you had a security detail when you've been out with Sam in the past?"

I think back. I've seen the men around but never focused on them. But now I most definitely would. Now I'd be hyperaware.

I plead with Sam. "It's not necessary. I know in my gut it's not necessary." Yes, she was pushing a threesome with Sam. But something tells me shock effect was her motive.

She had to know that once Sam saw her, there'd be no threesome. Maybe she's simply seeking attention.

Bill and Sam exchange a silent stare-off.

Sam reaches out to touch me. "Will you consider moving in with me? I know it's early in our relationship, but I know I'm ready for that step. You've been staying at my place anyway. And it would mean I would know you're safe."

"And if I move in with you, I won't need the security detail?"

"That's right. We can work with mine. Continue what we've been doing."

This isn't my dream way of being asked to move in with Sam. It is quick. But I've been wanting to move, anyway. And I'm serious enough about Sam that I wouldn't go through the hassle of finding another apartment. Signing a new one-year lease doesn't make sense. Moving in together will take our relationship to a whole new level. Nerves rumble as I pause before answering. "Yes. I'll move in with you."

Bill's stern voice interrupts. "She will still be in danger when she's not at the apartment."

Sam ignores him. "I'd have my driver drop you off and pick you up from campus. We'd continue having someone trail her." His voice turns cold when he references her. He turns to Bill. "Olivia will be safe. If she's living with me, she'll be safe. Ms. Ray won't make a move on campus. Security cameras are everywhere."

I add, "And now I know who she is. I'll be aware."

"Sir, she doesn't need to move in with you. There are other options to ensure Ms. Grayson's safety."

"There are other options, but this is what we want." His tone dismisses Bill. The discussion is over.

Bill knows Sam well enough to hear what's not said. "I can revise the security detail contract for Ms. Grayson to be based on her living with you. I'll keep security on her until the move."

I'm confused. "Wait. I thought we agreed to no security detail?"

Sam's still holding my hands, and he squeezes them. "How do you feel about packing a bag and moving in with me today? We can schedule movers for the rest of your stuff."

Today? I was already planning on staying with him tonight. I can do this. It's crazy, but I trust Sam. More than trusting Sam, I trust myself. Even if Sam and I don't work out, I trust myself to be okay. I look Sam in the eye. "I can do that."

I start to tell him we need to order in, and I need to work tonight, but the tension vibrates in the room between Bill and Sam, so I refrain. Sam tightens his hold on me as he speaks to Bill. "She'll be moving in with me for all intents and purposes today. No need for a full contract. We'll continue as we have been, with general monitoring of Ms. Ray's whereabouts. We should also explore legal options. See if my restraining order can be expanded to include Olivia, or if we can get her own restraining order."

The muscles along Bill's jaw line ripple. He doesn't say a word. Like an obedient military man, he nods and gives a brief, "Yes, sir," before leaving the room.

Chapter 26

Olivia

I sit down at the table, staring at the unusual food I selected from the line at The Little Beet. A fresh vinegar smell cuts through the air. I sent out an SOS to Delilah and Anna, telling them if at all possible, they needed to meet me for lunch today. A random Tuesday. They selected this place near their office.

It's a quick lunch spot with windows everywhere. Clean white tile covers select walls, adding to the modern, bright aesthetic. We have a table in a corner, which is ideal, given all I have to unload on them.

As they join me at the table, I struggle with where to begin. I go big. "I moved in with Sam."

Anna's eyes go wide like saucers. Delilah smirks, pushes her plate away, leans back, crosses her arms over her chest, and says, "Okay. Let's hear it. That's the emergency, right?"

"Yes and no." Anna's speechless. Delilah rolls her hand, her lips in a flat line, motioning for me to go on. "It's so crazy, I don't even know how to begin. Sam has a stalker. She started stalking me. My choices were to move in with him or have him hire me a full security detail. Which is crazy, so I moved in with him."

Delilah angles her head. "Do you want this or not? Because if you don't want to move in with him, he can totally afford a security detail for you."

"How do you know how much a security detail costs?"

She rolls her eyes and huffs. "I do know a thing or two. And I don't know exactly how much one costs, but I know Mr. Megabucks can afford it. So, do you want to move in with him? Are you that serious about him? How long have you been dating?"

Anna finally stops staring at me and turns to Delilah. "Hey, chill. Sam's a good guy."

"I am chill. I'm asking a question. An important question." Delilah's voice rises and carries through the restaurant, over the hum of patron noise.

"Sshhhh." The last thing I want is to attract attention to our conversation. "I want to move in, okay? I mean, we both agree it's moving our relationship to another level, but I'm ready. And I was looking for an apartment anyway."

"When exactly were you looking for an apartment?" Delilah asks, skepticism dripping from every word.

"Well, it was on my to-do list." I answer defensively. I'm not sure what's going on with Delilah, but this is not the Dee I know.

"How long have you been seeing him? Like, two months? That's insane. How can you know he's the one after two months?" She's practically glaring at me.

I set down my fork and place my hands on my hips. "I didn't say he was the one. I said things are good, and this feels like a natural progression. And I love him." Holy shit. Where is this anger coming from?

Anna, ever the mediator, jumps in. She touches Delilah's arm and says, "Hey, calm down." She waits until Delilah turns and faces her. "It's okay. If anything goes wrong, we'll be there for Olivia, okay? And if this person could be dangerous, then she's right where she needs to be, and she's safe. Safe. Okay?" Anna's mannerisms remind me of my kindergarten teacher when breaking up a fight on the playground. The thing I'm lost on is exactly why there's a fight on this playground.

Anna removes her hand from Delilah's and crosses her arms, resting them on the table. "Now, tell us more about this stalker. And are you in danger?"

Oh, yes. That's the reason I needed to speak with them. "Well, you know that girl I met at school and she's hung out with us some? Lindsey?"

Delilah sets her iced tea down on the table and answers with a slow, "Yeah?"

I lift my eyebrows and for some reason whisper-shout, "She's the stalker. She's not a student at Columbia. She's been stalking Sam for years. We think she must have seen us pretty soon after we started dating. Well, actually, Anna, right after we had dinner at your place. He kissed me on the sidewalk before he put me in the car. We think she must have tracked me down somehow, because I met her a few days after that."

Delilah squints. "But how would she know who you were if she just saw you on the sidewalk with him?"

I had thought of that too, but it seems she follows him everywhere. "I don't know. She doesn't have a job. She spends tons of time sitting outside watching. It's bizarre. She has some money from her parents' life insurance. Sam has a restraining order against her. They are looking into getting one for me now, but at this stage, it's probably not possible. She hasn't threatened me specifically. But, if you see her, go the other way. She goes by Tiffany, not Lindsey."

"Holy shit," Anna responds. "That's insane."

"Do you think she'd hurt you?" Delilah asks. She no longer seems angry, and judging from how she's leaning closer to me, she's intrigued and possibly concerned.

"I don't think so. Did either of you get that vibe from her?"

Anna shakes her head, but the wrinkles forming around the sides of her eyes express concern. Delilah sits back against her chair and smirks. "Well, her Halloween costume was 'sweet but psycho.'" Then, as if she just remembered, she slaps her palm down on the table. "Wait, didn't you make out with her that night?"

Anna's mouth drops open. I point my finger at her. "Close your mouth. And yes, we did. But, honestly, now that kind of makes more sense. She was feeding me drinks that night. And! She came on to me. I was so hammered anyone could have come up to me and pressed me against the wall."

Wrinkles form across Anna's brow. "Did you cheat on Sam?"

"No. Halloween was before our first official date. I don't count your house." And besides, even if you want to count that, we hadn't committed to each other then. I've told myself that only ten thousand times since Halloween.

"Does he know?"

"Yeah. I told him right after Halloween. Obviously, I didn't know Lindsey was his stalker." And I haven't actually made it clear that Lindsey is Ms. Halloween, but he knows *about* Halloween.

"How did you figure all this out?" Delilah asks.

"She approached me at the coffee shop, which I wouldn't have thought anything of, because I see her there all the time. One of Sam's security guys keeps an eye on her, though, and he saw her talking to me. Then Sam told me everything." I rub my hand over my face. "Crazy, right?"

Delilah nods. "Yeah, it is. But, you know, if this has been going on this long, she's seriously obsessed. And remember, some stalkers have definitely lost it, killed the object of their obsession, so you need to be careful. And you should probably tell Sam she's been pushing for a threesome, in case it's important to know for any reason."

"He hooked up with her," I blurt.

Delilah nods as if she expected that. "That may be what kicked the obsession off. But who knows? Do you remember that stalker who killed that girl on that TV show? *My Sister Sam*?"

Anna jumps a few inches in her seat. "Delilah, please!" She then looks at me and pops Delilah's head. "Jesus! Empathy!"

I throw my hands in the air. "All right, all right, all right," I say, in full imitation of Sam. That thought relaxes me.

"Wait, when did you move? And is our old apartment empty?" Anna jumps to the second question, her tone tinged with concern for our singles' pad, our home right after college. I just told her about a stalker, and she's envisioning our old place empty.

"I've only moved a couple of suitcases of stuff. You can help me tag stuff this weekend if you want. Sam's sending movers to get the rest of what I want out and to donate unwanted stuff."

With sad, puppy dog eyes, she asks, "The futon?"

"Anna, it's time to say goodbye to that futon."

*****

"Wait, if you're tossing this, can I have it?" Anna asks, pressing an old t-shirt dress up against her body.

It's Saturday morning, and Anna came up to our old place with me to help me pack. Sam offered to have movers do everything, but I decided I should go through my closet and purge items I don't want. Packers will pack everything. If I'm going through the moving hassle, I should reap the benefits of a more organized closet.

"Yeah. Of course." I hold up a pair of gold stilettos that have seen better days. "These are too worn, right? Time to go?"

Anna reaches over to grab them, running her finger over them. "Maybe…Aren't they uncomfortable as hell?"

"Yeah." Definitely. I hate walking in this particular pair. It cuts across my foot, but I like how they look on.

Anna shakes her head with a disapproving face. "Donate."

I've scheduled Goodwill for next week to pick up my furniture. It's all crap from college. They'll take everything, except for the mattress and futon. My plan is to leave those items on the sidewalk. That's one of the great but weird things about Manhattan. People leave things like sofas and mattresses out on the sidewalk. Within an hour, someone will walk by and claim it.

Going through all my shoes while emptying out my closet is giving me serious déjà vu. Less than two years ago, Anna and I went through this same exercise, only that time I was moving to Prague. I push a packing box onto the bed and sit beside it.

Anna is down on her knees, pulling out shoes, when she glances back and sees me. "You okay?"

I stare out the window at the view of the northern section of the city, mainly random high-rises of various heights. A view we've seen on snowy, rainy, and clear sky days and nights. A view neither Anna nor I will see again, since I'm letting my lease go. The building manager found someone to take over my lease without any issue.

"Do you remember the last time we were doing this? Moving me out of the apartment?"

Anna gets up and drops a few more pairs of shoes into a moving box on the floor, then squeezes my knee. "Things were a lot different then."

The sky is overcast, not quite gray, but not blue either. "Yes and no. I mean, I was heartbroken then and running. Now, I'm happy, but in a way, I'm still running."

"Are you really running?" she asks with her head cocked to the side.

I exhale loudly. "No. No, I'm not. If I didn't think I was ready for this step with Sam, I wouldn't do it. That's one thing spending eighteen months on my own and helping to manage an agency gave me—confidence. And I know myself better now. Much better than I did back then."

Anna's lips curl up into a gentle smile. "I agree.

My phone bings on the side table, and I reach for it. It's a text from Delilah. She's been a little MIA since I told her I was moving in with Sam. I never pegged her as being particularly judgmental, so I'm not sure what's up.

Delilah: Hey, do you want to meet up this afternoon?

I look around the place. I'm almost done here. Movers will pick up my boxes on Monday. Goodwill will get everything else. Then, sometime after that, Sam and I will

267

come back and drag out the mattress and clean up the apartment. I have two more weeks on my lease, so it's not a rush.

Me: Sure.

I turn to Anna. "Want to hang out with me and Delilah this afternoon?"

She sighs as she tapes up one of the garment boxes that's now full. "I wish. I told Jackson I'd go for a run with him this afternoon. Not sure why I promised that. I'm so much better doing morning runs than afternoon runs. I spend so much of the day dreading an afternoon run." I understand, given I'm not an avid runner. Neither was Anna until Jackson convinced her to take it up for the health of her dog.

Delilah: I'm going shopping for a gift for my Dad. It's that watch place I told you about. The guy sells super nice watches for less than retail. Small shop in diamond district. Want to meet there? You might be able to find a birthday gift for Sam, since I guess you're not taking Lindsey up on her offer. lol

I smirk. Yeah, ménage with a stalker? Not happening. God. I can only imagine what a nightmare that would have been if I'd taken her up on that, not knowing she was his stalker.

Me: Sounds good. Text me the address.

******

The cab turns onto Canal Street. There are a few large delivery trucks taking up space along the street, so I direct the cab to drop me off at the corner. As I step out of the cab, I inhale the pungent odor of uncollected trash. Graffiti lines the buildings. This isn't my favorite part of Manhattan, not by a long shot. And it's not even the real diamond district. The diamond district is officially on 47th Street in midtown. But there are definitely some smaller jewelers along Canal and Bowery.

I meander along the sidewalk, trying to locate building numbers so I can figure out where I'm supposed to go. I come to a glass door, framed in black metal with graffiti etched all along it. It's a bit grungy, but it fits. Places like this sell way below retail. Customers are willing to visit sketchy, temporary locations to get the real deal. Way below market price. Presumably better prices because of lower overhead. But I've also heard theories that the lower prices are because it's stolen goods.

I buzz on the number she texted, and the door vibrates. I pull it open. Trash litters the stairs. This place would definitely have lower rent.

I text Delilah that I'm here and headed up. I can't believe she was willing to come here alone. This place gives me the creeps. If I'd known how creepy this building is, I'd have asked Sam to join us. But I had been thinking I might buy him a watch for Christmas, so I didn't ask him to come or tell him what I was doing. He's watching the game with Jackson, anyway. His beloved Longhorns are playing.

I walk down the hall. There are four apartment doors. Nothing near any of these doors indicates one is a business. I pull out my phone to check again. Did she say B or D? None of these doors have letters.

As I look at my phone, I feel a sharp pain below my shoulder. The sting burns. I reach behind me, trying to touch the source of pain. Did something bite me? I can't quite reach the pain, but the tips of my fingers rub across what feels like a metal object. I spin, trying to reach the object. As I spin, the room blurs, and my eyes grow heavy.

I fall to my knees. I stare at my phone, indecisive. I need help, but who should I call? The police? Sam? I hit the green phone icon on my screen and stare at my list of favorites. I slide down to the floor as a heaviness envelops me.

I hear footsteps down the hall. The click of heels on the vinyl floor. The nasty vinyl floor catches my attention. A grayish black film covers the faded green squares.

A hand grips my bicep. The pain in my back increases, as if someone pushes on the bite on my back. I turn my head, trying to see behind me. Black cotton fabric falls over my face. It's not tight. It's loose enough that when I breathe, the fabric flows away from my face. When I inhale, the fabric floats to my nose.

I want the fabric off. I try to raise my arm. Get it off. My hand lies listless on the floor. I focus on raising it, but it barely moves.

The person behind me grips my wrist, places a foot on my ass, then grips my other wrist. Something rough wraps around both my wrists. I try to move them. A sharp object pushes onto my ass. It hurts.

An arm slides under each of my armpits. My body is raised. I'm pulled backward. The click of a doorknob opening sounds, and I'm pulled along, my legs dragging behind me.

My eyelids are heavy. My chest heaves like someone is sitting on it. It's hard to breathe. So hard to breathe. Just breathe. Breathe.

Chapter 27

Sam

The Longhorns win. 24-17. Hell, yes! I check the time on my watch and notice it's almost 6:00 p.m. I pull out my phone. No text from Olivia.

Jackson gets up and heads to the kitchen to toss his empty beer bottle. "Man, I can't believe you watch all their games."

"Well, how else am I gonna keep up with my Horns?"

He laughs. "I just meant, I figured you'd have more productive things to do with your time."

"It's Saturday afternoon. A man's gotta have some time off. And I don't watch all their games. Just the ones that are on at a convenient time."

He makes his way to the closet to get his coat, so I follow to walk him out.

I slap him on the back and say, "Thanks for coming over after your three-mile run." That man is like a machine. From what I can tell, exercise and Anna are the only two things that occupy any of his nonwork time.

I close the door and immediately dial Olivia. It goes to voicemail, so I text her.

Me: Hey, what time do you think you'll be home? Need me to pick up anything for dinner?

It was her idea for us to fix dinner together in the apartment tonight. She's probably at the grocery store now.

She wears an Apple watch, though, so she should see me calling.

I walk into my office and sit behind my desk. Flip open my laptop and scroll through email. I get lost reading through my inbox until the clock at the top right corner of my screen catches my eye. 7:15 p.m. It's dark outside with the exception of an array of city lights.

Where the hell is Olivia?

My phone sits on the desk beside me, screen faceup. I haven't received any messages.

I call her again. Again, it goes to voicemail.

I call Jackson. "Hey, man, Olivia hasn't gotten home yet, and she's not answering her phone. Has Anna seen her?"

"I don't think so. Let me ask."

I hear him ask Anna if she's seen Olivia. She reminds him they were together this morning. I hear her ask Jackson what's going on. He tells her. Then there's a shuffling sound.

"Hey, you. Look, I haven't seen Olivia since I left her at her apartment around lunchtime. She was going to meet Delilah. Have you called her?"

"I don't have her number."

"Here, let me call her for you."

Anna hangs up, and my gut twists as nerves fire off. Yes, it's our first week living together, and I'm still getting to know her, but Olivia has always been pretty reliable with plans and timing. We'd agreed on cooking dinner and staying in tonight. She was going to be back way earlier than this. Maybe even watch the game with me. This doesn't sit right.

I clear out the beer bottles for recycling, telling myself I'm worrying for nothing. Any moment, Olivia's gonna open the apartment door loaded down with groceries.

I'm pacing between the kitchen and living area when my cell rings. I answer on the first ring. "Hey, Anna."

"Hey, I couldn't reach Delilah on her cell. But this is the weird thing. I texted her, and she answered from her laptop via iMessage. She said she can't find her phone. She thinks someone stole it."

"Was she mugged? Was Olivia with her?"

"No, she hasn't been with Olivia all day." Anna's voice sounds strained as she repeats herself. "She hasn't been with her at all today, Sam."

I can tell I'm still missing something important. "Why did you think she was going to be with Delilah? Is that what she told you?"

"Yeah. She got a text from Delilah asking her to meet her. I couldn't go. But she was texting Delilah beside me today, making plans."

My pulse quickens. "Wait, are you saying she was lying to you about who she was texting?" Why the hell would she do that?

"No, no, that's not what I'm saying. I was standing beside her. I saw Delilah's text. I think whoever stole her phone was texting her, and that's who she met up with. It's the only answer. What time was she supposed to be home today?"

My hands go cold. Fuck. Damnit. Why the hell didn't I get her security?

"Anna, I gotta go." I don't wait for a response. I hang up and call Bill.

"Bill, something's happened to Olivia. Do you still have a tail on Ms. Ray?"

"Slow down. What happened?"

"Tail. Do you still have someone watching Tiffany? Lindsey?" I'm yelling, and I don't give a fuck.

274

"I'll send a text off and see if we have eyes on her. What's going on?"

"Olivia was supposed to be home this afternoon. She went to go meet a friend, but we found out that friend's phone was stolen this morning. It wasn't her friend who was texting her."

I think I hear a low "fuck" come from his end. Yeah, correct response.

"Let me check in with the weekend detail. I'll be back in touch."

"Wait. Should I contact the police? The FBI?"

"No. Let me make some calls." There's a pause. "How long has she been gone?"

"Anna last saw her around noon. She was going to meet whoever stole that phone, and we both know it's Ms. Ray."

"It's not long enough yet to contact the authorities. Stay calm. Don't contact anyone. We'll get her back."

Stay calm? Seriously? Why the fuck didn't I get her security? Helpless. I'm standing like a helpless god damn fool waiting for the phone to ring. A glass on the bar catches my eye, and I pick it up and hurl it at the wall. The loud crash followed by glass shattering almost soothes me.

I'm eyeing the wall, halfway considering punching it, pacing back and forth, when I hear knocking at my door. With long, quick strides I head to the door and swing it open, hoping with everything in my being it's Olivia.

Jackson and Anna push in. Anna has a few tears running down her cheeks. Fuck. Her tears suck the air out of me. My insides knot. This is happening. That lunatic has her, and who the fuck knows what she's planning on doing.

Anna lifts her arms toward me, as if she is going to pull me in for a hug. I dodge her arms and spin back to the living area. I can't handle being touched. I'm a live wire. I'm not about to tell them to leave, but I'm also not about to hug and cry.

I glance at the broken glass near the kitchen. I pound my fists down on the kitchen table. Focus on breathing. I'm a smart guy. I need to start thinking.

"Okay. My security guy is checking with the weekend detail to see if anyone has eyes on Ms. Ray. They are supposed to, so in theory, we could be jumping the gun."

Anna's lower lip quivers. She nods. Jackson comes to stand behind her, placing his hands on her shoulders. She places her hands over his.

"Can I tell her uncle?" Anna's voice breaks as she asks.

"Why?"

"He has resources. If she's been kidnapped, he can help. Timing is important. Or at least, that's what they say on TV."

I run a hand through my hair. I know she's right. A text comes through on my phone.

Bill Withers: Ray never came out of her apartment this morning.

More bubbles show. It looks like he's typing more. I turn to Anna. "Call her uncle. We'll take any help we can get."

Bill Withers: Headed to security apartment. Meet me there.

The security apartment is one floor below mine. It's where the security detail stays when I'm home, because I didn't want them in my apartment.

Me: K

My chest hurts. A tightness constricts, making it hard to breathe. All I can think is Olivia is in danger. I'm helpless. Relying on others.

Anna has walked off to the end of the room to call Olivia's uncle. Jackson asks, "Should we contact the police? At least get paperwork started?"

I close my eyes and rub my forehead. Damnit. "My head security guy said no. Not yet. Not enough time."

"You haven't had any ransom calls, right?"

I turn my head left and right in slow motion. Even I know that's not a good sign. This crazy-ass lady might not be after money at all. She may be making good on that threat.

If I can't have you, no one can.

When had she sent that? Ages ago. Way before I met Liv. That note had been a key piece of evidence when I went to get a restraining order. Right around the time we found out she had gun licenses from New Hampshire, Minnesota, and New York. Shit. Why didn't I take this psycho more seriously?

Chapter 28

Olivia

I'm surrounded by black. I inhale. Fabric touches my nose. I exhale. Fabric floats away. Light glimmers through the fabric. Weighted eyelids close.

I hear a voice. A woman. Far away.

"Fuck you!" she screams.

"I did it my way."

"She hasn't seen me. What the fuck do you take me for? I know what the fuck I'm doing!"

I only hear the one voice. Familiar. No screaming now. Talking, but I can't decipher the words.

I try to move. My limbs are heavy. Like my eyelids. I try to twist. Something holds me down.

"Hold on."

Footsteps sound.

"Tranq starting to wear off, huh?" Fingers glide over my shoulder and trail around my breast. Knocks sound. Rapid knocks. I hear footsteps. A moment later, I hear the muffled sound of her voice. I can't tell exactly what she's saying, but she's talking to someone. Anger. The voices are far away. Is she in another room?

I'm completely still. I don't know where she is, but I have to believe she can see me. It's Lindsey. I know it's Lindsey. But who is she talking to? I lie still. Frozen. Waiting.

Click. Click. Click. The sound of heels crossing the floor. "Seems you need a bigger dosage. More than a mountain lion."

A sharp pain radiates in my thigh. A burning sensation spreads through the muscle. Bloodshot eyes come into view. Inches away. My eyelids droop, heavy. Everything heavy. Hard to breathe. I struggle to breathe. Open my mouth. The thin black cloth over my face moves forward and backward. When I inhale, the fabric enters my mouth.

"That should be enough. You shouldn't remember any of this. Don't worry, I won't kill you."

She strokes my cheek. Down my neck. I'm wearing a sweater. She tugs up on the sweater. Cold air hits my stomach and breasts.

"Let's see what you're working with." My bra falls open. "Let's check out these breasts. I know what they feel like. Didn't get a good look before." Cold fingers fondle my breasts. A wetness encapsulates my nipple. "Hmmm…you know? I don't think these are better than mine. Not sure what he sees in you that he didn't see in me."

She tugs on my jeans. I want to twist, to fight, but my body won't respond.

"While I'm checking things out, let's see…have you waxed recently? Let's see how well you maintain yourself. Because, me? I'm a well-maintained girl. Sam deserves the best. Don't you think?"

Goosebumps prickle my cold skin. I shiver.

"You taste good. Want to know how I know that? I sucked all your juices off after I fingered you. Yum, yum, yum."

Nausea climbs from deep within to the back of my throat. *Please don't let me vomit.* If I vomit, I can't move my head. She has me tied on some board or table. I can't move. My heart races.

Pressure falls against my face. She whispers against the side of my head, "You taste so good. Do you think that's why he likes you? Because you taste good? Or do you have a tight pussy?"

Psychotic laughter rings through the room. "I'm pretty sure I'm not that tight. Maybe that's it. Maybe you have a *very* tight pussy."

Heavy footsteps thunder across the room.

"Tiffany, what the fuck are you doing?" A deep unfamiliar voice vibrates. Angry.

Shouting.

Breathing. So hard to breathe. The nausea intensifies. I struggle to breathe. Like I'm drowning. No water. Can't get air. Darkness falls.

Chapter 29

Sam

The security apartment is a one-bedroom on the fourth floor in my building. The den includes a wall with monitors. The monitors show feeds coming from a variety of locations. Outside my building, the lobby, the hall to my apartment. The street outside my apartment building. Many angles from my office building, office, and street.

I'm sitting here watching the incessant switch of camera views. It's crystal clear how much my security team knows about my life. I refused to have any cameras in my home. That felt too intrusive. I've been so sensitive about all this shit.

That's why I didn't push Olivia on a security detail. I know what it entails. How disconcerting it is to know that every time you leave your apartment, someone is watching. It's not easy to dismiss that knowledge. But damnit. Now look where we are.

Bill and two of his security guys are leaning over computers. One guy types at a rapid pace. Another appears to be reviewing feeds. Bill's on the phone, too far away for me to hear what he's saying, but I know he's working his connections. He's a former Navy SEAL. He's worked with men on Erik Prince's team, the genius behind Blackwater. I've authorized him to spend as much as it takes to pull in whoever and whatever he needs to find Olivia. He has an unlimited budget and one objective. Find Olivia.

After this is over, Olivia's going to have two full details. Fuck privacy.

There's a knock on the door to the apartment. The other three men are busy, and I'm the useless one, watching. The guy viewing footage glances over, and I raise my hand, so he knows I'll get the door. He needs to be working.

I open the door. Anna stands before me, and three men in suits stand behind her. Jackson stands behind them. Anna turns to the man standing closest to her. "Sam, this is Jordan Grayson, Olivia's uncle. Jordan, this is Sam Duke, Olivia's boyfriend."

He extends his arm. When we shake, his grip is firm, and he looks me in the eye. A moment later, he turns to the two men behind him. "John Morgan and Owen Smith. Both are FBI. John is a personal friend of mine. Can we come in?"

I give each a terse nod then direct them down the short hall. "My security team is right that way."

Jordan and the FBI men walk down the hall, while Anna and Jackson lag behind them. Anna looks like she wants to say something, but I head down the hall to make introductions. Anna and Jackson follow.

When I enter the den, I hear Bill say to whoever he's on the phone with, "I need to go. I'll call you back." He walks toward the kitchen table.

Bill angles his head in a silent question. He wants to know who I invited into his investigation.

"Bill, this is Jordan Grayson, Olivia's uncle. When he learned of Olivia's disappearance, he contacted his friend, John Morgan from the FBI. He and his colleague, Owen Smith, are here to talk about the case."

The muscles along Bill's jaw flex, as if he's grinding his teeth. Before I can say anything, Bill speaks, extending his hand to the newcomers.

"Bill Withers. Head security for Esprit Transactions. Also owner of Withers Security Company. The men you see here are employees of mine assigned to Sam's personal security detail. They are assisting in searching for Olivia. I've also been calling in additional resources."

Jordan stands tall, his eyes bouncing between the monitors on the wall. "What do you know right now?"

"Not much. We haven't been able to track her phone. We believe she has been taken by Tiffany Lindsey Ray. Sam has a restraining order against her. She's been obsessed with him for about two years and did make threats against him. We suspect she stole Olivia's friend's phone and used that to text her and make plans to meet her. We are working on locating them right now. I have others in another location looking through New York City feeds. Anna mentioned the diamond district, so our focus is in that area."

"You think she's in midtown?" Jordan asks, deep lines forming between his eyebrows.

"We do not have any visual leads yet. Only what Anna told us. There are any number of small jewelers located on 47th Street. I have men searching those stores now. Anna last saw Olivia close to noon today."

The reference to time forces my wrist to rotate. 10:30 p.m. We are pushing eleven hours now. Eleven hours a psycho has been doing god knows what to Olivia.

John Morgan steps forward. "We can help. I'd like to bring my team in to assist with the search."

Bill shakes his head in a jerky motion, his lips set in a firm, straight line. "Glad to know additional resources are available, but I've got a lot of wheels in motion right now. I do not doubt we will locate her within hours."

I step forward. I know what this is. It's a damn pissing match. And I'll be damned if I'm going to let Bill get fucking territorial right now. "Look, Bill, take all the help you can get. The FBI has resources you're not going to have."

Bill grinds out, "No, I can do more than they can. My guys don't have to follow the letter of the law. We'll have her soon." Bill taps my shoulder. "You put me in charge of this for a reason. Let me find her. I can't get bogged down bringing these guys up to speed and hand-holding them."

John and Owen share a silent exchange. They remain silent as Jordan reaches out to me, his hand wrapping along my elbow. He tugs my arm and leads me across the room.

In a low voice, he says, "We won't interfere in the ongoing investigation. The FBI will conduct a separate investigation. If we learn anything new we think will help Withers's team, we'll let you know. We would appreciate it if you would do the same. Stay here and keep us informed." He reaches out and takes my phone. I watch as he enters his contact information.

Bill charges over to us. Shoulders back. He looks angry as hell. I get it. He sees this as someone doubting his work. I slap my hand on his shoulder. "Hey, I've got this. These guys are gonna be leaving. I'll see them out. You get back to work finding Olivia." I'm staying calm. Doing what I do best and managing resources. Inside, I'm a fucking mess, and I want to lose it on Bill's childish attitude. Fuck.

Bill takes my bait. Walks back to the far corner of the room where he was standing before we came in, pulls out his phone, and calls someone.

I catch Jordan's eye, and we lead the way down the hall. Once we are all outside of the apartment and standing before the elevator, I place my hand on Jordan's shoulder. He stares at my hand the way someone would stare at a scorpion, with a look of disgust and caution. I remove it. So, we're not that familiar yet. Got it. "Look, I appreciate you doing anything you can do. Do you guys want to go up to my apartment? You can work from there. It's one floor up. My office is fully outfitted."

John smiles. "Thank you, but we'll be at the FBI offices. Can I ask you a favor?"

"Anything."

"Stay with Bill. As much as you can, stay with him."

I pause, running through the implications of his request. "Why?"

"Just a hunch. And besides, you're the only hope we have of knowing if they get any leads."

I raise my eyebrows. Now that, he is right about. Bill's not someone I'd call a friend, but I do place a lot of trust in him, spend a lot of time with him, and I know he's a competitive fucker. He's gonna want to bring Olivia home on his own. And in this ball game, we've gotta be a team. Remove anyone with an "I" mentality. I nod and look John in the eye. "I got you. I'll be there. Any leads, I'll share them with you." Almost to myself, I add, "We're a team."

They leave, and Anna takes my hand. "How can we help?"

I exhale. "I don't know. You guys want to go up to my apartment to wait? Or you can head back to yours, and I'll let you know if we find anything."

"We'll wait in yours. That way, we're here if you need us."

I walk back into the apartment. I sit on the sofa so I can hear Bill's conversation. Anna's words hang in the back of my mind. I flip my phone over and text Ollie. I won't ask anything from my family. Not right now. But I'll let them know a bit of what's going on. After I text Ollie, I text Jason. He knows Olivia. He may have even seen Tiffany, or Lindsey, on campus. Any information he might have might help these guys. After I explain the situation, I send over the most recent picture of Tiffany Lindsey Ray, the one of her in a motorcycle jacket.

Chapter 30

Sam

Bill stands at the far end of the den, pacing and alternating between making phone calls and reading and sending texts. Members of the security team have been coming and going. Checking out different locations. Coming back. Two men are talking in hushed tones, leaning over a computer.

I hear bits and pieces. Every store on 47th Street is clear. Footage on 47th Street from last twenty-four hours on NYC cameras, no sightings. Ms. Ray left her apartment through the vendor entrance. Located her at several subway stops. Working on tracking her through an endless maze of NYC cams.

I stare at the ceiling. I'm so fucking helpless. I've been losing confidence in Bill and his team as I watch them. Bill's face has gone pale. Perspiration runs down his temples. It's, like, sixty-five degrees in this apartment. He keeps lowering the heat. None of these are good signs.

My phone dings. I grab it from the table.

Jordan Grayson: Come up to your apartment.

I stand. I catch Bill's eye from across the room and toss my head in the direction of the door. I wave and mouth, "I'll be back." Not sure why I'm being silent.

This has to be good news. They found something.

I walk down the hall and open the door. Someone grabs my arm. A man in full SWAT gear places a finger over his lips and makes a soft "shhh" sound. I'm pushed farther down the hall. Approximately six men in SWAT gear are standing in the hall. Jordan stands at the end of the hall, beside his friend John. He's wearing a bulletproof vest over his suit.

It's 3:00 a.m. My emotions have been all over the fucking place, and my brain's in slow motion. Fogged. I step closer to Jordan.

From behind me, I hear one of the men shout, "FBI! Freeze!" I whip around, and the hall is empty, the door to the security apartment still open.

Jordan's hand falls on my shoulder, and he squeezes to get my attention. "We found Olivia. She's en route to a hospital. We need to go. Now."

"Is she okay?"

"Let's go."

I turn back, pointing at the security apartment. No noises come from the apartment as we walk by to the elevators. I'm so fucking confused. "What's—?"

"Your security team was behind Olivia's kidnapping." Jordan answers my obvious question.

We are in the elevator as the words hit me. "All of them?" I ask.

John answers. "We don't know that yet. Bill Withers, definitely. At least one more. We've been following each of the men when they leave this apartment. It does appear they were searching for her. She may have gone rogue. Or FBI involvement complicated their plan. We found her by following one of Bill's guys. Withers's security firm has run into financial issues, so we were immediately suspicious. The FBI is still investigating."

Holy shit. We're speed-walking to a car waiting for us. We all climb in. Jordan and I sit in the back. John takes the passenger seat.

The car takes off down the street. John immediately turns, his arm over the seat. "Did Bill pressure you to increase security?"

I run my hand through my hair. The first thing that comes to mind is how hard I fucking fought against my own security detail. I hired Bill for Esprit Transactions security based on a recommendation. He handles all non-technical security. But then he kept pushing for me to hire a personal security detail. I remember how pissed I was that day he came before the board to explain the stalker. The meeting where they pressured me to agree.

I grind my teeth and clench my fists. I have to focus my thoughts. "Why is Olivia going to the hospital? Did they hurt her?"

"They gave her a tranquilizer. We're not sure what it was, exactly. She wasn't conscious."

"Is she okay?" I stare at Jordan.

He responds, void of emotion. "No update yet. We're on our way to the hospital now. I know this is tough, but please answer John's questions. We have Olivia, but his team is still working the case."

John repeats his question. "Did he pressure you for additional security?"

I swallow. "Yes. I fought the security detail for me. He went before the board. There was this stalker. Ms. Ray. I've had a security detail for almost two years."

"Twenty-four-seven? Multiple men?"

"Yeah, full contract. Three shifts. Security apartment because I wouldn't let them in my home."

"Did he want Olivia to have a contract too?"

I nod. Rub a hand over my face, trying to corral my fractured thoughts. "The stalker. Her name was Tiffany Lindsey Ray. Was she in on this?"

John answers. "She's in custody. She'll tell us everything. We're looking into her bank accounts, but we're pretty sure she was on Withers's payroll. We suspect he didn't tell her to kidnap, though. If I'm right, he wanted her to scare you enough to sign another contract. If Jordan hadn't involved us, he might've gotten away with it."

So, Bill's bad. Fuck. He manages security for my entire fucking company. I pull out my phone and call Ted. He's COO. A groggy "hi" sounds across the phone.

"Ted. Sorry to wake you. I'm headed to the hospital."

"Wha—?"

"Bill Withers was behind kidnapping my girlfriend, Olivia. FBI has him in custody now. You need to handle from Esprit's perspective. He didn't have his hands on anything from a technical perspective. I don't know how many people on his team are with him. I don't know who we can trust."

"Is Olivia okay?"

"I don't know." I rub my sweaty palms against my jeans to dry them as my chest burns. I don't know if she's okay.

The car pulls up to the hospital, and Jordan jumps out. He charges toward the hospital entrance, not waiting for me. I jump out and run.

Chapter 31

Olivia

Beep. Beep. Beep. The sound is constant. I turn my head toward the noise. My head sort of flops against a soft object. I open my eyes and immediately squint. Bright yellow lights hurt.

"Hey, there you are. You're okay. You're okay." Sam's face comes into view. His hair's a mess, sandy brown chunks of it flopping forward. A few chunks arch backward, and random pieces stand straight up. His gorgeous blues are bloodshot. Deep lines I've never noticed before mark his face. He lifts my hand to his lips. That's when I notice the taped IV coming out of the back of my hand.

"What?"

"You're in Mount Sinai Hospital. Tiffany shot you with a tranquilizer. The kind of tranquilizer you'd shoot a bear with. Thank god we found you when we did. She didn't know what she was doing. She gave you too much."

His voice breaks, and vertical lines form around his lips as he grimaces. I remember the hall. I remember the pain in my back. Heavy muscles. Difficulty breathing. My fingers trace along my face and touch the plastic lines bringing oxygen to my nose. I look to Sam, questioning.

"You're okay now. They figured out what she gave you. They had the reversal drug here at the hospital. Naloxone or something like that. It doesn't matter. What matters is you are going to be okay."

"Do they have her?"

He nods. "Yeah, yeah, they do. You're safe now."

The door opens, and my uncle walks in the room. "Uncle Jordan?"

He looks straight to Sam. "You were supposed to come get me when she woke up."

Sam leans back in his chair but doesn't let go of my hand. "She just woke up."

Uncle Jordan looks me over then glances to the monitors showing my heartrate. "I'll go tell the nurse you're up." He walks out.

I focus on Sam. "Why is he here?"

"He helped find you. Got the FBI involved."

"How long was I missing?"

"Less than twenty-four hours. Thanks to your uncle." He rubs his fingers through his hair. "There's a lot to tell you. What matters is you're okay."

A nurse walks into the room, followed by my uncle. The nurse checks me over, looking at the monitors on the machines. She shines a light into each of my pupils. With a kind smile, she asks, "How are you feeling?"

"Okay. Tired. I was having trouble breathing. Before. But I can breathe now. My lungs still feel…" I pause, searching for the best word. "Tired. Like I ran a marathon."

"That's good. To be expected." She checks an IV drip hanging from a metal pole near me. "I'm going to let your doctor know you're awake now. The effects of the drugs should be wearing off. He'll probably want to keep you overnight for observation. Are you warm enough?"

"I'm cold." Freezing. Goosebumps cover my skin.

"That's normal." She turns to a closet and pulls out two blankets and spreads them over me. "I'll go get the doctor now." She's speaking to my uncle, not to me.

My uncle pulls up the unoccupied chair by the end of my bed. He sits and squeezes my ankle. "Glad you're okay, kiddo. You had us worried."

Sam intertwines his fingers with mine. "Turns out you never told your uncle about us. This isn't the way I wanted to get to know your family, but at least now you don't have to worry about introducing us."

He looks so tired. It's not that I hadn't wanted to introduce him to my family. I squint, the word *family* making me question. "Who all did you meet?"

Uncle Jordan squeezes my ankle. "Your parents were here earlier. In the same room, if you can believe it. They left once they knew you were going to be okay." I focus on the framed poster on the wall. Of course they left. "But, hey, they'll be back this evening. They knew Sam and I were here. They will be back, okay?"

The faded poster features a fern in a ceramic bowl. Uncle Jordan. Forever keeping the family together.

He continues. "Anyway, I've decided I like this guy, here. You should have brought him around earlier. Or at least let me know you're living with him now." His declaration is tinged with a distinct fatherly tone.

"I only moved in a week ago."

His lips turn up into a slight smile, and he squeezes my foot through the blankets. In a softer tone, he says, "It's okay. I'm teasing you. Anyway, I wanted to see you before I left. I'll be back this evening too. Your aunt's going to come with me. If they release you this afternoon, we'll stop by to visit you at your new home."

My new home. If Sam wants me there. Now there's no stalker. No crazed lunatic. I shudder, remembering my inability to move and those wild, bloodshot eyes.

The doctor comes. My uncle leaves. Then, finally, the doctor and another nurse leave. They may let me go home this afternoon. Waiting for some final lab results to come back.

Once we're alone again, Sam sits on the edge of the bed and rubs my cheeks. His touch feels warm on my cold skin. I can't get warm. No matter how many blankets they put on me, I'm cold.

Sam's blue eyes glisten. "I almost lost you." A single tear falls down his cheek, and I force my sore muscles to move. I lean over to press my lips to his neck, inhaling him. A hint of the cedar soap he uses replaces the sterile ammonia hospital aroma. The rough, hard growth of the stubble darkening his face and neck chafes against my cold skin. I welcome the sensation. It means I'm alive. His arms wrap around me and hold me close.

We sit there, holding each other for I don't know how long. The vibrations of his heartbeat calm me, heal me.

Eventually, he sets me back on the pillows. His fingers run through my hair. "You need to rest." He reaches for my other hand, so he's holding both mine in his. "How do you feel?"

He sits on the bed, leaning forward so we are close.

I take stock. "Relieved. I was so scared." Tears well in my eyes, and his warm hands cover my cold ones. "I can't even begin to describe how scared. To not be able to move. I was conscious. Sort of conscious. It was this almost dreamlike state. At first, I wasn't scared. Then as time wore on, and when I couldn't breathe, I started to think. I started to think…" Tears run down my cheeks unchecked. Sam wipes them away.

"Shhhhh. You're okay now. You're okay." He keeps repeating this until my tears have passed.

"I thought I wouldn't see you again," I finally admit. "I also remember thinking I'm too young to die. But, if it had been the end, at least I gave us a shot."

"Oh, baby." Tears run down his cheeks. He presses a firm kiss to my lips, then a soft kiss to my forehead, and he pulls me in, holding me tight. "I can't believe I almost lost you. And my security team was responsible."

A soft knock on the door interrupts us. Professor Longevite stands at the door. Sam wipes the remnants of tears from his face and settles me back on the pillows but doesn't shift away. He stays close, like he can't bear to be apart from me. I feel the same way

Jason enters the room and stops at the end of my hospital bed. "Glad to see you're okay, Olivia. You gave us quite a scare."

"Pull up a chair," Sam offers.

Jason slides the one chair that's across from my bed to the side. He sits on it and leans forward. "Ollie's flying in. He'll be here tonight. Your parents wanted to come too, but I convinced your mom she'd probably be more helpful once Olivia's back at your place. There's nothing worse than loads of people packed in a hospital room."

A look of understanding and compassion crosses Sam's face. "Thanks, man."

Jason sits back in his chair. "Okay, tell me. What the fuck happened?"

Sam and I both laugh. The light sound echoes through the room, bringing a welcome shift in mood.

While holding my hands, Sam shares the whole sordid story. It turned out Bill Withers earned a salary as head of security to Esprit. But Bill also had his own security company. He had grand visions of building up a solid private security business, but the security industry is a highly competitive market. Bill had a Navy SEALs background, not a business background. He thought since Erik Prince did it, he could do it too.

The security detail contracts were quite lucrative, but the expense of running the business was also high. The men he needed to hire, the security equipment he needed to buy, all added up to expenses he needed to cover.

At first, he had legitimate security detail contracts. Several of Esprit's board members were his clients. Then he had a tax bill he hadn't anticipated.

Bill came up with the idea of a stalker to convince Sam he needed a security detail. He thought one more contract was all he needed. But he spent that money to pay taxes and other expenses. And yet he still had the expense of providing Sam's security detail. After two years, his security business still struggled to get out of the hole. With his full-time job at Esprit, he didn't have enough time to focus on marketing his services and acquiring leads, so he decided he needed just one more lucrative contract.

Sam wraps the story up. "We're still figuring out details. It does seem the kidnapping wasn't Bill's plan." Sam straightens one of my blankets. "The FBI's on it. Right now, my focus is this one." His blue eyes glisten, and the muscles in his jaw tighten

Jason listens intently, concern etched on his face. "How're you holding up?" His hands grip the armrests of the chair as he studies Sam.

"I'm a whole lot better now that Olivia is safe."

"It's not your fault. You know that, right?"

Sam bites his lower lip and nods in agreement. "Yeah. I still can't believe it, though. The one guy I put so much trust in." He shakes his head, the frustration evident. "I can't even begin to tell you how much that guy knew about me. About my business."

Jason stands. "Yeah, well, he'll get his due. You focus on you. And this lovely lady." He then directs his attention to me. "You take care of this guy, okay? Make sure he doesn't wall himself off because of this." Then, as he gets up to leave, he adds, "Text me when she's home. I'll stop by. I'm going to be heading out of town tomorrow, but if you need anything, let me know."

Sam interrupts. "I'll let you know if I need anything. Thanks, man. Where are you off to?"

A smile spreads across Jason's face. "Chicago."

"You ever going to let me in on what's going on with you?"

Jason chuckles. "When I have good news, yes. Wish me luck." He slaps Sam on the shoulder and says, "You take care of this one, okay? She's got a tough accounting exam coming up." He chuckles when I grimace.

After he leaves, I turn to Sam. "What's going on with him?"

"He still hasn't told me everything. But it seems you were right. Some things have been going on with an old friend."

I reach out to touch his face, but the IV line pulls on my skin, so I rest it on the comforter.

Sam leans forward and covers my hand with his. Lines frame tired eyes, his jaw muscles taut. He's exhausted, but there's more. Something still bothers him. "What are you thinking?"

He fingers the unruly mass on his head as he exhales deeply. "My thoughts? Last few hours, they've been rampant. Emotions. A stampede." He lightly taps the silver railing on the side of my bed. "You see, when I was a kid, I trusted pretty much everyone. Then, after I became successful. Money. After that…" He grits his teeth. Stares at the wall. "I lost a lot of faith in humanity. Suspicious of everyone. You know, this whole thing. Bill Withers. Scamming me."

I squeeze his hand.

"Yeah. The one guy I put so much trust in. So much fucking trust. It makes me feel like…I don't know. Like I can't trust myself. It's not a great feeling." His eyes search mine. "It fucking sucks. I've been sitting here. Watching you. Unconscious. Thinking about all this. And I decided, I'm gonna lay it out. I need you to be honest with me. Always. I need to know I can trust you. If you are with me for any reason other than me. Please." His blue eyes drill into me. "Please tell me. I can't handle finding out I can't trust you. You, you're my everything. And I don't know how all that happened so fast. But when I was sitting out there, waiting to find out if the antidote would work, to find out how much damage the drug did to your central nervous system…" He studies the lines on his palms.

"Sam, you can always trust me. Always. I don't give a damn about money. Honestly, I think I've hated it for a lot of my life. I kind of blamed my parents' obsession with it for them being gone so much." I look out the window. It's narrow, gritty. It's an overcast winter day outside. "You know, the two of them, they hate each other. They should have divorced when I was a kid but didn't because it wasn't what my grandmother wanted, and my mom was afraid of losing access to her money. It's miserable to be around the two of them. That's why I didn't want to introduce you to them. I don't even know why they had me. To a large degree, they're like strangers. And that's fine. It is what it is. I'm kind of shocked they even came by the hospital." I squeeze harder on his hands until he's looking at me. "But you can always trust me. Money isn't what motivates me. I've seen what happens to people when money overrides their every decision. That will never be me." Our fingers intertwine, and I make a silent oath to always be true to him, to us.

He places soft kisses on my knuckles. "God, Olivia. I was completely helpless. Couldn't fly you to the world's greatest specialist because there aren't any doctors who specialize in tranquilizer overdosing. There's no Google ranking of doctors who deal with this. I'm not religious, and I prayed. I promised myself if you made it through, then I'm going to work like I've never worked in a relationship. To make us work. To be everything you deserve." He brushes a few strands of hair away from my face, and for a moment, I wonder what I must look like right now, but the warmth in his eyes tells me my appearance doesn't matter

I break the seriousness of the moment when I tease, "I'm just blown away someone like you, this gorgeous, brilliant guy, likes me. An intern." I emphasize the word *intern* and smile. My stomach flutters. "Are you sure you still want me to come home with you? The stalker's not a threat anymore. We can back things up if you want."

For a moment, he looks up to the ceiling. "You don't get it, do you? I love you. So goddamn much. The whole stalker nightmare may have moved us forward faster than we would have gone, but not by much. You belong with me. I belong with you. I've never been more certain about anything. About anyone. In my life." He pulls my hand up to his lips, once again kissing the back of my hand, carefully so as not to pull on the IV line. "Do you want to live with me?" Vulnerable blue eyes find mine.

"I do. I love you too." I rub the thick stubble lining his face. He's now close enough I can reach him. "So much. I still can't quite believe you're real. Coffee shop guys aren't really supposed to be real."

"Coffee shop guys?"

"Yeah. You know, love in a coffee shop? The guy you see from afar. Daydream about. Then he leaves. You were my coffee shop guy."

"Darling, if that's what a coffee shop guy is, then I hate to break it to you, but I'm not him. I'm your forever guy. I'm the love of your fucking life." He leans forward and presses his lips to mine.

I smile at him as he pulls back. "Promise?"

"Oh, baby. I've never been more right about anything in my life. This is it for us. Trust me."

Epilogue

Olivia

Six months later

It turns out Ms. Ray loved Bill. In her own way. Even after hours of interrogation, it's unclear what kind of relationship the two maintained over the years. It appears it was very much one-sided, with Lindsey caring far more for Bill than he did for her. She wanted to see him succeed. Didn't want his security company to go into bankruptcy. Bill had asked her to get to know me, as he suspected Sam wanted to date me. His plan was to raise concerns, at first to simply remind Sam of lurking dangers to increase security. Then, when our relationship did develop, he aimed to coax another contract. But Lindsey preferred to do things her own slightly irrational way. She thought they weren't being aggressive enough, so she took things a step farther. Bill had nothing to do with the kidnapping. But prosecution expects they will both be going to prison for a long time.

We're standing outside the courthouse now after providing our testimony in the case against Tiffany Lindsey Ray. We testified against Bill last week. Both pleaded not guilty to a host of charges. A handful of reporters surround us. There are a few flashing lights. Sam stands beside me, hand on my lower back, protective.

"Mr. Duke, how do you feel the case is going?" one reporter asks.

"Mr. Duke, are you surprised they plead not guilty?" another reporter asks.

"Mr. Duke, is it true that you had sexual relations with the defendant, Tiffany Lindsey Ray?"

"Are you and Ms. Grayson still living together? A source mentioned you had a fight in a restaurant recently."

Sam cuts his eyes to mine. One of Sam's lawyers steps up. "The case is ongoing. Mr. Duke will not be answering any questions or making any comments during the trial."

A few of the reporters nod, taking notes while a few flashes still go off. This is the response they expected. Sam isn't one of those pseudo-celebrities looking to comment to raise his profile level in the media. In fact, interviews with Sam are most frequently done by email. Handled completely by his PR team with business motivations in mind.

Sam's lawyer walks through the crowd and down the concrete steps onto the street, leading us to an awaiting black Tesla. Wes, one of Sam's regular drivers, stands with the back door open. He's wearing a *Star Wars* t-shirt and jeans. After the whole security debacle, Sam asked all his drivers to go casual. I don't think he wants anything around him that feels like a security guy is in the wings.

Sam thanks his lawyers, and we both slide into the back seat of the car.

"All right. All right. All right!" Sam slaps his hands together. "That's behind us. What do you say we head home?"

Home. His apartment is now truly our home. It no longer has a spartan, barely lived-in feel, although I'm sure his designer might cringe if she came over to visit. We have cozy throws in the den, and we've started a wall of candids of us and our friends and family. My favorite photo right now is of our first Christmas tree. Or maybe it's the one of us both riding a horse together, laughing, because we're riding bareback and Ollie snapped the photo right as the horse kicked out at a fly and we were struggling to stay on.

I grin. "It's four-thirty in the afternoon? You don't need to head back to the office?"

"Nope." He pulls me onto his lap and wraps his arms around me. "There's something else I need to be doing this afternoon." He wiggles his eyebrows and smirks, making me giggle.

I playfully take his earlobe and bite. He squirms, and I tickle him. He quickly grabs my wrists and gives me a fierce, playful glare. "Stop that."

I smile. Then I recall one of the questions I heard shouted. "Who do you think is going around saying we got in a public fight?"

"Who knows. Who knows if they even have a source. Thank god I'm not really in the public eye. I can't even begin to imagine how actors or politicians deal with that shit. It's like this moneymaking machine that doesn't even care which humans it grinds up to print money." His lips twist, a clear look of disgust across his face.

As I run fingers through his hair, I lean in to kiss his cheek. He lifts my hand and kisses it. "So, I've been meaning to ask you. Even though we may have to get security for our kids, and even though we have to sometimes deal with crap sources making comments to sell papers, are you still thinking you can do this with me?"

I lean back a bit so I can study his expression. "Do this?" I ask, a teasing smile playing across my lips.

"Yeah, this thing called life. You still up for sharing your life with me? Growing old with me?"

"Absolutely." I lean in and kiss him. Our tongues dance. He moans as my weight presses against his groin.

His arms wrap around me, holding me close. "That's a good thing. Because these last six months have been the best of my life."

I smile. "Mine too." I kiss him on the cheek. "Security for kids? I thought you were anti-security."

He roams my thigh with a light sensual touch as he shifts me on his lap. "I wouldn't say I'm anti-security. I just don't want to give up that freedom unless it's necessary. But our kids, that's a whole 'nother ball of wax. Keeping them safe. That'll be my number one priority. My muscles in my shoulders tighten thinking about it. That they could be the target for a ransom." He turns to watch the city glide by. "And they haven't even been born yet." He absentmindedly places light kisses along my knuckles.

"I don't think I've ever heard you talk about kids so much. Is something going on here? Is this your version of a proposal?" I don't even try to hold back my smile as I tease.

With his signature warm, shit-eating grin and in an exaggerated southern drawl, he says, "Darlin', when I propose—and I will propose—you'll know it's a proposal. This is just what I like to call testin' the waters."

I raise my eyebrows. "And what's your conclusion from your test?"

"I'm thinking the waters are mighty warm. Toasty. Trust me?"

Trust me. A lighthearted jest wrapping the crux of our relationship. We won't always be able to trust the people in our lives, but we have each other. I trust him with my soul. Instead of making me weaker, or vulnerable, he makes me stronger. I don't need a ring. He's my best friend, my confidante, and my future.

Acknowledgements

I originally wrote this before I'd even published the first book, *When the Stars Align*. It's all a little surreal, and I still have that feeling that I'm writing this section and few readers will ever read it.

Trust Me has gone through many iterations. Sections of it have been shared in a writing class. I've had many beta readers from Critique Match read some or all of it. Ada and Jenn, the same two beta readers who also read *When the Stars Align* read *Trust Me* and provided valuable feedback. AmyClaire Mager ripped it apart and helped me to piece it back together. Jenni Pezzano then read the revised version and helped me refine it. Which, I have to say, was so helpful, because, after so many changes, I wasn't even sure the new version, sans prologue, made sense.

Lori Whitwam took my unpolished draft, fixed all my errors, pointed out overused words and not only edited the piece but, just as she did with *When the Stars Align*, taught me so much. I'm looking forward to working with her in the future as I work to improve and grow as a writer.

Heather Whitehead copy edited *Trust Me* to find any comma or extra space errors and provided that one additional set of eyes to ensure a mistake-free manuscript.

Adlina Hamid-Yeow designed the book cover. She's been amazing to work with. She immediately "got it" and has also provided valuable insight as, she too, is a prolific romance reader.

Huge gratitude and appreciation goes out to the poet Becca Lee for providing permission for me to feature her poetry. I found her poem on Pinterest, and for me, it encapsulates the experience when Olivia ran away to another country after heartbreak, earned her own success, then returned stronger and in a better position to move forward with her life.

My husband and daughters, and my extended family, have gathered around to continue to support me on this crazy little endeavor. At Christmas, both my daughters gave me gifts that showed their support and brought on the tears. My husband and I continue to attempt to figure out the world of book marketing. As always, I'm forever grateful for his support and encouragement

Last but not least, a heartfelt thanks goes out to my cousin, Sarah Smith, who read my first book after it was published and bowled me over with her incredible enthusiasm. She let me know at a freak out moment, and I'll never forget how much her positivity meant. In some ways, she helped me to continue moving forward with this whole writing venture.

For Indie authors, every review helps. I've read this before, but never understood exactly how true it is until I released *When The Stars Align*. If you liked *Trust Me*, please consider leaving a review.

About the Author

After falling for a ginger in a kilt in *Outlander* and encountering Christian's hypnotic eyes in *50 Shades of Grey*, Isabel fell down the escapism rabbit hole. Inspired by a favorite Indie writer who said she started as an avid reader, Isabel decided to follow her high school dream and take the writing plunge. Through writing, she's found an outlet for the creative and passionate stories percolating in the deep recesses of her less than the safe-for-primetime mind.

Isabel has now written the first three books of the West Side series, a collection of romantic and erotic stories spanning time, friendships and exciting locations around the globe. The series has already received critical praise from early readers and critics alike, including first place in the RWA 2019 Four Seasons writers award.

Isabel lives outside of Charlotte, NC, where she splits her time between her two beautiful daughters, one charming yet clueless husband, a dog, a cat and an unquenchable desire to entertain, delight and share this passion with others like her.

If you've made it this far, please consider signing up for my newsletter. You'll get to hear me ramble on about

fun and naughty things I find, be alerted to new releases be- fore others and get to participate in whatever giveaways and contests I come up with. You can sign up at https: //isabeljoliebooks.com

You can connect with me on:

https://isabeljoliebooks.com http://twitter.com/isabelJoliebook
https://www.facebook.com/isabeljoliebooks
https://www.instagram.com/isabeljoliebooks
https://www.pinterest.com/isabeljoliebooks

Subscribe to my newsletter:

https://isabeljoliebooks.com

Also by Isabel Jolie

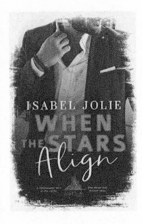

**When The Stars Align
(West Side Series Book 1)**
From award-winning romance writer
Isabel Jolie comes the first second-chance,
friends with benefits romance in her new
West Side Series - "When The Stars
Align."

Can Jackson and Anna put the past
behind them and take their second
chance at happily ever after—or are the
stars aligned against them once again?

Made in the USA
Monee, IL
23 January 2021

58452525R00184